BANKERS' GAME

A TALE OF GREED, LUST AND REDEMPTION

BANKERS' GAME

A TALE OF GREED, LUST AND REDEMPTION

ASHUTOSH MISHRA

JAICO PUBLISHING HOUSE

Ahmedabad Bangalore Bhopal Chennai
Delhi Hyderabad Kolkata Lucknow Mumbai

DISCLAIMER

This is a work of fiction. Names, characters, businesses, places, events and incidents are either the products of the author's imagination or used in a fictitious manner.

Published by Jaico Publishing House
A-2 Jash Chambers, 7-A Sir Phirozshah Mehta Road
Fort, Mumbai - 400 001
jaicopub@jaicobooks.com
www.jaicobooks.com

BANKERS' GAME
ISBN 978-93-89305-28-9

First Jaico Impression: 2020

Page design and layout: Jojy Philip, Delhi

Printed by
Trinity Academy For Corporate Training Limited, Mumbai

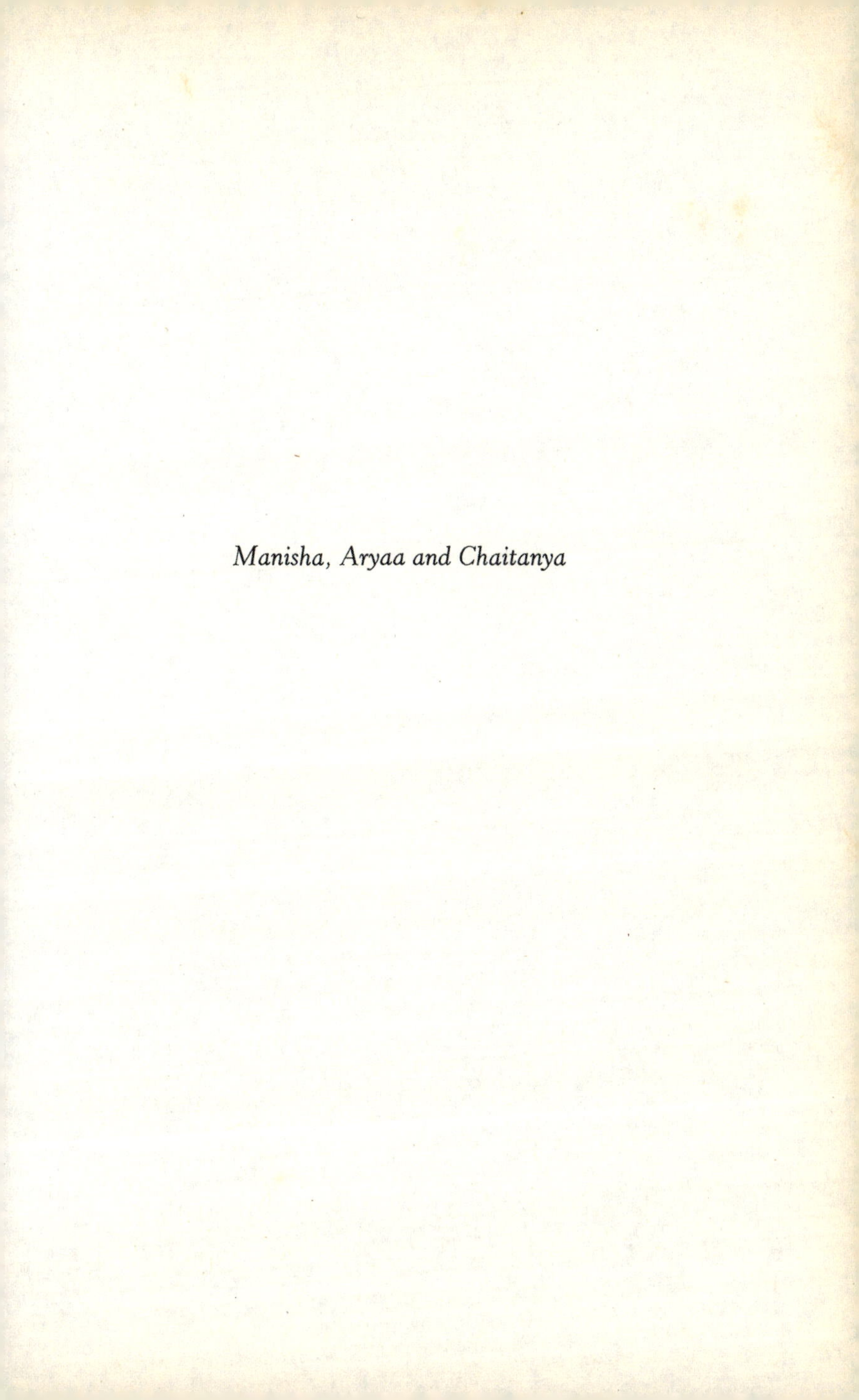

Manisha, Aryaa and Chaitanya

Prologue

As the sun went down, Mumbai's coastline was bathed in a rust red glow. Thousands of cars were lining up on the northbound lanes of posh Pedder Road, in the southern part of the city.

It was early evening. Brakes screeched as a car hit a middle-aged man, flinging him a few meters away. A large crowd gathered around the fallen body and traffic came to a standstill.

'Is this the Police Control Room?' a passer-by shouted hysterically into his mobile phone. 'There has been an accident on Pedder Road. A car hit a man and he is lying on the road. There is blood all around him.'

The voice on the other side was composed, as if nothing had happened. 'Did you note the number of the vehicle that hit him?'

'No, I just arrived at the scene. Please send an ambulance fast!'

'I don't have an ambulance nearby. I will message the closest patrol unit. Can you tell me the exact location?'

'Opposite the telephone exchange on Pedder Road, southbound lane.'

'Okay, give me a few minutes.'

A crowd was swelling around the man but nobody was willing to check if he was dead or alive. 'Call the police!' shouted someone. 'He is dead for sure,' said another. A few cars slid through the space between the body and the sidewalk, but none stopped to help or take the victim to a hospital.

A traffic police constable was the first to arrive. He examined the man—clothes soaked in blood, laboured breathing, no other signs of life. Meanwhile, a Mumbai Police van pulled up on the opposite side as it was impossible to approach the scene on the lane the accident had happened. It had taken them 30 minutes to reach; there is no concept of an emergency lane in a city where normal life unfolds like an emergency.

The police constable used his baton to turn the body over and threw some water on the man's face. The breathing had stopped by now. He took the wallet from the man's trouser pocket and pulled out a visiting card. The man was a bank official, though the bank's name looked alien to the constable.

Chapter 1

'Nitin, Nitin! Wake up now or I'll throw a bucketful of water on you,' said his mother, a middle-aged housewife.

'What, Ma… I was studying till three in the morning. Can't I just sleep for another hour?' Nitin pleaded with her.

'Not at all. Your class teacher has already struck out your name twice from the school records for being late and absent so frequently.'

'What's his problem! I score good marks and going to school is a big waste of time.'

'Enough boasting. You live in Jabalpur, you need to abide by the rules of the government high school.'

Nitin got up and went straight to the bathroom but the door was locked, as expected. He knocked on the door and his father, Shivlal shouted, 'Our prince has woken up now. Just wait outside, you wretched soul. You were not born in the royal family of Scindia with a mansion to live in.'

Nitin didn't want to hear the lecture his father imparted at every available opportunity—that he was the son of a Class 4 government employee, and was lucky to have clothes on his back, a roof over his head and admission in a school.

He reached school huffing and puffing. The morning prayers had just started and he could hear *itni shakti hamein dena data*. The teacher made him stand in a separate queue with the other latecomers because Sharmaji, the principal, was especially fond of chastising latecomers with old-school methods. He had a fixed punishment of five canes on the palm for first time offenders and ten for the repeat ones. For more habitual and hardened latecomers and absentees, he took the creative liberty of deciding the punishment on the spot.

As he reached Nitin after caning a few students, he let out a sigh, 'Not again, Nitin. You are really testing me. Okay, pick up your bag and run ten rounds of the playground. Sunil will keep an eye on you and report to me.'

After a disastrous start to the day, Nitin passed his time in class after class sitting on the back bench and fiddling with his pen. He would have to study everything on his own anyway to score state-topping marks. His teachers often wondered how a back-bencher was a topper.

In the evening, he showed his father his broken shoe, implying that it was time to buy a new pair of shoes. Shivlal erupted again, 'Rascal! Just go to the cobbler and get this stitched for two rupees. I could use this shoe for another two years, if not more.'

'Okay,' was all he could mutter. He silently took two rupees from his mother.

After an hour, he made a solemn entry, 'Actually, I got the shoe repaired and kept it safely in a bag on the cycle. But when I reached home, I couldn't find the bag.'

'What? I know you very well. This is another ploy to get a new pair of shoes. I will make you regret this.' Shivlal picked up the other shoe and started beating him.

Nitin yelped in pain. 'No, no. Let me go, leave me, leave me—'

Suddenly, he felt someone shaking him. 'Nitin, what's the matter? Wake up now, it's time to go to work.'

It was his wife, Vani. He opened his eyes to Vani's sweet voice and saw her fresh face, a few drops of water still on her cheeks.

'Is it one of your nightmares? Why don't you share them with me? What happened?'

'Nothing, Vani. I just felt a bit suffocated and then you woke me up.'

'Oh, come on now, you are getting late.'

'Looking at you, I have other ideas.' He took Vani in his arms. She looked beautiful in her light yellow cotton dress. Her slender body belied the fact that she was a mother of two as she took special care to maintain her figure with Pilates and aerobics.

She placed her head against his chest for a moment and then pushed him away, 'It's seven already, Nitin. Let's save this for the evening.'

'As you say, Madame.' Sensing that he was late for work, he went straight to the bathroom. Half an hour later, he joined Vani for breakfast. As she buttered her toast, she asked, 'All set for the day?'

'I have been doing this for 15 years now, I'm almost on autopilot.'

'Wow, you have been in banking for so many years but I am still not sure what exactly you do.'

'You know I work with Markets or the treasury function, right?'

She nodded. He explained the details to her one more time, 'Look, Markets refers to the esoteric world of high finance. We have some of the sharpest minds performing financial alchemy.'

'This is even more confusing!'

'You see, we use simple financial instruments like stocks, foreign exchange, bonds and commodities and devise complicated deals called derivatives.'

'Maybe you need to take a full day off to explain all this to me. But why do you call it financial alchemy?'

'Just like an alchemist creates gold using the philosopher's stone, we use these derivatives to create money for our clients and for the bank.' He chose not to mention just one minor detail—that his swollen pay check and the bonus was also a result of this process.

Still, Vani caught on, 'But you guys get paid well too!'

Nitin explained that it took some large investments in computer systems and an extraordinary knowledge of mathematics and programming to come up with these products. The grunt work was done in big financial centres like New York, London and Hong Kong by the highly paid quants or the rocket scientists. The banks charged their clients an arm and a leg to sell derivatives, which promised easy money. He winked, 'Smart people need to be paid well.'

'You have to be joking. Rocket scientists in a bank?'

'No, it's not a joke. These guys actually trained to become rocket scientists but joined this field to make quick fortunes.'

Using the tools they developed, the bank's branches in lesser developed markets like India concocted their own sweet potions designed to serve clients and, of course, make some money in the process. He didn't think it necessary to touch upon the huge risks these instruments created for the clients, the banks and the global financial system.

As he finished his breakfast, he looked at his watch. It was 8 am. Just enough time to reach work at 8.30 sharp. He told his driver to bring the car around to the porch.

The swanky new Audi Q5 sailed in and he hopped into the rear seat. 'To the office,' he said and opened *The Economic Times*.

The car left the plush building where he had a flat paid for by the company in Malabar Hill, just metres away from the Chief Minister's residence. As he travelled down the Walkeshwar slope with the sea on one side, he glanced over the south Mumbai skyline dotted with many landmark skyscrapers. It felt good to have come so far after the challenging childhood in a small city. His engineering degree and the subsequent MBA from IIM Ahmedabad had obviously helped.

Nitin worked at the British Bank as Head of Sales for the Markets function, a fairly senior and well-paid position. British Bank was one of the largest global banks, headquartered in London with branches in more than a hundred countries.

Chapter 2

The car dropped him in front of the huge colonial-era building that housed British Bank in Mumbai's Fort area. The building was more than a hundred years old and British Bank had leased it from the government for a 99-year term. It was 2006 and the lease had 70 more years to go. The ornate façade of the building betrayed none of its plush interiors and the high-profile dealings in international markets that took place inside.

Nitin stepped out of the Audi in quick, precise movements and headed straight to his office. His six-foot frame looked dapper in a dark grey Hugo Boss suit and he had a fair complexion and a square jawline. The guard at the entrance gave him a salute and he nodded back curtly. The time he regularly spent at the gym showed in his muscular but slim body.

His office was on the second floor, where the Markets dealing room was located. He walked up the white marble spiral staircase, taking in the cool rose-scented air of the office. The staircase and the corridor were lined with large Renaissance-era paintings. British Bank owned a huge art collection globally and had placed some of its choicest paintings here. Rumour had it that the value of paintings in the Mumbai office alone was more than three hundred crores.

The Markets floor was an open hall and had five rows of desks where the traders and sales staff were seated. The furniture, imported from London, looked right out of a sci-fi movie. British Bank believed in providing similar world-class working conditions to its staff in all countries. The contrast between the chaos of the dusty Mumbai roads and the cool, Wall Street-like atmosphere inside British Bank was overwhelming for newcomers.

As soon as Nitin entered the dealing room, he saw that his boss, Joe, the Head of Markets, was barking orders to the trading team. But none of Nitin's three salespersons—Rekha, Amit and Satya—had arrived yet. Nitin and Joe privately referred to these three as schmucks. During one quarterly performance review meeting, when Joe had asked, 'Who's behind on their revenue target?' the three of them half raised their hands, as if displaying the election symbol of the Indian National Congress party.

Joe had erupted, 'Oh man, I don't understand! What kind of schmucks would be behind their targets in such a booming market?' This proved to be the naming ceremony for Satya, Amit and Rekha. They swallowed their pride, as always, to protect their jobs, and silently accepted the title, getting anointed as schmucks.

Nitin was visibly annoyed at being the first to arrive among the sales team while the trading team was buzzing with activity. Just then, Rekha and Amit walked in.

Amit whispered, 'This asshole is always in the office before us. We need to reach a bit earlier.' Rekha pretended not to hear anything. They took their seats at the long desk opposite Nitin and started dialling into the morning conference call. Joe had instituted this call and attending it was sacrosanct for all the sales and trading staff. They used it to update each other on the overnight developments in the fascinating world of foreign exchange, bonds and commodities. This helped the traders make money by buying and selling these financial instruments, and the salespersons could also sell these to their clients with a nice profit margin.

The open architecture allowed the staff to hear most conversations regarding news and pricing, leading to a smooth flow of information. The diktat to the Markets staff was clear—beg, borrow or steal but make money, and don't get caught. The famous line from their global CEO was imprinted in everyone's brain, 'Banking works on rules. Some can be bent and others can be broken.' The rewards for making money were huge and expectations of the B word—a big Bonus—kept everyone on their toes.

Chapter 3

A black and yellow taxi stopped just outside British Bank. Satya handed five hundred rupees to the driver and didn't wait to receive the change, leaving behind a hefty tip. The tip was unintended but less valuable than every minute that he could save.

Another maddening day. He was late for the morning call. Nitin, his boss, monitored the latecomers closely. Satya hated that he needed to be at work at 8:30 when the Indian currency and bond markets opened at 9.

Joe glanced at him as he entered the dealing room but didn't say a word. But he noticed Joe looking at Nitin, who walked over. 'Let's have a quick chat,' Nitin motioned for him to come to the glass-walled conference room close to the sales desk.

'Satya, why don't you take the morning call seriously?' Nitin had given him so many warnings already.

'My car is getting serviced and you know how difficult it is to get a cab in the morning,' Satya mumbled.

Another lame excuse. 'You know the rules, Satya, and this is not the first time.'

'But Nitin, I tried really hard to reach on time.'

'I don't care. We don't pay top dollar to our staff to hear excuses. Make alternative arrangements—get a replacement car for God's sake!' Nitin dismissed the meeting.

It was a soundproof cabin but as soon as they stepped out, Satya was met with wicked smiles from his colleagues. The chat was short but its contents were no secret. Satya had a feeling that Joe was quite relaxed about his coming in late but Nitin didn't have the word 'mercy' in his vocabulary. He believed if he allowed a few minutes' grace to his staff, people would start stretching it and office attendance would be in tatters.

As soon as Satya switched on his computer, Amit, who sat next to him, looked over at his screen. Satya hated the easy access provided by the glorified open hall called the dealing room. The chaos and the noise actually reminded him of a railway sleeper class waiting room.

Thanks to the late arrival and the almost public chastising, Satya had only five minutes to catch up on the news and prices. At two minutes to 9, he called up Narayanan, the treasurer of a large conglomerate. Narayanan's ego was larger than the company he worked for and the trick was to call him and keep chatting with him till the market opened, so that he might do a big deal with you at the opening price. But everyone in the trade knew this and it was almost impossible to get through his phone at this time.

Satya's hypothesis turned out to be true; Narayanan's number was busy. As he put down the receiver, Nitin threw him a dirty look. An eternal optimist, Satya tried to catch the next big fish. That was also in some other bank's net. No problem. He tried the third and voila! He had one.

He shouted into the phone, 'Sir, the rupee has opened lower

due to the overnight action by the US central bank. Our traders feel that it will go higher from the current level. Do you want to buy some?' The client replied, 'Satya, I agree with your view but I am in the local train. I will reach my office in next 20 minutes. Can you call me after that?'

Satya was not going to miss his prized catch just because he was in a train. How else could he save face in front of Nitin? He insisted, 'Sir, the opportunity will be gone by then. Please buy now.'

'Okay, please—...,' the client replied.

'Sir, I can't hear you. Please say that again.' Satya could feel his blood pressure rise with his desperation. The entire dealing room was watching him. He felt like a circus elephant who was about to drop the ball—and the ringmaster would whip him with an electric hunter if he did.

The client spoke, 'I am...—... in...—, the signal...—' And the line went dead. Satya's third call had been aborted. Today was not his day.

Nitin was monitoring the situation closely. It was five past 9 and his salesperson covering large corporates was still struggling to close the day's first deal. Satya felt the perspiration on his forehead even though the air-conditioned office made most wear sweaters and jackets to keep warm. On the other hand, Amit's face betrayed immense joy as he had already closed a couple of bond trades with other banks.

Nitin pounced on Satya, ditching the courtesy of inviting him inside the conference room, 'Satya, your deal book is looking like India's Olympic medal tally. It's five past 9 and you haven't closed any deal yet.'

'I am trying...' Satya tried to murmur something, but Nitin tore into him, 'No wonder you are behind on your revenue target. Look at Amit, he is doing so well!' Nitin towered over Satya as he was a good six inches taller.

'But this comparison is not fair, Nitin. Amit covers banks and a bank is supposed to buy and sell all the time. The same cannot be said about my corporate clients.'

But Nitin gave him a stern look and turned and walked away, driving a knife through Satya with his silence. British Bank's culture thrived on the three C's of comparison, competition and criticism.

Satya's heart was pounding. *This loser, Amit, has an easier job. In any case, he is more interested in reading my emails and spying on my deals. Oh God… please get me out of here soon.*

That was true and Amit made no effort to hide his intrusion. Satya actually had to step out to type sensitive emails on his Blackberry. The other day, Amit taunted him with 'I can't believe the credit risk officer turned down your request so strongly!' He had read the latest email in Satya's inbox even before the intended recipient had.

Satya had ordered a special screen cover that prevented people from reading the screen from the side. In fact, Reuters, their information service provider, had even gifted them a device that gave an entirely new meaning to the term 'watching over your shoulder.' It was a small round convex mirror, similar to a rear-view mirror, that could be attached to the computer screen. It gave you a good view of what was happening just in case the boss or a colleague sneaked up behind you.

Chapter 4

Rekha was the newest member of the sales team, hired to provide structuring expertise to Nitin, Amit and Satya. Structuring referred to the art of producing complicated financial products also known as derivatives.

Suddenly, Rekha felt something shift in the office. All the men—and it was largely men in there—became attentive and alert, and were staring in the same direction. Jenny, the CEO's secretary, had just walked in wearing a short skirt and her trademark Chanel No. 5 perfume. But everyone knew that the good vibe would last only till she opened her mouth and laid into someone.

Jenny headed to Rekha and slammed a bunch of papers onto her desk. 'Is this what you call briefing notes for the CEO? I want these properly drafted and submitted to me before you go home,' she shouted.

Rekha, a tigress in the dealing room, instantly turned into a meek lamb. She didn't even consider defending the quality of the work. 'But the meeting is day after tomorrow, right?' she asked, implying that the redrafting could be done the next day.

Everyone could see Jenny fuming but she checked her temper and snapped, 'Rakesh prefers his briefing memos two days before the meeting, understood?'

'I have other stuff to take care of, Jenny.'

'Now, don't get me started. I heard you went to Wharton.' *Don't they teach multi-tasking there?*

'Enough, Jenny. I will get these to you by the evening.'

You better. After trampling Rekha, Jenny vanished from the scene leaving behind only the distinctive scent of her perfume. Amit, who was sitting next to Rekha, tried to sympathise with her and said, 'Jenny is so rude.'

'I think Rakesh leaves the hard talk to Jenny and comes across as extra polite himself,' Rekha said.

'Is Rakesh really so diligent?'

'Not at all. I once accompanied Rakesh for a meeting and in the car, he was still fumbling through the files to get the right memo. Finally, when he did get it, instead of reading it, he asked me to summarise the note in two lines.'

'I always suspected him to be a big show-off.'

Shortly thereafter, she received a call from Smita, a relationship banker, to discuss an upcoming deal.

'Hey, Rekha! Just wanted to update you on my meeting with Gloria Chemicals. Do you have a minute?'

'Good timing, Smita. I am actually a bit stiff sitting here all morning. I could do with a cup of coffee. Let's go out.'

'Sure.'

At a nearby café, Smita asked, 'You seem a bit weary. What's the matter?'

'Nothing yaar. I'm sick of Satya and Amit palming off their work to me. Every now and then, they just announce that they are heading out for a client call and ask me to work out the next deal idea. What am I supposed to be? A sponge that absorbs everything and still maintains its composure? I am going to complain to Nitin about it.'

'That's nothing serious, Rekha. At our bank, that is part of the job. Instead, I will advise you to tackle them indirectly. Direct complaints, though true, are seen negatively. Get into the good books of Nitin and Joe. That's the way to screw your enemies' happiness.'

'Yeah, I don't think Nitin has a high opinion of both of them anyway. Satya provided the morning's entertainment by walking in late. Joe has been silent so far and left it to Nitin. But I'm sure he will crack the whip himself next time.'

'You need to notice these small things and use them to your advantage,' Smita continued her counselling.

'You know, Amit has been cribbing about the lack of new products for his clients. The worst part is that he never came to me to talk about it or to ideate. He made some noise in front of Nitin but I am sure there is more to it.'

'Is it? Did you try to find out?'

'Actually, since I joined, people in the team have been jealous of my supposedly big pay package and the sign-on bonus.'

'Really?'

'Yes, Satya had remarked on my second day, "Let's see what value you bring to the table. I have heard that you are an expensive hire." I told him that his comment was not funny and how I wished the rumours about my compensation were true.'

Smita giggled, 'Rekha, everyone knows. Stop being defensive about it.'

'You are right, I don't need to be defensive. But what should I do?'

'The best way to deal with any gossip from the grapevine is to never deny it vehemently. The stronger your denial, the more reinforcement the rumour gets. Just a slight protest is fine.'

'While I negotiated to the last penny possible, I was still limited by my imagination.'

Smita smiled, 'Life is always one step ahead of you. Better luck next time!'

While walking back, Rekha recalled her journey to British Bank—it had been a tough one. After her MBA from Wharton, she had slogged for eight long years at BNP Paribas at a modest salary, where she learnt cutting-edge product knowledge. Then this job came up and she knew she had to monetise the opportunity while the industry was booming. She had negotiated a good jump in her salary and sign-on bonus.

I deserve every bit of it and more. Let people burn in the fire of jealousy—it only makes me happier.

But after she had started at British Bank, she heard about the money being pocketed by Joe and Nitin. *Here I am, short-changed again.*

Chapter 5

As soon as Rekha returned after venting her heart out and getting some fresh air, Satya looked at Amit. That meant a cigarette break for Satya and tea for both at the roadside stall. Satya told Rekha, 'We are stepping out for a few minutes, please handle the client calls while we are out.'

'I need to go for a meeting in exactly ten minutes,' replied Rekha.

She watched them walk out together as if they were co-conspirators. The short pot-bellied Satya and the tall and thin Amit looked like an odd couple and she grinned as she noticed the contrast. The only thing they had in common was a severely receding hairline.

Outside, Satya lit his Marlboro Lights. 'What's it between Rekha and Jenny?'

'Jenny is a bitch with everyone.'

'No, I think she is especially harsh with Rekha.'

'It could be the usual women thing, you know.'

'What's that?'

'Rekha is the only woman in the bank who can rival Jenny when it comes to attracting male attention.'

'You are right,' Satya said. 'Rekha is pretty, has a good figure and dresses well too.'

'Yup, her long, flowing hair is the icing on the cake.'

'Ah I see, you seem to be checking her out,' Satya said. *I am not the only one ogling her.*

'No, no. Nothing like that. She is attractive no doubt but I have a strict no romance at work policy,' said Amit. *Sure, I like to check her out but from a distance.*

'I agree, it can only lead to trouble. Anyway, their fights don't affect us.'

'Right yaar. We need to stay away from trouble. Speaking of trouble, do you know why Nitin behaves like an asshole with us?'

'Why?' Satya asked.

'I overheard Joe telling him, "Man, you just got promoted to the Head of Sales. Now, you are one of us." Nitin puffed his chest and kept nodding.'

'I'm not surprised. They think cracking jokes and laughing with us will downgrade their seniority,' added Amit.

'Yeah, it's what Joe told him. He advised him not to socialise freely with people who were his colleagues before he got the promotion. Empathizing with his team would make him look weak as a manager. His juniors would not respect him and he would not be considered senior management material.'

'Hmm. I have seen people like this at my previous job. What more did he tell Nitin?'

'He left it at that. I guess he let Nitin decipher what would happen to his next promotion and bonus in case he disobeyed,' Satya chuckled.

'What does Joe even do? He has become so hefty sitting at

the desk the whole day, and he smells like a bulldog.' Amit was referring to the paunch Joe had developed.

Satya was agitated as well. 'You know, Nitin is always on the prowl to hear about my large deals.'

'And without discussing the deal's details or its probability, he informs Joe,' Amit shared his grievance.

'I see, his motive is to quickly put his stamp on your deals.' Satya was puffing away, flicking the cigarette to sprinkle the ash on the footpath.

'Yes, he subtly tells the management that he advised me to have a conversation with the client on an idea or that the client agreed to do it based solely on his recommendation.' Amit slurped the hot cutting-chai.

'I'm yet to suffer like that, but Nitin is capable of doing it to me.'

'You will feel the pain when this happens to you. When the deal is done, Joe crowns Nitin with all the credit behind closed doors.'

'Grow up yaar,' Satya patted Amit, 'This is part of corporate life.'

'I don't mind him taking the glory but they should at least give some meaningful credit to us!' Amit was ranting now. 'If the deal doesn't materialise, I get the blame for faulty execution and not capitalizing on the great ideation.'

Amit was extremely animated, 'Yesterday, after lunch, I had to go to the washroom but one of my clients was supposed to call back to close a big-ticket deal. I wanted to be around to close it.'

'I remember, you were looking forward to it.' Satya was making perfectly circular puffs with his mouth facing upwards.

'But I couldn't wait and I dashed to the loo. I relieved myself in a hurry and rushed back to the desk.' Satya's puff hit Amit, as he was taller, but he chose to ignore it.

'So, what happened?' Satya lit another cigarette.

'I saw Joe patting Nitin's back and congratulating him. As

expected, my client did call and Nitin closed the deal, losing no time in informing Joe.'

'That's cold, but not unexpected. These guys are like hyenas, they specialise in snatching up prey.'

'Again, one month of hard work down the drain. The bank made money, but what about me? These moments will come back to haunt me on Bonus day.'

Satya had a solemn look on his face. 'Bonus day reminds me of Judgement Day. All the dead wake up and stand beside you.'

'I agree. Spending the whole year in high-action mode and seeing everyone happy around you, we are led to believe that this year is different.'

'Believe me, this is my tenth year in this profession and not once has this feeling been met with an equally rosy bonus letter. These guys just don't want to see the schmucks happy.'

'Look, I will confess that my bonus numbers in the last couple of years have been plump, but what about Nitin and Joe, who get fatter cheques just for screwing my life?'

'The other day, I looked at the fancy cufflinks Joe was wearing and asked, "What does the 'Ω' mean?" He gave me a dirty look implying I was a scumbag of the lowest order. He said, "It is the symbol for Omega, the well-known luxury brand!"'

Satya burst out laughing. This was proving to be an entertaining session, even if it was at their expense.

'The summer trainee sitting close to us jumped in and flaunted his Omega watch, "My dad gifted me this Omega watch when I passed my 12th standard boards." Joe looked at his watch and smiled, "Yeah, that's the Omega Seamaster. That's a great model, Jay."'

'I get it. This bloke is the son of the chairman of a large public sector company.'

'Nobody gave me even a Swatch even though I scored more than 95 percent.'

'Nitin offered this trainee a summer 'internship' to get some business from his dad's company.' The internship merely offered a whole summer in a cool office with free internet, and occasional free lessons in finance delivered by lesser mortals like Amit and Satya.

'Yes, but I don't think we will recruit him for a full-time role. Thank God for small justices,' Satya tried to console Amit. The real summer interns at British Bank were recruited from a proper campus selection process at top B-schools around the world.

Satya lit the next one.

'This summer trainee is a minion. What do you think of Rekha's situation?' Amit steered the conversation to the real enemy. He still remembered the day she joined the team as a product expert—the floor was abuzz with the rumours of her hefty package and the sign-on bonus she had been paid to lure her away from a large investment bank.

'Oh yes, the kind of numbers people were talking about had me squirming.' *It is high time that I got an extraordinary offer from another bank and I never look back.*

'Same here. I could not sleep for many days,' Amit relived the pain. *I couldn't even muster the courage to share it with my wife or she would kill me for being such a loser, only working hard and getting paid nothing.*

'Don't worry, man; every dog has his day and ours will come soon too!'

As they walked back to their desks, Amit asked the office boy to serve his lunch at the desk. This was characteristic of the Markets department. The world would fall apart if traders or salespersons stepped away from the desk for lunch. People barely registered their meal as they spent the entire day hunched in front of multiple computer screens. The sales guys got two screens, unlike traders who could hoard eight screens or even more. And the more exotic the graphs and data displayed on your screen, the more intelligent you looked to your colleagues and bosses.

Chapter 6

Rekha was relieved that the duo came back in 20 minutes. They were capable of spending a full hour loitering outside if Nitin was not in the office. For now, she needed to work on the next big deal that Nitin had referred to her. If it went through, Joe and Nitin would more than take care of her.

Working on this new deal, though exciting, took the life out of her. It was already past 8 in the evening but she had not been able to tie various ends together. She needed to speak with the compliance person urgently but he was long gone. If she waited till the next day, it would be too late to show the final presentation to Nitin. Then, he would be at his sarcastic best. The little noise Amit had made would only get louder. She tried the compliance officer on the mobile but there was no answer.

If Nitin called her on her phone even after work hours and she failed to pick up the call, she would have it. Last time, when she was at the hospital with Neeraj, her husband, Nitin had kept her on the mobile the entire time. And when she was unable to answer calls, they taunted her with endless snide comments: 'Some people have an amazing quality of life,' 'Mobiles are useless devices to be given to employees,' 'Youngsters nowadays want a European lifestyle.'

When she called her colleagues in New York or London after they had left for the day, there was no answer and no way to reach them. But here, everyone expected the employees to be walking zombies who answer calls on the first ring even at midnight. Whoever coined the term 'work-life balance' clearly hadn't worked here.

After finishing whatever she could, she called a cab and left for home. On her way, she couldn't help but think about that high-heeled, short-skirted, aggressive she-devil Jenny. *Creating unnecessary urgency is another hallmark of these self-obsessed secretaries. Using the CEO's name gives them enough power to pull anyone down. And it was so demeaning that the drama took place in front of the entire dealing room.*

Rekha knew that stooping to Jenny's level was not a choice. That would mean getting kicked out of her newly-acquired job and losing the money that comes with it. Swallowing her pride was the only option, saving vengeance for another day.

After the verbal scuffle, Amit had sympathised with her but she knew it was fake. *He thinks I am vulnerable and wants to use such opportunities to get close. He knows my marital status but workplace flirting has its advantages.* For Rekha, thinking seriously about any man other than Neeraj was a strict no. Still, she enjoyed her power over Amit and Satya. They were a great help despite their shortcomings. One just needed to know how to use them to one's advantage.

Whenever the pressure mounted, she knew she could have Amit and Satya fight over her. Their hierarchy of people to keep happy was their bosses first, then the girls around them and then maybe their families. The family members were already in their fold as they depended on these men, who took full advantage of this dependence. That's why she had decided to be financially independent and focused on her career.

A couple of years after she came back to India from the US, she started dating Neeraj. He seemed nice with cute looks and he was a senior consultant at a global auditing firm. When she told her family that she was considering marriage, her dad was not too happy. He didn't like Neeraj's lower middle-class family. He also expressed reservations about Neeraj's flamboyant attitude.

Rather than marrying her off to the son of another Punjabi businessman, her family had encouraged her to study and to do well professionally. Her dad's garments export business was doing well and paying her Wharton fees had not been heavy at all, either on the pocket or on the mind. When they heard that she had been admitted, her father had been thrilled. 'I want nothing but the best for my daughter,' he had declared to his wife, Asha.

But her parents were convinced that Neeraj was not the best match for her. When the families first met, the disconnect was apparent. Rekha's mother-in-law to be was very orthodox and expected her to quit her job, stay at home and take care of her husband and children.

After a little bickering among the parents, the prospective couple's wish prevailed and they decided to keep the families out of the relationship as much as possible. Asha also advised Rekha's dad to back off and let things take their course.

'Madam, we have reached your place,' the cab driver said, jolting Rekha back to the present. Asha opened the door and blocked the way with her tall imposing frame. She wore a peach coloured cotton Punjabi suit with a green dupatta to beat the humid Mumbai heat.

'Rekha, what is this? Both of you come home so late.'

An equally tall Rekha had to struggle past her into the house. Rekha had inherited her mother's features, along with her height and fair complexion. She looked exactly like a young Asha.

'I can't help it, Mamma. Don't want to talk about the same thing again.'

'You hardly meet Neeraj and spend any time with him.'

'I knew this was coming. Why can't you talk about—'

Asha cut her off, 'But how will it continue like this?'

Rekha raised her voice to get a word in. 'Mamma, the problem is not timing but intent. Neeraj makes it a point to reach home after I do.'

'Beta, I see you two growing apart, aren't you going to do something about it?' Asha added gently, trying to calm things down.

'I don't have all the answers, please let me change and relax for some time,' Rekha replied, still agitated.

'I knew you would try to shut me up. Neeraj is rude to me anyway. I will return home tomorrow.' Asha shook her head. *That's why I didn't want to come here despite her repeated requests. This situation is hopeless.*

'Please Mamma, I need you. Be here for a couple of days for my sake.' Rekha put her arm around Asha.

'I can see your health deteriorating, too. You are looking plumper than last year,' Asha resumed.

Rekha had no choice but to engage with her. She threw her bag aside and realised that she was still standing. She sat down and said, 'Mamma, you don't need to tell me that. Even though I try by joining a gym or a yoga class, I am not able to continue for more than a month or two.'

'I thought you had paid for a year at the gym near your office.' Asha got a glass of water for her.

'That frees me from guilt—at least I joined. The real culprits are my job and Neeraj.'

'Rekha, stop blaming others. You need to take matters in your hands.'

'Why, Mamma? I will blame Neeraj for sure. He earns less than

I do but still expects a king's treatment at home. Whether the maids do the work or I fill in, he refuses to move from that couch. He has an infinite capacity to keep lying down in front of the TV.'

'I have seen that myself, but that's how he is.'

'And you tell me my health is deteriorating?' Rekha paused to take a sip of water. 'Mamma, do you know how long he takes in the bathroom? 30 minutes! I suspect he watches sports on his mobile while he is relieving himself in the washroom.'

'Now, you are really making a villain out of him. After all, he is your husband.'

Rekha was finding it hard to figure out whose side her mother was on, but she continued, 'He also smokes in there. Our bathroom feels like the smoking room at the airport. I prefer to use the other washroom as it is impossible to correct this guy!'

'You knew about his smoking and drinking before marriage. Why are you cribbing now?'

'People do everything but within limits. He promised to quit smoking and reduce his drinking,' Rekha said. 'If the maid doesn't turn up in the morning, I simply cannot pack lunch for us. He insults me, "My mother always made sure that my dad carried lunch to his office. Food cooked by the lady of the house has a high nutritional value," and other such orthodox crap.'

'To hell with such comparisons with his half-educated mother who spent the better part of her life in small cities cooking aloo parathas,' Asha was now seeing the point. 'Did she ever earn even a single penny? You contribute equally to your home loan payments and daily expenditure.' Asha didn't know that Neeraj was eyeing Rekha's bonus to buy his Harley Davidson motorbike.

'Yes, Mamma. I am now very careful about my personal finances and maintain separate accounts.' Rekha was slumped on the sofa with her head thrown back as if she were talking to the ceiling.

'Hai mere rabba, all of this doesn't sound good. Why don't you resolve matters like adults? Where has the love gone from your love marriage?' Asha adjusted her dupatta and was looking increasingly hassled.

'I don't know if there's any love anymore. Neeraj has been commenting on my deteriorating figure of late. What a hypocrite!' Rekha found more ammunition to fuel her disdain. 'Why doesn't he look at his bulging cheeks and the big beer belly? His smoking and drinking is going to cost us big.'

'Did you ever try talking to him?'

'When I confront him, "Baby, when do you plan to start exercising?" his response is either, "Soon" or "When you also become regular."'

Her mother vigorously shook her head. 'I could sense that all is not well.'

'Then, the occasional arrival of his mother increases my pain. She lives not far away but keeps her distance, ostensibly because of me.'

'But what have you done to make her angry?'

'His mother's first comment on arrival, for the past six years of our marriage is, "When will we get the good news?" referring to the arrival of a ten-pound grandson of her dreams.'

'Such a predictable Indian mother,' Asha said.

'I don't even feel Neeraj is serious about me and I can hardly think of starting a family with him. It is too risky to take a break in my career to produce a smaller Neeraj.'

'May not be a bad idea, after all. I have seen men become serious about life after they have kids,' Asha was trying all means to secure a recovery of their relationship.

'Now you are being a predictable Indian mother,' Rekha knew this would hurt. Asha smarted at this stinging remark but Rekha did not stop, 'So far I have not felt any dormant motherly tendencies that need an outlet.'

'I'll leave it to you,' Asha said, trying to sound modern.

'His mother's next comment is as predictable, "Aww my son,

you are looking so weak." From which angle does he look weak? Is she hallucinating? I am sure he is weak from the inside but he looks like an overfed hippo from the outside.'

'I know he is spoiling his health but there's little we can do to motivate him to do some exercise.'

'The mere thought of this hippo attempting to run on a treadmill will send his mother's blood pressure to the moon. That's one of the reasons for people letting themselves expand sideways—extra love from their near and dear ones. Parents and relatives are too afraid to say the right things and risk spoiling their relationships,' Rekha needed this emotional outburst and started feeling better.

'Okay, enough complaining. You go change and let's have dinner together. It's eleven and there is no sign of Neeraj, yet.'

Rekha couldn't help but think about Neeraj's health, which she felt was equivalent to that of a 60-year-old. Due to his sedentary lifestyle, his health indicators were worsening every year. Rekha was present at his last annual health check-up when the doctor had told him that he needed medication for his blood pressure and cholesterol that were higher than normal.

The doctor gave him a semi-statutory warning, 'If you don't take these pills, your arteries will get blocked faster and you will be at a high risk for a heart attack in the next few years. Your fasting blood sugar is at the border, making you a prime candidate for diabetes.'

Neeraj was in denial, 'No doctor, it may not be that bad. Things have been a bit hectic at work recently and my lifestyle has been erratic. Anyway, I will take these medicines for sure.'

The doctor had continued, 'You need a complete lifestyle modification. A combination of light to medium intensity exercises for an hour every day and a healthy, homemade diet should be ideal.'

Rekha thought about the late night football matches, the rushed mornings with no time for breakfast and the daily drinking binges... if only the doctor knew.

Neeraj had made excuses. 'See doctor, it's very tough for me to find time for all this. I work in a multinational firm. I need to travel frequently and you know that the diet goes for a toss when you are on business travel. And my wife works in a large bank as well. I cannot get homemade food every day as the maids take frequent holidays.'

Rekha silently fumed. She knew that every evening, Neeraj had Domino's on speed dial and a beer in his hand, no matter who cooked what.

The doctor was not willing to give up. 'Look, I will refer you to a good nutritionist and a fitness trainer in your neighbourhood. You take it from there.'

Neeraj had spent a few thousand rupees consulting the nutritionist and then had thrown all her suggestions and recipes into the bin after a week of 'trying' to follow them. The fitness trainer lasted for a month. During the hour-long session, he spent 30 minutes getting Neeraj into the proper frame of mind. Neeraj would then follow the trainer's instruction for about ten minutes in the garden before giving up and collapsing on the floor.

The trainer would spend the last ten minutes motivating him that tomorrow would be a better day. After a month of babysitting Neeraj, the trainer vowed never to take on a client without a trial week.

Chapter 7

Amit woke up with the sun directly on his face, through the bedroom window. He softly poked Anu, his wife, 'Wake up, baby. It's already 8.'

Anu was enjoying the lazy start to the day, and an unexpected midweek day off from work. She cozied up under the soft quilt and dozed off.

Ten minutes later, Amit walked into the bedroom with a quickly assembled breakfast tray and some coffee. Anu looked like a baby, snuggling in her pink night suit. He couldn't thank God enough that he had met and married his soulmate. There was a mystical sense of purity about her. Dusky and beautiful, she had caught his eye as soon as they met during orientation at IIM Kolkata. He had spent the better part of the next two terms wooing her. Anu had found the soft-mannered lanky boy very different from the rest of the aggressive crowd. He was six feet tall and she was about ten inches shorter but they made a super cute couple, according to their batchmates.

She opened her eyes and was surprised to see Amit standing with the tray. She exclaimed, 'What is this? I haven't had this privilege for the last five years of our marriage!' Now, she was really feeling pampered. She yawned and stretched her arms while Amit smiled and enjoyed the feeling of giving her a nice experience.

They had a quick breakfast before dozing off again. They needed to catch up on sleep and on each other's gossip. Although Amit's job tended to be more strenuous, Anu's also took up a lot of time. Both of them were from IIM, but she had chosen to take up a mid-level job in a small company as they were planning to have a child soon. She wanted to devote a good amount of time to the child.

Unlike many couples who went their separate ways after graduating, they had decided to tie the knot. Both of them belonged to middle-class professional families. Amit's parents were doctors and Anu's were architects.

Amit's days were hectic in part due to his commute—30 kilometres twice a day. He stayed in Goregaon, a western suburb of Mumbai. Their home was right next to the Western Express Highway but it was a highway in name only and 'express' was misleading. The municipal corporation built flyovers that were needed 20 years ago and traffic on the highway never improved.

Nitin habitually called people to the office on holidays. Amit had tried to refuse several times, but you couldn't ask your boss to knock it off all the time.

Just last Saturday, Nitin called him while he was shopping for things for the house.

'Why do you waste your time with chores?' Nitin admonished. 'Dedicate time to bigger things and you will benefit. The deal we are working on has just gone live and one of the Tata Sons' directors wants to see our ideas over the weekend. Why don't you drop by the office quickly?'

While Amit was still wondering how to get out of that tricky situation, Nitin spoke again, 'I will see you at the office in 15 minutes.' But before Nitin could disconnect the call, Amit had managed an intelligent response, 'But Nitin, I stay in Goregaon. It will take me an hour and a half to reach the office.'

Nitin didn't skip a beat, 'Okay then, see you in an hour.'

Amit remembered, soon after joining, he told Nitin about where he stayed. But this detail had failed to register with Nitin despite many reminders. Amit guessed that the space in Nitin's mind was reserved for more important things.

Once, Amit asked him,' Where do you stay, Nitin?'

Nitin smirked, 'Mont Blanc.'

'Huh? Is that a new locality in Mumbai that just sprang up from nowhere?' thought Amit. He persisted, 'Where's that?'

'Oh, I see. You are not familiar with south Mumbai. This building is at Nepean Sea Road,' Nitin said.

After spending some intimate moments at home, Amit and Anu headed out for a movie around noon. They were pleasantly surprised to find no crowd at all. The movie theatre was sparsely occupied with middle-aged housewives, elderly couples and a few students whose parents thought they were at college.

They watched the movie feeling like royalty as they had the entire row to themselves. There was an occasional moan from the back where some of the couples were being naughty.

'Surprisingly, there was no cruel reaction from Nitin and Joe after I informed them of my sick leave,' Amit said as soon as the movie was over. He was checking his Blackberry once in a while but all seemed to be in order at work.

'I am amazed. Usually, your bosses make you feel that the whole bank will come crashing down and your clients will mourn if you are not at your desk,' Anu replied.

'But this important status somehow doesn't reflect in my comp.'

'What's comp?'

'Comp is short for compensation, that's my salary and bonus. I learnt this jargon on a call from our global head.'

'Wow, you bankers always come up with these interesting terms,' Anu said, as she followed Amit into a coffee shop. After the heavy snack during the movie, lunch was out of question; they decided to have coffee.

'Incidentally, he is visiting us next month. As soon as his trip was announced, I asked Nitin about what we were expected to present to Jorge.'

Amit paused, remembering the derogatory smile on Nitin's face. 'He sneered and told me that his name is pronounced Horhè and not Jorge.'

'That must have felt bad,' Anu said, impulsively.

'I was speechless. How was I supposed to know that Jorge is actually Horhè?'

Amit went on to narrate the whole incident:

That day, as Amit was licking his wounds, Nitin dealt the real blow. 'Actually you guys will not get a chance to speak to him,' he said. 'Only the seniors will present to him.' Then he called Rekha, Satya and Amit into a room and asked them to start working on this presentation. Collaboration among the three of them was next to impossible. They typically operated alone, off on their own paths.

As soon as he left, the three scrambled to claim the easiest part of the presentation. Rekha shouted, 'I will work on India's economic outlook.' Sure enough, that was the easiest part that entailed cutting and pasting from the economics research reports. Then it was Satya's turn. 'I will do the current state of business and the pipeline.' This was just a collation of readily available data from finance and business management teams

Anu was listening attentively and said, 'Let me guess, you got the least-desirable part?'

'Correct, you know me so well. I was left with the most difficult task of compiling the key asks or demands of the India team.'

'That doesn't sound too bad.'

'Yeah, it looked like the most relevant but I knew it was the most useless one. I have seen these BSDs drop by and listen to the local team's demands. They usually trash them at the first class lounge at the airport on the way home.'

'Hmm, what's BSD?'

'Big Swinging Dicks, a common Wall Street term referring to corporate honchos with big egos. I read it in *Liar's Poker*.'

'Just how many times have you read *Liar's Poker*?'

'Too many to remember now, Anu. It's the bible!'

Amit went on. The three of them decided to meet again in a couple of days to compare notes. The meeting was a fine example of corporate distrust. Each kept asking the others to show their work, hiding their own like skilled boxers. Anu was increasingly amused as she listened to the dysfunctional way of working at British Bank.

The day Nitin was supposed to review the first draft, they handed him their separate printouts. Of course, he was expecting this but he still reacted violently. 'What am I supposed to do with this?' he yelled, threw the sheets in the air and stormed out. Later, he sent them an email, copying Joe on it, warning them about their lack of teamwork. He gave them one more day to compile the three parts into an intelligent-looking deck.

Anu said, 'I wonder how these people expect you to work as a team when they promote fierce competition. I can imagine the three of you like dogs, tied to ropes short enough not to reach a pile of food kept in the centre.'

'You are spot on, Anu. All day we bark at each other, making sure the other two don't get to eat anything either.'

Fresh from the berating, they met again and put their respective outputs on a laptop. They combined the parts and agreed not to send the output to the boss till all agreed. The person sending the final output would sign for all three so that the credit would not be awarded to the sender alone.

To ease the environment, they decided to go for a couple of drinks. This ostensible bonding time was essentially an intense bitching session. Much gossip was exchanged but you believed it at your own risk. You also ran the risk of being misquoted behind your back if you spoke too much.

As soon as the beers arrived, they put up a show of solidarity and toasted with a loud banging of the mugs.

'And I thought one only drinks with the best of buddies!' said Anu.

'You are living in your dream world, baby, away from our corporate madhouse.'

Over drinks, Satya had kicked off the much-awaited bad mouthing, 'Nitin is such a prick. He told me that I need to learn from how well both of you were performing.'

Amit was shocked, 'Nitin told me the same about you and Rekha.' They didn't need to ask what he had told Rekha.

But Rekha began by articulating her dislike for Jenny, 'I am going to take revenge for every insult the day I leave this place.'

Amit laughed at this, 'You will walk out quietly the day you quit. You don't want to ruin your character certificate for a flunky.' The session had continued till rather late that night as there were a lot of suppressed emotions.

Amit had asked Rekha, for the sake of formality, 'Can I drop you home?'

'Hey thanks, I will manage,' she said and Amit didn't look back. He had learnt in the last POSH training that if a man went out of his way to drop a female colleague, his motives may be questioned. POSH was the bank's Prevention of Sexual Harassment Committee.

Back in the present, Amit boasted to Anu, 'So, I just received my car from the valet and drove off. I was lucky there were no checks for drunk driving on the way.'

Anu was sufficiently entertained but not happy to learn that Amit was driving after drinking. She pursed her lips and told him, 'Amit, haven't I warned you so many times against driving if you drink even a drop of alcohol? You promised me you wouldn't.'

'Okay baby, don't get started. I am so sorry, this will not happen again.' *Actually, she is right, I should not have done that.*

His early apology contained the situation and the relaxed midweek holiday continued.

Chapter 8

Nitin was at his desk, poring over a large document. It listed the terms and conditions of a complex financial deal between a large Indian company and a Korean pension fund. British Bank was just an intermediary but would pocket a big fee for arranging this funding for the Indian company. Through the deal, the Korean pension fund would earn a higher interest income than what they would earn investing in South Korea.

It seemed like yesterday that he was lured to British Bank by a high-profile head hunter even though it was five years ago. The bank laid out the proverbial red carpet and paid him a generous joining bonus. He joined the sales team reporting to Vikram.

Then, a year ago, around this time, while he was taking stock of the business, his phone rang, 'Please call me from one of the conference rooms, this is Ernest.' Ernest was Vikram's boss.

Nitin could feel his heart pound. It was unusual to get a call from one's super boss, even though Nitin was on good terms with him. Actually, better than good. Of late, Ernest was taking Nitin's feedback on important matters and had even praised him for a few transactions. Nitin had also taken the cue and shared the gossip from the India office with him. They inadvertently ended up bitching about Vikram, 'Don't get me wrong, Vikram is a great guy but he is getting a bit complacent. I think the Indian market has enormous potential and we need to be more aggressive to capitalise on it.'

Such words were music to the senior management's ears. They were always on the lookout to cull old bulls from the herd and send them to the gallows. At the same time, they were looking for younger bulls who could keep the profit generation going at a feverish pace.

In the conference room, Ernest had come straight to the point, 'Congratulations, Nitin. The day you have been waiting for has come. You are being appointed Head of Sales for India starting today.'

Nitin was pleasantly shocked. His hands trembled with excitement and the phone receiver shook. He felt a sudden rush of adrenaline and big dollar signs flashed before his eyes. It was bound to happen someday but he hadn't expected it so soon.

'That's really great news, Ernest! I cannot thank you enough for giving me this opportunity!' Nitin lost no time in giving Ernest the credit.

'Oh, you deserve every bit of it, Nitin. Moreover, you will break this news to Vikram and ask him to vacate his cabin for you. He will report to you and will occupy your erstwhile seat outside, on the dealing floor.'

Nitin took a moment to absorb this. They had made Nitin the boss and had demoted Vikram to a mere team member. As he searched for a response, Ernest blurted, 'I know it takes time to adjust but we don't have the luxury of time. HR will hand over the new employment letters for you and Vikram. Then, you can inform Vikram. Cheers and good luck!'

As soon as Nitin got both letters from HR, he went to a secluded conference room. First, he read his promotion letter. He would be a Managing Director. It had a more than a decent increase in salary and allotment of stock options. Then, with bated breath, he opened Vikram's letter. It was terse and made reference to some previous discussions with him. They had downgraded him from Managing Director to Director, with new compensation figures, naturally. Nitin wondered why he had to deliver the terrible blow to Vikram.

Perhaps it was akin to the induction of a new member into the mafia, Nitin remembered thinking. The rookie was given an assassination to finally test his toughness. If the target was eliminated successfully, the new member was given a hero's welcome and inducted as an equal.

He exited the conference room, kept his letter in his office bag and went to Vikram's cabin. He knocked but barged in without waiting for an answer. Vikram was on the phone and motioned for him to sit down. But Nitin preferred to stand, his feet trembling with apprehension. The second Vikram's call ended, Nitin spoke, half-dazed, 'Vikram, I was told by Ernest and by HR to convey a message to you.'

'Oh, is it? What was it that Ernest couldn't tell me directly?' Vikram was irritated as usual, and looked like he had a premonition of what was happening.

'Starting today, I am Managing Director of Sales in India and you will be a team member occupying the desk outside this room.' Nitin tried to pack all the information in one sentence. Vikram's face turned pale.

He handed Vikram the letter and hurried out of his room, giving him a few hours to move his stuff out of the room onto the new desk. Very soon the news would be public and it would be difficult for Nitin to hide his jubilation and for Vikram to hide his fall.

Nitin knew that few people survived without adding much economic value. Joe was one of them, but such people were high on the political quotient. The trick was to keep your political activity higher than that of your team members. This meant sucking up to the bosses to such an extent that they didn't have any bandwidth left for anyone else. *Vikram had faltered at this. It worked out well for me though—I had unfettered access to Ernest.*

While Nitin was still pondering over how he would face Vikram again, he got another call from Ernest, who was elated. 'Hey mate, well done. You executed my plan flawlessly.'

Vikram had just tendered his resignation and left the office. 'Cheers and congratulations again!'

As soon as Ernest hung up, it dawned on Nitin—the plan. They never wanted Vikram to stay in the bank in the new role. So, they made him an awful offer through a subordinate. They made Nitin humiliate him so that he, like any self-respecting Markets bull, walked out gracefully. Vikram was financially secure, though still gunning for more—maybe a fourth or fifth million-dollar property, a couple of holiday homes and a 40 feet yacht off the harbour near the Gateway of India. That had been the last of Vikram he ever saw.

Joe had been next to congratulate Nitin. 'Well done, man. I always knew you had it in you.' *I am ahead in the game, though. You better not play with me.*

Nitin had replied, 'Thanks, boss,' acknowledging his authority. Joe could breathe a bit easy as the new bull would take time to mature.

Embracing his new responsibilities had been exciting and punishing. He maintained his desk on the dealing floor as well as the cabin to give a hands-on impression to the team. It was important to keep an eye on the schmucks, lest they slacken the pace or tried to backstab him. The way he had displaced his boss to become the alpha male would serve as an example for ages; or at least till one of the calves in the room became sufficiently strong to challenge him. It was inevitable and he understood that. But he was determined to prolong the stint for as long as possible and earn as high a share as he could.

The strong whiff of a musk deodorant invaded his thoughts as Joe tapped him on the shoulder and brought him back to the present. 'Now that Jorge is visiting us, we have to put up a great show for him.'

'Sure, Joe. It goes without saying. Jorge is even more powerful now. I still remember when I met him for the first time few years back,' Nitin cringed as he recalled a painful memory, 'Can you believe it? I ended up calling him Jorge.'

'Oh man, I see, you too seem to have committed the mistake!' Joe laughed.

'Yes, my enthusiasm was crushed as he gave me an insulting glance, my hand still hanging out in the hope of being shaken. He looked at Vikram who quickly jumped in with a snigger, "Nitin, his name is pronounced as Horhè."'

'What? Vikram didn't tell you this before his arrival?'

'I meekly withdrew my hand and kept it in my pocket as if I was hugging a rejected child. Vikram had hidden the secret of his name's pronunciation from everyone and used it as a nuclear missile to wipe out any competition,' Nitin said.

'Ha ha, now I understand the seed of your hatred towards Vikram was sown that very day.'

'So, here I am, ready to welcome Jorge, nah Horhè,' Nitin had had the last laugh. *I just love being the undisputed king of sales and the power that comes with it.*

'Please show me the initial draft of the presentation soon. I am sure you will have a couple of tough rounds of review with your three schmucks.'

'I sure will. Getting any kind of quality work out of these people is so tough. They think that merely coming to office and booking a few deals and revenue is enough.'

Joe left for a doctor's appointment in the middle of the day—a perk of being a senior. And how they would scoff at any schmuck trying to run personal errands during a workday!

Joe understood that he could not keep everyone in the jungle hungry. Even a lion needs a council of ministers to rule. So, he had decided to create a close circle of insiders. They were like hyenas around a pride of lions; Nitin was one such hyena. He just left enough for these hyenas to feel important and motivated, to keep all the peripheral animals sufficiently scared. Joe had created such an atmosphere at work that people had to think twice before speaking.

Once, Satya had been invited to a tournament to be held abroad and sponsored by a client. He was particularly happy that Nitin was not invited by the client to that event. He assumed that this instance would show that he was doing all the client coverage independently, contrary to what Nitin claimed.

Satya went over to Joe's desk and flaunted the invitation card, 'See, I am the only one to get invited to this India-Pakistan cricket series in Canada.'

Joe gave him a stern look. 'So, have you already closed the large deal you were supposed to be working on?' He beat a hasty retreat.

Chapter 9

After drinking with Amit and Rekha that night, Satya had not been as lucky. He had barely made it to Marine Drive when his car was stopped by a pot-bellied constable. The constable gestured for him to lower the window. As soon as he did, the constable's head was inside the car, so close that both of them could smell each other's breath—the constable could smell the liquor and Satya, the tobacco-laced betel nuts.

He asked Satya, 'Sir, what's your name?' and, as soon as he opened his mouth to answer, his breath gave him away. He had taken the precaution of using a strong mouth freshener but apparently it had failed to do its job.

The constable asked him to pull the car aside and step out. Then he summoned his colleague. Sub-inspector Pawar ran over with the breath analyser, aware that it would be a big catch. The results of the breath analyser test were a mere formality because once you were caught, the absolute level of alcohol didn't matter. In any case, the machine usually exaggerated the alcohol percentage. Satya only had a few moments to take control of the situation. *Think, Satya. Think. Once these jerks write out a challan in your name, there is no looking back.*

He turned to the lady constable, who looked more reasonable, and mumbled, 'Wait ma'am, I am sure we can work this out. I only had a small drink.'

She smiled. 'Everyone says that.'

'No ma'am, I am telling the truth. I don't know how the reading on that machine is so high. You see I can walk and talk properly. Let me know what I can do to get out of here?'

The lady constable more than got the hint and walked over to her senior. They consulted in whispers. She returned, still smiling, and mildly chided him, 'Why do you educated and well-dressed people do such things?'

'I swear, I will never do this again, ma'am.' *Oh, just take some money and get it over with. There's nothing that money can't buy.*

'If I book you now, you will be arrested and presented at court tomorrow. My boss says we can let you go as you don't look like a criminal, but only if you promise not to do it again.' Satya knew that the last part of the sentence was merely a verbal moral policing to hide the guilt of accepting bribes. The case was settled for ten thousand rupees—a small price to pay considering that he would have to explain himself at work if the police registered a formal case. If things took an ugly turn, he could also lose his job.

There was just one hitch, he was not carrying that much cash. The kind policewoman allowed him to walk to an ATM nearby and withdraw the cash. However, she asked him to keep his mobile phone inside the car and lock it. *These guys are two steps ahead of the game. She doesn't want me to call a vigilance squad. Anyway, I am hardly in a position to afford such shit.* He just wanted to pay up and leave. He hoped he wouldn't get caught again the same night.

As he was driving away, his mobile rang. It was Kakoli, his wife.

She asked, 'Where are you? When can I expect you home? What would you prefer for dinner?'

He directed all his irritation at her, 'What the heck, Kakoli? I am driving and you are bombarding me with so many questions. I had an important client event and will be home in an hour.' He lived in Andheri west, about thirty kilometres from work. Yet another victim of the Western 'Express' Highway. *I don't care about dinner as long as I get to eat something.* He hung up without waiting for her response.

'Client event' or 'evening meeting' meant a free drinking license for him. It was too complicated to explain at home why he needed to get drunk so frequently with a few random people who just happened to be his colleagues. Once in a while there were genuine client meetings, where he ended up drinking a lot more even if the client drank very little or nothing at all. Such luxury billed on the corporate credit card was one of the many perks of the job that he enjoyed thoroughly.

Kakoli was from Asansol, a small city in West Bengal. Well-educated and multitalented, like most middle-class Bengalis, she was still adjusting to the ways of this maddening city and her husband's puzzling work life.

Her parents were sold on Satya the moment they saw the marriage proposal—that is, his salary. Their idea of a banker was more of a grey safari suit clad middle-aged man with thick glasses and a pair of black sandals. That banker would leave home at 9 with a three-boxed lunch, on his Priya scooter and would come back home promptly at 6 in the evening.

But here she had Satya, leaving home sharp at 7:30 in the morning with no fixed time of return. The only reason she did not complain was the fat pay package and the year-end moolah that Satya was collecting for their 'bright and secure future.'

She also put up with his many antics and irritable behaviour due to these perks. She had never seen such frequent drinking at her parents' house. Once in a while, her father would drink a couple pegs of whiskey with his colleagues. The days he would drink, he would not talk to any of his children lest he gave away the secret. His mouth would be full of betel leaves to camouflage the smell. The children understood and dared not ask baba anything.

Even with such infrequent drinking, her mother would not miss an opportunity to take pot-shots at him using the choicest adjectives. Baba decided not to speak to her as well on those nights, and he hit the bed snoring, wearing a vest riddled with holes, his belly moving up and down rhythmically. She remembered the way he snorted and breathed through his open mouth—it was enough to fill the room with gusts of air even in the absence of electricity. Back then, they would get electricity for only three to four hours a day. One of the things she loved about Mumbai was the uninterrupted power supply.

In the early days of their marriage, Kakoli's lower middle-class values prompted her to prepare good food for her husband and to wait for him to have dinner. But Satya's schedule was so erratic that she had decided to have her dinner by 9. She would buzz him at around 8:30 to find out when he would reach home and then proceed to finish dinner in case he was late. To her amazement, Satya didn't mind this at all. She suspected that it freed him from the guilt of coming home late so regularly.

But she was also worried that such frequent drinking and smoking would take a toll on his health. Satya blamed his smoking on his college friends in Kolkata and claimed that the drinking was required to entertain clients and bosses. Recently, she had also been upset about Satya's tendency to pick up expensive whiskey bottles from duty free shops while returning from his many trips overseas.

She did not know anything about these trips other than the destinations. Satya had explained that multinational banks often sent their employees to international financial centres like

Singapore, Hong Kong, London and New York for networking and training. And like all the other superficially explained aspects of his job, she had no choice but to buy this explanation.

Actually these trips, though disguised as training programs, were meant to get employees hooked on free business class travel, five-star hotels, booze and other freebies. As the young bankers gladly accepted these perks, they became increasingly dependent on their job. Over time, the bankers would book high-end resorts for their personal and family travel also as it became unthinkable to stay in a resort of a lower quality after tasting luxury.

Satya rang the bell thrice to indicate the tearing hurry. His bladder was almost bursting and he hadn't wanted to stop on the way home after the incident on Marine Drive.

Such routine drinking also caused him severe headaches the next morning but he quietly popped a pill and never shared the fact with Kakoli or with his colleagues—he feared the former's concern and the latter's ridicule.

As soon as Kakoli opened the door, Satya brushed passed her without a word and rushed to the washroom. She was used to him coming home in such a condition.

Satya returned and slumped on the sofa, unfastening his already loosened tie. 'Oh my God, what a day.' *I need to look exhausted to show her that I work hard.*

'Looks like you had a tiring day, jol khabo?' She asked if he needed water.

He nodded, drank the water quietly and asked her, 'And how was your day?'

Kakoli didn't want to burden him with the mundane details of running a household and just shared a few important things, like his dad's call. 'Baba was livid that you have not called them for over three weeks.'

Even though Satya carried a mobile phone, a Blackberry and had a ten-line phone at his desk, it somehow never occurred to him to call his wife or his parents. *But I am sending them more money every month than their government pension.*

'I will call him tomorrow. It is too late now,' he winked at Kakoli. *We hardly have an hour of quality time to spend with each other.* All her frustration and anger vanished with this romantic gesture from Satya.

'O baba, this rohu fish in mustard gravy is too yum, Kakoli!'

'Why all this flattery now? This is how I usually cook.' *He really appreciates my hard work. What else do I need?*

'No, it's tasting much better today. The mustard flavour is just right, a bit more and it would have been bitter. A bit less, it would have been tasteless.' *Appreciating a woman is the best way to ensure her dedication.*

'Now I am on cloud nine.'

'Even my mother can't make fish curry as good as this. But let us keep this between the two us,' he laughed heartily. Kakoli accepted the compliments and gave him a loving glance. She liked the quiet dinners at home. The praise was a bonus and an endorsement of what she had chosen to do.

Satya now observed how sensuous Kakoli looked in a cotton sari with a sleeveless blouse. *She is a dark beauty.* He said to her, 'And you look stunning too. I like the way you have maintained yourself even after five years of marriage.' Actually, she looked nothing less than a Bollywood starlet. As soon as he finished dinner, they found themselves rolling over each other in bed.

'Look Satya, I don't know much of what you do. We don't get to spend a good amount of time with each other, but I hope you love me and keep loving me.'

'I do, Kakoli and I will forever.' It was all she wanted to hear. Their marital bliss had not yet faded.

Chapter 10

The day had come. The three schmucks collated their disjointed parts of the presentation and gave Nitin the scrambled output. His response, at first, was meant simply to humiliate them—he gave a long, hearty, derisive laugh. Amit had a hard time suppressing his anger while Satya and Rekha, used to Nitin's thrashing, didn't get flustered.

'On page two, I don't like this sentence. What is this graph doing at the bottom?' Nitin proceeded to take it apart sentence by sentence, page by page.

The schmucks were staring hard at the polished wooden table. Whoever made eye contact would have to bear the brunt of Nitin's anger. By the end of the review, which had lasted 30 minutes and felt more like a biopsy, Rekha knew they were going to spend the night at the office with the presentation, pizza and coffee. Amit was mentally cursing Nitin and Joe while Satya was trying to be optimistic. *It's not too bad, it just needs a bit of editing and polishing.*

They decided to meet at 6 to rework the presentation.

At 8, Rekha started making her usual excuses. 'I am a bit under the weather,' she whimpered. 'I have tried to finish the amendments to my part as quickly as possible.'

She had a habit of chickening out of group tasks after contributing the minimum work possible. But Amit and Satya knew there was no point making her stay. She was the closest to Nitin among the three of them, so any complaints were likely to backfire.

Given that it was a lost cause, Satya tried to score brownie points with her by sympathizing, 'I see you look a bit down today. Why don't you carry on? Amit and I will finish and wind it up in the next couple of hours.' Amit nodded in agreement but wanted to kill Satya for this.

Once out of the office, Rekha made it a point to inform Nitin. She called him, 'Hi Nitin, I have incorporated all your feedback in the presentation deck. You know how it is with Amit and Satya, they are so inefficient! They are still scratching their heads. I had no patience and instead of waiting for their corrections, I took care of it myself.'

'Okay, what are they doing now?'

'They have decided to party in the office over coke and pizzas. I just hope they don't mix some rum with the coke.' He chuckled and asked her to leave… as if she was waiting for that.

As soon as she was out of sight, Amit snapped, 'What the hell did you just do? You allowed her to go? Now, we better do a good job or risk getting more of Nitin's criticism.'

'Fuck you man. Who offered his arm to her when Jenny skinned her alive? If I didn't politely agree to her departure, she would have gotten Nitin's permission anyway. Now at least we can claim the credit for whatever we produce.'

Little did he know that the credit was already taken.

On the way home, Rekha inadvertently started comparing Nitin and Neeraj. Nitin's great physique, his well-built arms and broad chest underneath the tight-fitting shirts were not lost on her. *If only Neeraj could work on his body a bit and cut that flab. I could have tolerated his bulging belly if he made it up through his behaviour, but even that is too much to ask for now. Our sex life is so dysfunctional. I can't remember when we did it last.*

In that moment, she decided she would try to rekindle the fire tonight. She may have to overlook certain things but she was determined to make a conscious effort.

She reached home around 9 and discovered a huge mess in the living room. There was a large bowl of popcorn on the table in front of the couch, with its contents strewn across the floor. A couple of beer bottles were lying flat on the floor, and she tripped over one and almost fell. On the verge of losing it, she reminded herself of the resolution she had made on the way home.

Meanwhile, Neeraj hadn't even acknowledged her presence. He stared at the TV, transfixed—Arsenal was playing Barca. 'Be careful and don't break my beer bottle,' he finally said.

That was it. All of Rekha's plans for the night vanished and she banged a beer bottle on the TV. The sound and the interruption to his viewing finally caught Neeraj's attention and he looked at her.

'Bloody hell, you've ruined my mood!' he shouted. 'I am heading to the Manchester United bar to watch the match.'

'Go wherever you want. I don't care. Get lost!' Rekha was in tears now. There was no point trying to communicate with him, she realised. He picked up the car keys and rushed out and she changed into an old nightgown, too tired for anything but sleep.

As she was brushing her hair, she noticed Neeraj's phone vibrating. Friend X was calling him but Rekha thought that the girl in the photo looked rather well-endowed to be friends with this jerk. She didn't answer the phone. However, she could not resist the urge to check his messages.

The next hour was the most excruciating of her life. She felt utter revulsion at the messages Neeraj had exchanged with his bevy of girlfriends. The sexually explicit photos, the late night conversations—she was almost impressed by how imaginative a sloth like Neeraj could be. She wondered how he was able to attract such beauties with his 44-inch waist and found an answer in the alerts from his bank about regular payments to unknown accounts.

Rekha was in agony. She considered confronting him right away but was afraid of how he may react. There was no one at home and he had a history of being violent. She shed a few tears for her marriage before giving in to exhaustion. As she lay in bed, her thoughts were swirling and she planned a course of action. *My decision to not start a family with this scumbag was a good one. I was right to hold on to my job and maintain my finances separately.*

She locked the bedroom door before she finally fell asleep. *Once you lose trust, you cannot stay in the same room.*

Chapter 11

When Rekha entered the office that morning, she found Samir and Alex hovering over her desk. This was a bad sign. Samir was the head of Debt Capital Markets (DCM), which helped clients borrow billions of dollars from international investors by issuing bonds. And Alex was a senior relationship manager. Both of them together in the dealing room indicated a major goof-up was about to happen. Samir was a good-humoured person of medium build, who was more interested in talking about his meditation escapades, running adventures and exotic salads than anything business related. Everyone wondered how he had survived so long in this dog-eat-dog world.

Alex was more like a banker than Samir, with a large paunch and a never-ending appetite for chocolate shakes and croissants. The bigger the deal he was working on, the bigger the calorie boost he needed to keep going.

Trying to hide her escalating anxiety, Rekha greeted them enthusiastically. But she was met with a dry 'Morning.' It was early in the day but Alex was panting and sweating profusely. Rekha asked, 'All well with you, Alex?'

She regretted asking it as soon as she did, however.

'Nothing's well this morning. I ran here from the parking lot—Samir has been calling me frantically all morning. In fact, we called you also.' Rekha frowned. This was about that large deal Nitin had entrusted her with. The client was acting funny. They had been sure they had got the deal because Nitin's presentation to the client—Rekha had crafted the idea—had been a hit. Samir was in charge of issuing bonds and Alex, the quintessential relationship manager, was keeping a tight leash on all parties.

Samir spoke with a slight smile, as if he was not very disturbed, 'The client bounced off our idea with another bank, which agreed to the same deal at a much lower price.' This was how innovation was rewarded in banking. Clients were also notorious for not paying any fee for the ideas and services, forcing banks to hide their margins.

Rekha was upset but also relieved that it wasn't her fault. If the deal fell through, she quickly surmised, they would blame Alex for not maintaining a close enough relationship with the client. Samir could also be blamed for tardy execution of the bond deal, delaying the whole process.

While the three of them were analysing the situation, Nitin joined them. 'God damn it, what were both of you doing, letting the client slip away?' It was a pointed question that made Samir and Alex visibly uncomfortable. Just then, an email alert popped up on Rekha's screen and she said, 'Come guys, Rakesh has summoned us to his room.'

Inside the CEO's sprawling office, everyone was on edge. Samir and Alex had already briefed him. Breaking the bad news to a superior has the disadvantage of you nearly getting eviscerated but it also allowed you to explain your side of the story and influence the boss to favour you. And senior managers were always short on time and wilful victims of biases.

Rakesh was ready to hang the guilty even without hearing out all the parties. He shouted, 'Nitin, your team has stuffed up again.'

'I didn't get you, Rakesh?' Nitin was surprised to see the tide turn against him.

'Why was the idea presented so late? Due to your delay, the bond deal was postponed and the client got more time to seek out the competition.' Rakesh was understandably furious because he would have the largest dent in his bonus.

Nitin submitted meekly, 'But we presented the idea very quickly, and in fact it was a very innovative plan.' In such situations, 'we' was a convenient way to take all the credit from your team members even though his only contribution was handing over the problem to Rekha.

But Samir and Alex had convinced him well. Rakesh gave his summary judgement, 'Nitin, you will pay for this.' It was beneath his dignity to comment on Rekha's role, separated as she was from him by three layers of the organisation. He swivelled to the side to face his computer and dismissed the meeting. There was no question of re-evaluation; Rakesh was already on his next case.

Nitin and Rekha sought Joe to discuss this and he told them, in no uncertain terms, that it was their fault. 'I don't care about the client or the deal but managing Rakesh and the system should be your top priority.' They heard him out. Such tips were hard to find in management books and if a senior shared them with you, you better listen up.

'Coffee?' Nitin offered.

'Yes, sure,' Rekha nodded and they went out for coffee.

Nitin started, 'I am utterly disgusted. How can Rakesh be so rash? Can't he see through the obvious lies Samir and Alex fed him?'

Rekha, though less experienced, still offered some advice, 'See, these seniors have very little time for a full-fledged inquiry. If they do, the cases will drag on like they do in Indian courts. They go by their preconceived notions.'

'Yeah, he has clearly been kept in good humour by others, and they are benefiting. We need to remember the consequences before we treat someone like crap, especially a senior.'

'Why do you say that? Is there more to this?' Rekha was curious.

Joe and Nitin were the star performers for many years. Rakesh had joined last year and they had snubbed him in every possible way. In his initial days, whenever Rakesh stepped onto the dealing floor, they pointedly ignored him. But Rakesh was a mature and battle-hardened player. During his long stint at Citibank, he had worked extensively on his political skills. He had also acquired an accent, as if he had lived in New York all his life. In fact, he had spent only five years abroad but it had given him an edge. He was also deft at tactical and strategic moves, making him fit to be CEO. When Joe and Nitin insulted him, he retreated and worked around the system to get them under his command. He began travelling to the regional head office in Singapore very frequently.

'You know, he impressed the management there with his Ferragamo ties, Zegna suits and his impeccable American accent,' Nitin rounded up.

Rekha giggled as she recalled the twang in Rakesh's voice. 'But these things alone cannot help in the long run, right?'

'Yes, true. He also provided some great analysis of the situation on the ground.'

'I can see that. It looks like he is here to play a long innings.' Rekha was enjoying this flow of useful information and wanted more. 'How do you know all this?'

'I am very close to Ernest and he told me about Rakesh's feedback to the global bosses—that the business heads in India were satisfied with sub-optimal performance and, as CEO, he needed direct command to get them to achieve more.'

'Really a lot to learn from this guy!' Rekha admired.

'It wasn't surprising when all the business heads in India started receiving direct orders from the top to keep Rakesh involved in all matters—minor or major. Such is the power of networking and business travel, if used properly,' Nitin said.

'I am beginning to learn these tricks through some rather unpleasant experiences.'

'We cannot be off guard even for a moment.'

'Right! Today's client email arrived at 1 am, informing us about the developments. Samir and Alex read the email first, strategised and got Rakesh on their side.' *Keeping the Blackberry handy at night is another skill I need to master, even if it ruins my sleep and peace of mind.*

'But Rakesh has always been partial to them. From the moment he joined, Samir and Alex—below average performers from a revenue generation perspective—made him feel all important.'

'So, there is a reason for what happened today.'

Nitin gave a slight nod. 'Whenever Alex met Rakesh, he had comments and observations prepared—like "Hey Rakesh, dandy shoes! Where did you pick them up?"'

'What? That's sycophancy at its worst.'

'Yes, but Rakesh loves this. An opportunity to talk about his shoes from his summer in London.'

Rekha was amused. *A lesson to master. If your business performance is not great, you do need to compensate with flattery.*

They decided to go out for a drink in the evening to talk more at leisure. They enjoyed each other's company, but they needed to be back at their desks soon or tongues would wag.

But back at her desk, Rekha found it difficult to focus on work. She kept returning to the pictures of Friend X on Neeraj's phone. The girl's curvaceous figure and sultry lips troubled her even more when she caught a glimpse of herself in the mirror. Over the years, she had developed a small tyre around her once-slim waist and she looked five years older than she was. She was angry and irritated with Neeraj but was upset with herself as well.

Adding to the frustration was the trouble at work. She was used to such turbulence but this time it rattled her. In her many years in banking, she had never felt that she would last long. One's survival depended on so many factors in addition to performance that it was difficult to fully fathom. This anxiety always kept her on guard and she felt like a lamb lined up for slaughter. She realised that she needed to learn to use her charisma to survive in this corporate jungle.

Chapter 12

Around seven in the evening, Rekha and Nitin went to a bar a little away from the office, in the old commercial district of Mumbai. The place was dimly lit and already smelling of smoky whiskey thanks to the early drinkers. They sat in a far corner.

Nitin was tapping his fingers on the dark wooden table. 'I really like the way you think, Rekha. You are so much better than Amit and Satya. They refuse to learn their lessons and keep involving me in trouble along with themselves.'

'Ah, don't know about myself but those two are born losers. Their professional aptitude is mediocre and they fail to make it up with any extraordinary efforts.'

'Joe has been pressing me to teach those two a good lesson.'

'I have had the ill-fortune of working with them on the presentation for Jorge. And I will get the brickbats too for the poor quality of work.' Rekha was sharpening her political skills. *I have to crush them if I want to become Managing Director one day.*

By that time, they were down a couple of beers each and the mood was light. Nitin touched her on the wrist and said, 'You don't worry about it. I have to treat all of you the same in public but I fully understand who is contributing what.'

Rekha felt a nice tingle but was a bit surprised at the touch. It had been a long time since any man had touched her like that. The only contact she had at home was occasional run ins with Neeraj near the refrigerator or while grabbing the TV remote to change those sports channels.

Nitin pressed on, 'So, when it comes to rewards, both Joe and I will take care of you. This year's promotion cycle is around the corner and if you play your cards well, I will nominate you.'

Rekha wondered if he was suggesting she would have to get closer to him to get this promotion. *Why did I go for the expensive MBA and slog night after night if I was going to be an object of lust? For God's sake, I was top of my class at Wharton and no less than any man. Why should I have to stoop to get ahead in my career?*

While she was evaluating the situation, Nitin kept making his advances. They ordered the next round of beers and Rekha decided to be direct, 'Are you flirting with me or suggesting that I need to get closer to you to ensure my promotion?'

Nitin didn't look offended. 'Rekha, don't get me wrong. I confess, I genuinely like you. Your promotion is not in any way dependent on any favours. Work aside, I am still attracted to you.' He threw an arm around her for a gentle sideways embrace.

Rekha pulled herself away, trying not to offend him. 'Hey, I also like your company but given that both of us are married, let's maintain some distance.' She winked and chuckled to lighten the situation.

Nitin was confused whether it was a no or an indication to move ahead gradually. In his experience, girls specialised in the art of keeping men on standby. If need be, she could increase the intensity later. Still, they ended up having a good time and called it a night at ten.

On the way home, Nitin got to thinking about his days at IIM Ahmedabad. The girls from big city colleges didn't pay him any attention because of his modest beginnings and the resulting lack of polish gave him away. He used to watch the girls and boys flirting and longed to have a girlfriend. After graduating with top grades, he landed his dream job. With time and money and hard work at the gym, he acquired the polish, physique and power that made it difficult for girls to ignore him. *This is my time and I will make the most of it.*

Nitin explained the outing at home to Vani as the usual 'unexpected client meeting' while Rekha didn't need to explain anything to anyone.

Chapter 13

Jorge's visit was now just around the corner. It was late in the evening and Nitin was sitting at the head of the table with the three schmucks, getting restless with every revision of the presentation. For the last few days, they had been advised to drop everything to focus on getting it right.

The last version of the presentation that Nitin showed to Joe came very close to getting approved. 'This looks better but I am not getting that AHA feeling. Let me suggest some more improvements,' Joe had said. *If I manage to impress Jorge, I will secure my position for a couple more years.*

But everyone knew that the presentation would keep getting revised till the last moment. Joe and Nitin were trying to outguess Jorge—they kept thinking of new ideas and continued pushing the schmucks to update the presentation. Joe would suddenly have an issue with the font size, style and design while Nitin would change his mind about the structure. 'This looks run of the mill. Even monkeys on the street can give this output. I don't know why we hire MBAs and pay them so much! Where's the EDGE in this, guys?'

'Guys' was the most civilised noun he had used for them so far. He had exhausted all the expletives that could be used without provoking bullying lawsuits against him and the bank. Just last year, an employee had sued her boss at the bank's New York office for calling her a black monkey. The accused had been fired and the woman had received hefty monetary compensation.

Thus, the bank's management was scared of any lawsuits based on racial or sexual discrimination and bullying. The bank's anti-bullying policy defined bullying as 'creating a fearful and severely intimidating work environment.' But by that definition, most of the time spent at work could be classified as bullying.

Nitin had realised, however, that Indian courts and laws made suing the bank a much less attractive proposition than that overseas. In India, the judge may as well joke, 'What's wrong if your boss called you an idiot or a chimpanzee? You must have behaved like one.' Such thoughts and no possibility of getting a fat compensation or another job after the lawsuit kept employees in India away from such misadventure.

Satya was jolted to the present by someone moving his chair vigorously. It was Nitin, who had been rebuking them for a long time while Satya had been day dreaming

Satya mumbled an apology but he was livid because he hadn't been able to go out for a smoke in the last two hours. The other two kept themselves alert with tea and coffee but his mind refused to focus without its constant nicotine supply. His frequent requests to be allowed to go for a drag were met with sarcastic comments by Amit and Rekha, neither of whom smoked. And he didn't want to risk stepping out alone.

It would cost him dearly if Nitin found out that he was loitering on the street while the other two worked. Nitin had left instructions for the next revision and they had to get to it right away. He would be working at his desk till they showed him the output while Joe had left work but was awaiting the presentation before going to sleep.

As soon as Nitin stepped out of the room to take a call, the three of them heaved a sigh of relief. Satya broke the silence, 'People, our minds seem to have numbed sitting in this moronic conference room. We need some fresh air, let's go down for a five-minute break.'

Rekha reacted predictably, 'I didn't know cigarettes were a source of fresh air. But anyway, I think I can do with a break too.'

Amit didn't want the two of them together as they might hatch some conspiracy against him. Whenever a project was on its way to go horribly wrong, every member concentrated more on how to cover his ass instead of trying to salvage the situation.

He said, 'I also want to go out. I'm feeling nauseous thanks to the strong musk smell. I think he overdid it today.' Everyone had a good laugh and the mood lightened.

The cool breeze on the street soothed their nerves for some time. Fort's famous street vendors were winding up their stalls and, in the distance, the magnificent Chhatrapati Shivaji Terminus stood, bathed in yellow light.

While Satya finally lit his cigarette, Rekha and Amit ordered tea for everyone. Rekha said, 'Nitin may come back and think that we have sneaked out. We should have invited him for tea also.'

Amit and Satya choked on their tea. 'Oh, tell me you are joking!' Satya spluttered.

'Why?'

'Nitin and Joe order from the gourmet coffee shops,' Amit said. 'They would never drink our street-shop masala tea.'

Satya added, 'They don't want to have anything to do with the low-ranking people. If Rakesh ever saw them standing at the street tea stall with us, it would kill their reputation, possibly even their careers.'

They returned after tea and got down to the presentation. It took them one more hour to complete all the changes and show it to Nitin. He was also tired, even after guzzling a couple of large americanos from Barista. Nitin shook his head. 'For now, I will send this to Joe. Tomorrow, we will finalise the stuff.'

His comment didn't reveal whether he thought the presentation was good, bad or ugly. They figured it was fine since Nitin was sending it to Joe, but they could never be sure. The bosses' philosophy was that as long as they were paying them a salary and the bonus, they need not confer other soft rewards like compliments or encouragement.

Those were the heady days of 2006, when the global markets were scaling one peak after another. The bank had healthy revenues and its bonus pool was better than ever before. It made sense for the minions to not worry about compliments and ignore the abuses in order to keep receiving the money.

The financial markets worldwide had become incredibly sophisticated and well-connected. Investors were taking massive risks, buying and selling large quantities of financial instruments and pocketing smart profits. Unlike in the real economy where entrepreneurs created industries, manufactured goods or delivered services, in the financial world, people played with money. The industrialist would borrow money, set up large factories, mobilise raw material, hire people, set up a distribution network and then hope to make some profit. But here the financial whiz-kids created money out of thin air, and got paid millions.

When Nitin left work, they decided to hit a bar close by for a quick beer. Satya was in an analytical mode. He twirled the few remaining strands of hair on his head and said, 'I can't figure out why these global heads get paid millions of dollars.'

'Bonus is nothing but a glorified term for the commission on the profits they produce,' Rekha sighed.

'But what about the risks they take? There are already some murmurs of a crash in the markets.'

'No one is paying attention to the risks. If there is a crash, the banks will lose much more than what they have earned in the last few years put together.'

'My brother-in-law is a hedge fund manager in London. I heard even he is reaping the big bucks. What exactly is a hedge fund?' Jealousy was getting the better of Amit.

'Hedge funds manage large chunks of money, as in billions of dollars, for wealthy clients, pension funds, insurance funds. They are big investors in all types of financial assets or securities,' Rekha responded.

Amit said, 'Hmm profits are pouring in, but I can tell that we are sitting on a ticking time bomb.'

'If *you* know this, then all the finance wizards must also know. Why are they still playing with fire?' asked Satya.

'For easy profits and big bonuses, you fool. The CEO of Citibank recently told the world, "This is a game of musical chairs, we must go around until the music stops."'

'Okay, Okay. I accept that. Now, answer one final question. Why is Jorge coming to India? He is the head of Asia. Why India?'

Rekha was irritated by his stupid question. She waved her hand in Satya's face as if waking him up, 'Hello, can't you see that this global risk-taking trend has brushed onto Indian companies as well?'

Indian companies had become large players in the foreign exchange and derivatives market under the guise of managing their business risk. They were striking large derivative deals with banks, making good profits and becoming bolder with their bets. Banks in India were pocketing big commissions.

'Jorge wants to put his stamp on this profitable business and push us to do even more,' continued Rekha.

'Is it good for us?' Satya asked.

'Who cares? Take your money and leave, that's the mantra in Markets. It is good for the job market.'

After a pause, Rekha said, 'Jorge is also coming here to sniff around. He doesn't want his shop to be robbed by the new entrants in the game.' India was attracting large investment banks like Merrill Lynch, Goldman Sachs and Lehman Brothers.

'Ah, now I know,' Satya was finally satisfied.

Rekha reached home around midnight and was greeted by the familiar sight of her portly husband lying drunk on the couch in front of the TV. After her discovery from the other day, she had stopped trying to correct Neeraj's behaviour. Instead, she was considering how to broach the subject without letting Neeraj know that she had gone through his phone.

Her first thought had been to call her mother. She was her best counsel and understood her well. *Mamma's prediction is coming true and our marriage has real problems. But calling her is fraught with complications. I don't think she is prepared to hear all the shocking details that I have unearthed. She may not react rationally or provide any useful advice.*

Breaking the news to her mother would also mean the point of no return. *Am I sure I can't handle this on my own? If I call her to be with me while I broach the subject with Neeraj, she may lose her cool with Neeraj. Perhaps I should do this on my own.*

Neeraj was still busy in the living room. Rekha went to the kitchen and brewed a cup of green tea for herself. It helped soothe her nerves and cleared her thoughts... whatever clarity was possible in this horrible situation. She sipped the warm tea and sat with her back supported by pillows on the bed. *All said and done, Mamma is the only one I can call for emotional and physical support.*

'Mamma, all is not well between us, my marriage is in trouble,' she didn't give too many details to avoid scaring her mother too much.

Asha was calm, as though she had seen it coming, 'You come over for a few days and talk it out with me.'

'Mamma, it will help if you can come here so I can gather the courage to speak to Neeraj. I have been postponing it because of work and also because I fear his reaction. You know he is volatile and may even resort to violence.'

Her mother reluctantly agreed to visit her. In the past, she hadn't particularly enjoyed her visits to their home. Neeraj's behaviour towards his mother-in-law was cold to say the least. He ignored her presence in the house, looked through her, and never addressed her directly, if at all.

Chapter 14

Joe was about to hit the bed when his Blackberry made a sound. He checked it immediately—he had been waiting for the presentation. It was 11 pm, he told his wife to go off to sleep and went into his study. Slightly apprehensive, he opened the presentation. He could not believe his eyes. The schmucks, under Nitin, had done a fabulous job.

Joe decided that he didn't need to comment as it was all in order and joined his wife in the bedroom.

The next morning, as Joe entered the office, Nitin and his team straightened up in their chairs. They were sufficiently prepared for more abusing and insults. He summoned them inside the conference room and asked them to be seated.

Joe said, 'So, I got the presentation last night and reviewed it. I will accept it in the current form because Jorge will be in the office tomorrow and we don't have time for further improvement.'

Despite his implication that the presentation was far from perfect, they took it as a tacit approval of what they had produced. If the work was truly not up to the mark, they knew that Joe would have made them work on it till the last moment.

The three of them had no idea about Jorge's itinerary so Amit paid an innocuous visit to Joe's secretary, Gita, a friendly enough lady. Amit liked to maintain a good relationship with her as secretaries could help where bosses refused to. He made light conversation with her about the weather or the crowd in local trains while trying to get a good look at her computer screen.

Luckily, Jorge's schedule was open on the screen and he could make out that Jorge would arrive at half past nine after having an early breakfast with Joe. He would then spend an hour on the internal presentation before going out for client meetings. In the evening, he would address an all-staff meeting and then a slot was marked for drinks and dinner with the entire Markets team.

Nobody had informed them about the evening's plan—it was characteristic of Joe. He would probably send the invite the same afternoon depending on Jorge's mood.

But it was a predictable schedule. The senior guys in the department always had the privilege of a meeting at the beginning of the visit. At breakfast, they would sufficiently brainwash the visitor even before he entered the office. Joe would likely reinforce his key messages about the business scenario and update Jorge about the next few guys he planned to fire in Markets to ensure a healthy 'churn.' He might also keep him informed about a couple of better performers, which would help in pushing through their promotions when the time came. All in all, Jorge's actual visit would be over before he even came into the office.

Chapter 15

The next day, everyone in the dealing room was dressed in crisp white shirts and ties, their jackets hanging on the back of their chairs. The traders were more relaxed and a few of them didn't wear a tie. A couple of the juniors were giving away their position by wearing a tie *and* a jacket.

Nitin got a text from Joe, 'The eagle has landed.' It meant Jorge would soon be escorted by Joe into the dealing room and be introduced to each person at their desk. It was a pointless exercise because there was no way Jorge would remember their names, but it had to be done.

Joe introduced Nitin briefly and then headed to the sales desk. Satya said, 'Hello Jorge, I am on the Corporate Sales team.' Proud to have pronounced his name correctly, Satya puffed up his chest.

Jorge punctured it just as swiftly, 'Hey, I just got to know that we are in terrible need of a few more deals from you.' That was the signal for Satya to hide for the rest of his visit.

Amit said a brief hello and didn't risk a wrong pronunciation or a fate like Satya's. Jorge returned his greeting and moved on.

Rekha knew that her professional talent and performance needed to be cemented by the right amount of kowtowing. She fell at Jorge's feet as he started praising her, 'Ah, so you are Rekha. I have heard a lot about you, of course all positive! Please continue the good work.'

This brief interaction had defined the pecking order in the sales team. While Rekha would definitely be promoted and paid well, Satya was close to the firing line. Amit was in the neutral zone and could still work on improving his performance.

The evening town hall, where Jorge was going to address the staff, was packed with people from across the bank. Rakesh opened with a brief introduction and said, 'We are thankful that you visited our office and took stock of the progress we have made so far.'

Jorge followed with a flamboyant speech in which he declared, 'We have done very well in our division this year and the bank has also met the profit projections globally.' He thanked everyone for their contribution and requested them to keep firing on all cylinders.

Hiding deep in the audience, Satya wondered how these global visitors always claimed the organisation was doing very well. All of this confidence vanished as soon as the employee demanded anything. Then, they would be reminded of cost pressures and business downturn. Such hypocrisy. Satya had come to understand, though a bit late, that everything need not be taken at face value. Everybody made statements that suited the situation and moved on.

All the minions on the dealing floor were invited for drinks and dinner with Jorge. Everyone pretended to be busy until about half past seven, as Jorge seemed to be transacting important business inside the glass-walled conference room. People kept glancing at it regularly to see if he was looking at them. He wasn't. He was busy reassuring his mother back home that he was safe and would not be mugged on Mumbai's streets.

Finally, the wait was over and Joe escorted Jorge out of the office. Their car left for the night's venue—the luxury restaurant Indigo, located close to Gateway of India in Colaba. Everyone else was ready to leave but nobody wanted to be the first to reach such a party because it would be construed as joblessness.

Around 8, Satya and Amit entered the large dining hall that Gita had reserved. It had an elegant white marble bar counter and an open area to accommodate 15-20 people. The authentic wooden flooring gave it an earthy feel that was complemented by the dark grey stucco walls. But Amit and Satya were embarrassed to be the first ones there and obviously the most ill-informed. Nitin had motioned Rekha in the office to stay and go with him a bit later.

Before the two of them could decide to exit and hide in their cars, they were greeted, or rather scoffed at, by Jorge. 'Wow, the team is already here!' Jorge's initial impression of Satya was reinforced—this prick was not performing well and was too eager to start gulping down alcohol at the bank's expense. Satya was cursing his luck. But soon, all looked well as the whole team arrived. While the sales team chatted with Jorge, he said, 'I compliment Joe and Nitin on the excellent presentation. Great job, guys!'

Nitin and Joe accepted the praise with a slight bow and smile. They didn't think it necessary to mention that the three standing right there had been instrumental in preparing the presentation. Of course, Jorge knew that but everyone was determined to feign ignorance.

People gathered around the large antique table in the room's centre while Jorge admired the large Mughal-style chandelier hanging above it. The lights were dimmed and the bartender distributed champagne flutes to all and handed Jorge a chilled bottle of Moet. 'It was fabulous to hear about your business plan. I am sure that the business in India is in safe hands,' Jorge declared as he popped the champagne.

Jorge raised a toast to the success of British Bank and the team drank to good times. Satya, not used to drinking bubbly, gulped it down and burped loudly. Joe was embarrassed and glared at Satya but Jorge laughed it off. The others delicately sipped their bubbly.

As the evening wore on, the alcohol flowed. Jorge was notorious for getting people drunk while holding onto his single glass of red wine. He ordered rounds of shots continuously and the employees figured that refusing to drink would be disrespectful. Rekha was already down a couple of Long Island iced teas in a bid to impress Joe and to also drown out her thoughts and personal troubles.

Satya was in great form and used this opportunity to make an impression. Emboldened by multiple shots of Laphroaig single malt whiskey, he approached Jorge, 'Hey Jorge, can I offer you some Cuban cigars?' They were prohibitively expensive but Satya knew he had the bank's credit card. Jorge was excited, 'Wow! You get them here? I wanted one so bad.'

'You get everything here, but at a price,' Satya winked.

Amit joined in with his wine glass, 'Are you liking it here?'

'Not bad, actually,' Jorge was enjoying himself. Both the schmucks were keeping him company and making sure he got whatever he wanted.

A small group started shaking a leg in the area in front of the bar. To everyone's surprise, Jorge joined them. Amit pulled in Rekha, though she was not in a mood to dance. As the dancing got wilder, most of the people came to the floor and it got crowded. Rekha was dizzy with alcohol and the pictures and messages on Neeraj's phone started flashing before her eyes. She felt uncomfortable with so many men around her and, though drunk beyond her capacity, she pulled herself away from the centre.

Satya and Amit had created a bit of a rapport with Jorge and had managed to salvage their reputation. Jorge was engaging in drinking games with them and the loser had to honour the bet by taking shots of whiskey.

Soon, the bets in the drinking game were raised and the loser had to climb onto the high bar counter and dance. Amit got the dubious honour to perform on the bar and Jorge thoroughly enjoyed it. He was drinking more now—he had saved his drinking appetite for later, unlike the amateurs who were crashing one after the other.

The party reluctantly ended at two in the morning. Jorge ridiculed the bill. Despite their best efforts, the bill had not exceeded a couple of lakhs, which was a mere five thousand US dollars for Jorge.

The seniors left in their chauffeur-driven vehicles. Rekha was almost unconscious and mumbling incoherently. Joe sent her home with the saintly Gita, who had not touched a drink all evening. None of the bank's male staff, senior or not, dared escort a drunk lady colleague anywhere.

Chapter 16

Satya, as usual, decided to ignore that he was drunk. He stepped out of the restaurant and called the valet with a hiccup, 'Aeyyy boss, can you get my caarrrrr?' The valet heard him slur and realised he was drunk. 'Sir, we have drivers available for hire. One can drop you home for a small fee.'

'Just shuttt uppp and get the caarrrr.' Satya could barely stand. The valet resolved never to give unsolicited advice and he brought Satya's car and opened the door for him. Satya staggered to the car, paused at the car's door and gave the valet a dirty look. 'You think I can't drive? I will show you.' He was certain that he could drive safely and drove rather well that night for a person who had had more than half a bottle of whiskey, numerous shots and Cuban cigars.

As he picked up speed on the Western Express Highway, he was blinded by large flashlights. He barely made out a faint figure waving in front of the car and his car rammed into a police barricade.

The policeman who had been waving at him to stop managed to jump out of his way at the very last minute.

He was surrounded by a battery of men in uniform but he could not make sense of what had happened. One officer opened the door of his car and asked him to step out. Satya could hear voices echoing as if from far away and the lights shone too brightly for him to see anything. The hollow voice boomed again, 'Sir, please get out of the car.' Once out, he tried to stand upright but staggered and fell flat on his face. They took a breath analyser test for the records and sent him to a government hospital nearby for a blood test.

Unlike in the previous cases, Satya didn't get any time to arrange a 'compromise' as he was drunk beyond any limit and also had nearly killed a policeman. At the hospital, they took his blood sample, confirmed the alcohol content and sent him to the police station. He was locked up inside a cage-like room with a small hole in a corner to be used as a toilet. It was filled with mosquitoes and the stench of urine.

This is a nightmare. In all the drama, he had also lost his mobile phone somewhere. *What would Kakoli be thinking?* He had told her he would be later than usual that night and she should not wait for him. But knowing her, she would definitely try to reach him. He cursed himself repeatedly but soon was fast asleep along with the other snoring bozos in the cell.

Satya was woken up by a heavy blow. It was the police constable, waking up the occupants of the cell like a shepherd does with his sheep. All of them were to be produced before the magistrate at the city court. Satya had a throbbing headache and the mixture of food and different types of alcohol he had consumed made him queasy.

Satya struggled to get on his feet. He wanted to pee badly and had no choice but to relieve himself in the corner that was already dirty beyond imagination. Before he could, however, he found himself bent double, puking all over the urinal and himself.

His clothes were now dirty and a terrible smell emanated from them. He felt a little less queasy but his headache was worsening. And he was terrified that now there was little difference between his appearance and that of the petty criminals holed up with him. *The judge will not be inclined to show any leniency with me looking and smelling like a pig.*

Desperate to ease the hangover, he asked the constable, 'Can I have some lime juice please?' The constable laughed heartily and spat his pan masala in a corner inside the police station. 'Looks like your first time here. Just shut up and follow the instructions. Don't act smart with me. There is a tap in the corner if you want to drink some water.'

Satya didn't want to contract cholera or jaundice, so he chose to remain dehydrated. The headache was killing him. People around him looked more at ease and happy. One of them was whistling and seemed to enjoy his time in the lock-up. Soon, the cop asked them to march towards the exit.

Satya heard a woman's voice calling his name. Kakoli was there. All his plans to make a flimsy excuse to keep this episode a secret were shattered. His mobile phone and wallet had been confiscated by the police and, when Satya didn't reach home that night, Kakoli tried his number, the inspector answered and told her the story.

She had been imagining that Satya had met with an accident and was dreadfully hurt. When she heard about the arrest, her fear turned into relief and joy before giving way to anger. She had warned him so many times not to drive if drunk.

Satya was terrified about what would happen at court and later with Kakoli. She was crying but spoke calmly, 'Hope you are fine. I was getting all kinds of ideas.'

Satya nodded, 'I am sorry you had to come here because of me.'

'Let's hope you are freed soon,' she maintained her cool, saving the fighting for home. She followed the police van in a taxi. They reached the court and Satya was made to sit in a line with the others to be produced in front of the judge.

A friend had advised Kakoli to hire a local lawyer on the spot. Sure enough, she was approached by a lawyer who seemed to understand the entire situation. He started, 'Here you are. Another sophisticated and high class person caught in this dirty system. Don't worry, I will get your husband out with a warning and a small fine. Does he have a history of drinking and driving?'

Kakoli didn't know of any such incident and Satya confirmed he was clean. All his other cases had been settled by paying cash, leaving no trail in the system. The lawyer advised him to admit his mistake and commit to never driving in a drunken state.

At 11, the judge, a middle-aged lady, entered. This court was very different from the ones he had seen in movies. There was no box for him to stand in and the staff were not wearing antiquated uniforms. The judge sat on a rickety chair that seemed too weak to bear her weight. Her desk was a cheap metal table with files piled high. In fact, tall cabinets filled with dusty files lined the walls—no wonder millions of cases were pending in Indian courts.

The inspector read out the charges against Satya while he stared at the rugged floor. The judge asked, 'Are these charges true?'

'Yes ma'am, but I am sorry for what happened. I was driving very slowly and could not see the police barricade because of the flashing lights.'

'Hmm.'

'I promise it will never happen again,' Satya said, looking genuinely apologetic. *I better convince her that I am sorry or she will throw me in for six months. What will happen to my job and my career?*

The judge seemed to know the drill. She fined him ten thousand rupees and issued a stern warning. She added that, if caught again, he would be put behind bars for one year and his driving license would be cancelled for life. With this brief proceeding, he was set free.

But his troubles were just starting. Nitin had also called his mobile to check whether he had reached home safely and had heard the story from the inspector. Moreover, in the taxi on the way home, Kakoli burst out, 'What is all this? In the name of your job you have been drinking incessantly. I am calling your parents now to tell them everything.'

Satya, his head now in excruciating pain, shouted, 'This is between us, Kakoli. I am admitting my fault. Why do you want to drag my parents into this?'

Kakoli was crying bitterly, 'I need to tell them because this is about your conduct. You could have crushed a pedestrian last night.'

Satya was defiant, 'If you call them, it will be the last time you see me. I am telling you it's not a big deal. It's not a criminal offence, just a civil offence, and I am out now.'

'So you are not sorry about what happened! I am sure you will do it again.'

Satya knew he needed to keep this episode under wraps and a secret from his parents. Just to calm her down, he said, 'I am sorry Kakoli, it will never happen again. Just give me another chance.' With this ability to sound genuine and repentant, he convinced her to believe him and she calmed down.

Chapter 17

An alarm pierced the early morning silence. It was quarter to five and still dark. Samir turned in his bed and pushed himself to get up. He kept the alarm clock far from the bed so that he could not press snooze without getting up. He had learnt that if he got up from the bed without thinking too much, he could wake up early and there was nothing better than starting the day two hours earlier than the average person.

After freshening up, he did his yoga exercises for an hour followed by twenty minutes of meditation. He was finished by the time he was supposed to wake up the kids for school. He had been following this early morning routine for the last 15 years and would do anything to stick to it. Every week, a couple of days he did yoga, a few days he ran or jogged and the remaining days he hit the gym. He had devised his own holistic well-being program.

When the kids were off to school, he came and hugged his wife, Amrita from behind. She was preparing breakfast in the kitchen and greeted him with a 'Good morning, Sam!'

'Love you, Amu!' he said, placing his cheek next to hers.

'Aha, I like this romance but you need to get ready fast or you will be late for work,' she said, unclasping his hands from around her.

Amrita, a postgraduate in History, worked as a lecturer at Mumbai University. Her academic career allowed her to be flexible and take care of the household. Both Samir and Amrita were not in favour of jobs that took over their home and personal lives. Amrita wanted to care for the kids herself and loathed the idea of leaving them with babysitters or in the day care centre. Luckily, Samir's banking career was going well so far and provided them financial security.

Samir came back down to have breakfast and she asked, 'Are you fine? You were looking a bit disturbed last evening after coming from work.'

'Nothing much, Amu. You know, I work in an environment where nothing is okay even for a minute. People are working extra hard to make each other's lives more difficult.' He laughed, 'Actually, modern organisations thrive on this.'

Amrita had been hearing his office stories for many years, 'Why do they do this?'

'Companies promote 'healthy' tension among people and departments. They think that if everyone pushes each other, the company will achieve the best outcome.'

'But isn't it counter-productive? If employees have uneven relationships with colleagues, won't they end up wasting a lot of time and energy in internal issues rather than on productive work?'

'You are right, but unfortunately that's the way companies work. As far as possible, I like to keep it straight for my team.'

He explained how aggressive people hog all the limelight and get themselves promoted over others who may be introverted but performing better.

Amrita found it hard to appreciate what Samir was telling her. 'But managers need to trust the people they hire,' she protested.

'The company works on the premise that everyone is inherently lazy and has to be kicked regularly,' chuckled Samir.

'But how can they promote people only on the basis of extroverted and sycophantic behaviour?'

'That's the way it is, Amu.'

'So you mean there is no future for introverts in the corporate world?' she asked.

'It's not like that Amu, you know I used to be far more introverted earlier but I did try to change. I realised that I had to ensure I get due credit for my work. For that I had to be vocal and get noticed by the seniors.'

'I agree, Sam. Actually, I am happy to see the transformation in you.'

'Thanks to you too for that. You have been a great support and advisor in this journey.'

'At work, I have overheard people making fun of the way I focus on my well-being,' Samir added.

'Why? Is taking care of oneself bad?'

'It's not bad but people do have biases. The other day, Rakesh was stunned when he learnt that I am going for a ten-day meditation course. He asked me what I gain with such old-fashioned stuff.'

'So, what did you tell him, Sam?' Amrita said, tying her flowing hair.

'I told him that it was needed to develop mindfulness, to live in the moment completely. Otherwise, the running from one goal to another is going to make us lose our sanity.'

'I wonder if he liked your lecture. Won't it affect your career, Sam?'

'He responded with his usual smirk, "Maybe you need it!" I don't mind people's taunts as long as I am convinced of the benefits. And these things help me combat the stress at work.'

He added jokingly, 'But I am yet to learn any techniques to

manage the pressure given by the boss at home.' Amrita got the joke and hit him with a cushion.

He continued, 'Just take last evening. There was a late night party thrown by our global boss. I excused myself early and I hope he will understand but most others hung around till early morning.'

'Oh my, Sam, that's why you were a bit tense when you reached home,' Amrita caressed his shoulder.

'But now I am just fine and ready to tackle another hectic day at work,' Samir smiled and gave Amrita a bear hug before picking up his office bag and leaving.

Chapter 18

Satya took the day off as he was just not in a state to go to work. He needed to recover from the hangover before he could think or talk about anything. Reporting sick at work and sleeping through the day was the only option. He kept on ingesting water and all kinds of juices whenever he woke up. That and two tablets of disprin helped him recover by late evening. He was happy that he would be able to go to work the next day but was worried about Nitin's reaction. Would he report the incident to management? Would he use this to squeeze favours out of him or would he get him fired summarily?

The next day, as Satya entered the office, he noticed people giving him strange looks. He was convinced that the story of his drunken driving and his nearly killing a policeman had already spread in the office. Ten minutes later, Nitin called him into a conference room.

Nitin came to the point quickly, 'I got to know from the police inspector. Do you know you can be fired for getting involved in such a case?'

Satya stared at him blankly, imagining the consequences.

'First, the bank will suspend you, conduct an inquiry and then in all probability, let you go.' Satya nodded and looked down, the phrase 'let you go' reverberating in his mind.

Nitin continued, 'Satya, you have done okay so far at work, so I have no complaints. I got to know about the incident by chance. I will keep quiet about it and leave it to you how you want to handle it.' Satya felt a rush of relief at this unexpected offer from Nitin. He didn't care about what Nitin would ask from him in return, he was just happy in the moment. He supressed his joy, however, and keeping with corporate etiquette, he smiled and said, 'Thanks a lot Nitin, for this.'

He was not good with words, so he could not express his gratitude properly. Someone like Rekha would have spoken for five minutes to ensure that Nitin fully understood that she appreciated the favour. He was sure Nitin would extract his pound of flesh some day for this gesture.

But, for now, Satya was at peace and sat at the desk. The people around him seemed to act normally after all. It had all been in his head.

He tried to focus on work but couldn't. *If anything had gone wrong at office, I would have had a tough time explaining it to Kakoli. She would have cried for many days, to say the least. Her crying is a weapon that knocks me out any time. Maybe she understood this early on and makes it a point to cry whenever she feels I am not empathizing with her.*

He also suspected that her mother had advised her to use that tool. Maybe not. Kakoli's tears were so natural and innocent, it was difficult to imagine they were fake. Whatever it was, he was stuck with it. He was willing to live with it as long as most other things were taken care of and there was sufficient love between them.

Love among couples in an arranged marriage is a strange phenomenon. Though he fell very much in love during the few months of arranged courtship, he realised after a year of marriage that love was just beginning to develop between them.

The first year of their marriage was a breeze; they were lost in each other for most of it. Satya didn't care about work too much and Kakoli didn't worry about home and other issues. After the wild fire of passion subsided, they slowly started facing the grim realities of life.

Now, Satya understood that love was when Kakoli kept everything aside, ignored all his shortcomings and looked forward to spending some time with him. And for Kakoli, love was when he set aside his office stress, got over his fatigue and took her into his arms. They would postpone problems and issues and not wait for every little nagging thing to get resolved before experiencing love.

With the police matter behind him, Satya began to look forward to a romantic evening.

Chapter 19

Amit called Nitin at eight in the evening, 'Boss, can I take a minute of your time?'

'Yeah, sure.'

'The large deal that we are working on for the Delhi-based client has hit a glitch.'

'What's that? Can you ever give me some good news?'

'The client is insisting that we give him written assurance about potential profits,' Amit explained. Giving any such assurance was against the bank's policy, especially when the deal was very risky and the client could potentially lose a lot of money.

'Okay, let me sleep over it. Talk tomorrow,' Nitin hung up. He was amazed that Amit was taking this small problem so seriously. He had the solution ready in his head but didn't want to share it immediately. He wanted to let the schmuck think that he actually worked on the solution overnight. *Otherwise, how can I get my team to respect me more?*

The next day, as soon as Nitin entered the Markets dealing room, he heard a loud commotion. There was a large group of people standing around Vicky, the chief trader. Nitin knew it was a serious matter because Joe was also the part of the crowd. He waded through the crowd and asked Amit, 'What's happening here?'

'Hey, we just noticed that Vicky is wearing his new Hublot Big Bang watch. People are excited to see such an expensive watch,' Amit replied. Nitin's face turned red. 'What, Hublot Gold? That damn thing costs ten lakh rupees. Are you sure it is not fake?' Nitin had wanted to buy an expensive watch all his life but just couldn't get around to spending that much on one watch even though he had the money.

Joe asked Vicky to take off the watch and inspected it for authenticity. Once satisfied, he handed it back to Vicky lest it fall on the floor and break its sapphire crystal dial. Finally, Vicky had to agree to order coffee for everyone. A couple of thousand rupees was a small price to pay to get them off his back. Nitin also congratulated Vicky and wrote his coffee order on the paper.

Coming back to his desk, Amit remarked, 'I didn't even know of this brand of watches, let alone the price!'

Joe overheard and smirked at him, 'Oh man, you are still to hear a lot of new things!'

Picking up business from where they left it the previous night, Amit asked Nitin, 'Boss, did you think of any solution to the problem?' Nitin took Amit to the glass conference room. 'I thought hard about this. In my view, we can work out a solution.'

Amit's eyes widened in anticipation.

'You know Amar? We hired him from IIM Ahmedabad as a management trainee? We can send the email to the client through him,' said Nitin.

Amit was shocked, 'You mean, we use him to do something that is absolutely not compliant with policy?'

'Don't start acting holier than thou. You have indicated lucrative profits to the client over the phone. What's the problem in sending the email?'

'But—,' Amit could not think of how to counter his boss.

'No ifs and buts. This is not a business for the faint-hearted. Each of us is expected to make a hefty profit. We cannot possibly do that year after year if we are so harsh on ourselves. Just call Amar right now and tell him what to do,' Nitin was losing his patience.

Nitin had trouble reconciling that people had sky-high ambitions for income and standard of living but didn't want to take risks to achieve them. According to him, this was the biggest difference between a middle-class mindset and the mindset of the wealthy.

'Amar, can you come to the small meeting room?' Amit instructed. Amar promptly reported and awaited instructions. Nitin had left by now. He didn't want to witness the dubious discussion.

Amit explained to Amar, 'We are discussing a large transaction with this client. They have liked the idea and want to do the deal with us. They have asked for a short email to be sent to them indicating the potentially huge profit they will make on this transaction.'

Amar nodded. At this stage in his career, his performance was measured by just one parameter—obedience. If you asked too many questions, you ran the risk of getting thrown out. Amit dictated the text of the email to Amar, who noted it dutifully. Amit didn't want to send the text to Amar via email or anything that could be traced back to his desk in an audit.

Amar sent the email to the client and marked a copy to Amit. Now, Amit was irritated. He brought it up with Nitin, 'Boss, Amit sent out the email as we discussed but the fool has marked a copy to me.'

Nitin was his usual semi-angry, semi-sarcastic self, 'You can't get a simple thing done without complicating it. Anyway, what has happened has happened. Just leave it at that and don't reply to that email.'

Amit didn't know how to respond.

'Just call the client and close the deal.' Every time Amit talked to Nitin, his self-confidence took a beating. He ended up wondering, 'Am I really so bad at handling any task? What does Nitin gain by making me feel bad?'

Amit called the client and repeated the terms of the transaction and, as expected, the deal was done. Nitin couldn't hide his happiness. They had pocketed a large profit and they exchanged the customary handshakes and high-fives. For ten joyous seconds, Joe and Nitin made Amit look like a real hero.

But Rakesh happened to enter the dealing room and when he heard the news, exclaimed, 'I had dinner with the owner of this company last week and asked him to increase their business with us. See, they have done just that!'

Bastard. The CEO is also in the queue to take credit for the deal. I am far behind.

Amit didn't know what to make of the whole situation. He chose to believe that the email to the client would never be discovered. He knew that he should not have done what Nitin asked him to do, but he was not sure of the consequences.

If he had declined to obey his order, Nitin would have blacklisted him and got him fired at the earliest opportunity. He would have waited either for a small mistake from Amit or for the performance appraisal to screw up his rating, paving the way for his eventual exit. Even though there were elaborate whistleblowing policies in place, Amit knew that they existed only on paper. The stakes for people like Rakesh, Joe and Nitin were too high and they would not let any whistle-blower get away easily. He had to let things take their own course. He was a pawn in the larger system after all.

At 7 pm, Amit rushed to Frangipani, the slick restaurant at The Oberoi. He was meeting a client for drinks. The corner table, with a thick white pure cotton cover, was reserved for them. A few flowers arranged in the Ikebana style were placed at the centre. The place was dimly lit and the smell of the freshener was overpowering. The air-conditioner was blasting cool air, leaving no trace of the hot and humid weather just outside on Marine Drive.

Amit stood up to receive the client. The waiter placed a tray of assorted breads and an exotic double-barrelled olive oil dispenser.

'Two Talisker double please,' Amit ordered.

The waiter politely asked, '10 years or 18 years?'

'18 years, please.'

Choosing the 18-year whiskey meant almost double the price but Amit didn't care. It was a client entertainment meeting and the corporate credit card was meant for such days.

The client, a mid-level manager at a large finance company, looked approvingly at the glasses. They picked up the drinks, clinked the glasses and exclaimed, 'Cheers!'

While Amit was smelling his single malt whiskey in a sophisticated manner before taking a sip, the client remarked, 'Actually, I like my whiskey with soda.'

Amit couldn't believe his ears. What a waste of a premium single malt, which is supposed to be had with a just a little bit of water. But the client was used to drowning himself in the oxymoronic Indian Made Foreign Liquor (IMFL) Royal Stag whiskey diluted with soda.

He could hardly contain his disdainful smirk and called the waiter, 'Some soda please.' The waiter was also visibly disturbed at this plan to butcher the single malt delicacy.

However, the client had his way and mercilessly poured copious amounts of soda in his glass. Amit looked the other way, he didn't want to see a crime being committed. They ordered a few more rounds. Amit was at his versatile best. As opposed to his conversations on art and museums around the world that he had with the senior clients, he adjusted the subject to the bad weather in Mumbai and the menace of traffic jams every evening. He kept the client sufficiently engaged through the evening, trying to get a sense of the next big bond deal.

But as the client drank more, he became more closed off. He obviously understood why he was being plied with expensive alcohol and was on his guard. Amit asked for the cheque and they ended the evening there.

He took a cab home. It was a waste, entertaining these people. He had heard how clients in Japan and Korea rewarded their bankers after a nice evening, although entertainment in those countries meant a lot more than alcohol. But this was India and those options were not easily available.

At one of the bank's offsites, his Korean colleagues had told him wild stories of client entertainment in Seoul. They would start drinking at 'civilised' places early in the evening and have their dinner. Post dinner they would head out to the more exotic entertainment places that specialised in a legal supply of booze and women. The banker would pick up the tab of this after-party on his personal card as the return on investment was almost guaranteed. The Korean guys were notorious for their drinking capacity. They would finish up more than a bottle of whiskey each and could report for work directly after the party. They carried an extra shirt and tie with them so that the clothes stinking of alcohol and cigar smoke could be changed. The client would reward the salesperson with a large deal the same day, turning a blind eye to the profit being pocketed by the bank

A sudden jolt of the taxi in the pothole-riddled roads of Mumbai brought him back to India. Most clients here were smart enough to drink to their heart's content and still not compromise on their company's interests. At best, they may give hints or be a little lenient with the salesperson when they were fiercely bidding out any the transaction to 35 banks

Chapter 20

Rekha's mother advised her to talk to Neeraj and take a call about the issue. Even though the evidence was quite conclusive, it was conventional wisdom to hear out the other party. One evening, Rekha broached the subject with Neeraj, while Asha sat inside the bedroom, ready to come to her daughter's aid.

Neeraj was slouched on the sofa as usual and was absorbed in the TV. She had to strain to be heard above the TV, 'Can we talk for a few minutes?'

'Huh,' Neeraj muttered and took a sip of his beer. 'What now? This match is at an interesting point. Can't you wait?'

'There is always some match or the other, we need to talk now,' Rekha tried to take hold of the remote but Neeraj snatched it back, refusing to turn off the TV. He wasn't pleased at the interruption and slouched further, 'Okay, what is it?'

'I have been thinking of asking you for some time. What's

happening? You come home late, drink beer and watch TV. Do we have a life in common?'

'I don't know what you are talking about. You are busy with your job, there is no fixed time to come home. Why are you asking me all this?'

'Many couples have this issue but they make it work. We could coordinate our timings; we could share the home chores. Anyway, I wanted to ask you where you have been spending so much time. Has your workload suddenly increased or have you no desire to spend time with me?'

'Women like you place their career above family and then complain about their husbands. Why don't you understand that we needed to start a family yesterday, and you need to think about taking a break from work to do that.'

Rekha countered him for whatever it was worth, 'Women have the right to build a career. If I am working and contributing more than equally to our household, why am I expected to be a servant in the house? Why can't you also shoulder some of the housework, like buying groceries at least?'

'Shut up, Rekha. I am a busy professional. I don't owe an explanation to anyone. If my mother asked my dad such questions, he would have slapped her.'

After five years of marriage, Rekha knew that Neeraj had inherited his father's values and behaviour but she didn't think that she was supposed to conform to those. They had married on equal terms. She realised that the indirect talk was not helping and came to the point, 'So meeting those voluptuous girls and doling out money to them is part of your job? I demand an answer and you dare not treat me like your father treats your mother, understood?'

'What do you mean? Who has filled your mind with filth?'

But Rekha was armed with data from his mobile phone. She said, 'See, no point in hiding this stuff, I have some phone numbers and details of your bank transfers.' And she slammed a sheet of paper on the table.

As soon as he realised that his secrets were out, he became wild, 'You crazy bitch, you have been spying on me!'

'This is enough to put any self-respecting person to shame but you are shouting at me?'

'Oh you... wait... I will teach you a lesson,' he lunged towards her.

Rekha was terrified and shouted, 'Mamma!' Asha ran into the room and threw her arms around Rekha. Neeraj backed off and started shouting his complaints, 'This woman is always busy with her job and she treats me like her last priority. She has not even agreed to start a family with me and keeps a separate bank account.'

Asha had to think quickly before someone got hurt. She shielded Rekha and whisked her away to the kitchen. Neeraj charged towards the kitchen but Rekha locked the door to keep him out. She was trying hard to remain calm enough to call the police helpline.

Chapter 21

Joe and Nitin were discussing the sales budgets and planning for the next year. Emboldened by the 50 percent growth delivered by the India branch over the previous year, the management had proposed a steep increase in their revenue target.

'The budget for 2007 is 60 percent more than last year's revenue. How on earth are we going to achieve it?' asked Joe.

Nitin was cool about it, 'Come on boss, we know that management keeps pushing the targets in line with performance.'

There were some automatons in the strategy team whose only job was to keep punching numbers into their Excel sheets to churn out targets. These analysts, though young, had a say with all the right people in the bank. The actual decision makers wanted to focus on their politics to protect their seats and multi-million dollar bonuses. When it came to decision making, they relied on the inputs from this team of mid-level advisors.

Joe was surprised at the insights offered by Nitin, a relatively new senior. He concurred, 'I am happy that you have understood the practical issues so quickly.'

'I just wonder why the seniors take such shortcuts for crucial decisions.'

'Senior managers at global banks are notorious for their indulgences and for spending very little time on official matters.'

'But they worked hard to reach there, right? I guess only people like us who are not able to reach that level crib about this.' *The rewards of reaching the top are so high that people don't really care about crushing anyone or anything that comes in the way. Would I mind such a life?*

'Yes, and the risk-reward is pleasantly skewed. If you are in the top seat during the economic upswing, the banking business generally does well. The large banks produce gazillions of dollars and their top executives get paid in tens of millions.'

'Yeah, that makes perfect sense. Anyway, let's look at the ways of making sure that we achieve the seemingly impossible target. We also need to collect a small share of the pie,' Nitin winked.

Nitin proposed a break up of sales targets for each of his team members and for himself. At British Bank, they encouraged managers to have targets of their own as well. This ensured that the manager was producing revenue and the rest of the team looked up to him. However, it also promoted unhealthy competition between the team leader and the team members.

Recently, Nitin had been feeling jittery about Satya's large deal. He called Satya one day, 'Hey man, what's up? How's the MaxCorp deal going?'

'It's going well, Nitin. We are midway through the negotiation. In fact, the company CEO is going to be involved from now on as the deal is critical to MaxCorp.'

'Exactly the point I am coming to, Satya. Since the CEO is going to be involved and the deal is critical to our team achieving the full year targets, I am going to take charge of this transaction.'

'But... Nitin...,' Satya stammered.

'Don't worry, Satya, I am not asking you to dissociate yourself from the deal. You will work closely with me and I will give you due credit for it.' Nitin had cut the call.

Satya had been devastated. He considered this transaction career changing stuff. He could have staked a claim to a senior role after delivering on this. Nitin's assurance of 'giving due credit' meant nothing. British Bank's culture was fiercely individualistic and only one person was rewarded for a particular deal.

The global head of Markets, Nick, had a philosophy of ascribing credit for a transaction to one lead banker, never a team of people. Nick also wanted healthy tension and an environment of hustling across the departments. Bankers were encouraged to poach their colleagues' clients and demonstrate that they could cover them better. Nick felt that it helped maximise the bank's revenue and hence its shareholder value. Nobody could argue with him as long as he was delivering the profit numbers.

Satya's thoughts were meandering. *Now, Nitin will be all over the place. All my dreams of managing the client's CEO on my own are trashed. If the transaction goes well, Nitin will book the revenue in his name and I will not be able to do anything about it.* Indeed, that was the last time Satya thought about the deal. He provided the required information to Nitin whenever he was asked for it. Nitin asked Rekha to assist him for that transaction and Satya was phased out.

Joe and Nitin concluded the budget setting meeting after deciding on a few marketing initiatives and a task force for implementing them. Joe called for a meeting with Nitin and his team.

'Guys, I want to brief you on the most important marketing initiative this year. As you would have seen already, the budget numbers for next year are aggressive to say the least,' Joe was trying to pump some energy into his speech to emulate the overseas visitors.

Nitin added, 'This initiative is an overseas offsite for our important clients. We are confident that the offsite will help take our business to the next level. We need to work out some details like the list of clients to be invited, the proposed location, itinerary, agenda and the cost.'

Satya, Amit and Rekha looked at each other and their faces lit up with excitement as they anticipated free travel and entertainment. They still wanted to hear more before saying anything and risk Joe's reprimands.

Joe didn't expect them to speak unless explicitly asked to. He said, 'Can I suggest that we take the clients to Mauritius this year? It is an exotic location and I am sure our clients will reward us for this gesture.'

Satya knew that Mauritius would be a disastrous location for the offsite but he was too low in the hierarchy to counter Joe. He looked at Nitin helplessly. Nitin got the hint. Being a seasoned salesperson, he knew how to select a good location. He spoke to Joe, 'That's a great suggestion, Joe. Mauritius is a great place. I went there for my honeymoon; have fond memories.'

Satya squirmed in his seat. *What's wrong with Nitin? Instead of opposing Joe, he is encouraging his bad choice.*

Having aligned with Joe by supporting him, Nitin came to the point, 'But there is one small problem with Mauritius. It's a beach destination and our clients are generally not interested in sun-bathing on the beach. They are more likely to enjoy sightseeing and a night life.'

Amit was waiting for this opening, 'Can I suggest Bangkok?' Rekha immediately made a face. There was pin-drop silence.

Joe never let go of any opportunity to insult a team member. 'With your down-market choice of Bangkok, we know what kind of entertainment you want to offer the clients,' he said.

Amit didn't give up easily, 'But Bangkok has a rich cultural heritage, many ancient Buddhist temples, royal palaces and the historical capital of King Rama, Ayutthaya.'

Satya also took pot-shots at Amit, 'Why don't you tell Anu that you want to visit Bangkok alone and see her reaction?' Everyone burst out laughing. Having sufficiently belittled Amit, the focus was back on the choice of location.

Satya, the better travelled of the lot, proposed Vienna. Before Joe could come up with another stupid option, Nitin supported Satya for a change, 'Wow, that sounds great. Vienna offers the right mix of cultural heritage, historical sites and entertainment options.'

Joe also nodded. His choice of Mauritius was cleverly out-manoeuvred by his team without he being snubbed. 'So, Vienna it is. Nitin, please instruct the team to work with Sapphire Events and get cracking. We need to have a great offsite to kick-start the new year with a bang.' He left the meeting, leaving the details to the schmucks.

Nitin closed the meeting with operational directions, 'It will be a three-day event and it needs to be flawless. I need a list of clients to be invited by tomorrow evening.'

All nodded.

'Rekha, please take charge of coordinating with Sapphire. Satya, come up with a list of places to visit and the client entertainment options. Amit, do some research on the topics for the conference.'

Joe put up the proposal for the offsite for business and compliance approvals. Spending a quarter million US dollars on the event was not a problem for British Bank as the offsite promised to supplement its revenues by over ten million dollars.

'The schmucks better make sure that the commercial angle works out,' Joe told Nitin.

Later, Amit asked Satya, 'How come they always give the contracts to Sapphire? How do they know Sapphire's cost is fair?'

'Look, there are rumours in the bank that the CEO of Sapphire Events, Aden, is a close friend of Rakesh. Aden also has Nitin and Joe in his pocket,' Satya said. All of British Bank's events were contracted to Sapphire and minor hiccups and major cost variations were, of course, supposed to be overlooked. But Satya didn't realise that Sapphire was playing the same game that British Bank played with its clients.

Chapter 22

Satya called Mr. Pandey, the CFO of Angelo Industries, 'Sir, how are you? I have some good news for you.'

'Good news for me? Tell me fast!'

'We are organizing an overseas offsite at Vienna for our important clients like you. Kindly make yourself available during the third week of January.'

He expected Mr. Pandey to jump at the offer but the client was cold, 'What has happened to large foreign banks like you? Even the Indian banks are inviting me to these mass events. They are taking clients to places like Paris, Barcelona, Istanbul. Why don't you guys do Las Vegas? I am telling you, it will be a big hit.'

Satya knew that was not possible. Perhaps if their business increased tenfold or the bank's compliance officer was drugged, Las Vegas would be a likely destination. He persisted, 'Sir, even that will happen with your good wishes. For now, I request that you come with us. It's an all-expense paid trip. You just need to give my travel agent your passport and a few documents and we will arrange a visa for you.'

Mr. Pandey's ego was well-inflated after years of flattery by a multitude of bankers. He said, 'What do you think of me? I have a valid multiple entry Schengen Visa. I will be there just because you insist.'

Fearing that he may be left behind in the race to gather clients, Amit called his client, Universal Finance, a small finance company, 'Hello Mr. Vijayan, how are you?'

'All well, Amit. How are things at your end?' After exchanging a few more pleasantries, Amit asked him, 'Sir, did you look at the trade proposal I sent you last week?'

'Not yet, Amit. I have been busy preparing for our board meeting. It is scheduled for next week. I will look at your email after that.' Clients almost never looked at emails from the banks unless they were followed up.

'I understand that, sir. There's only a small hitch. I was making a list of clients to invite for our international offsite. It will be held in Vienna in the third week of January. It's an all-expense paid trip for our esteemed clients.'

Now he had Mr. Vijayan's attention, 'So, what's the hitch?'

'I want to invite you but I don't have any business with you so far. If you could look at my email and close the transaction by tomorrow, I will be able to justify your name for the offsite.'

Amit imagined Mr. Vijayan's eyes widening with excitement and he wasn't wrong. Mr. Vijayan suddenly found time, 'I am actually very busy but since you are insisting, I will look at your proposal. We will close the deal if it is in my company's interest. Please call me tomorrow afternoon.'

Amit was used to hearing such malarkey. 'Company's interest' meant his own gratification. Though, most of the time, managers looked out for their employer's interest, they didn't see any harm in benefitting on the side. Why not make some money for the company and get invited for a free foreign trip? Amit duly called Mr. Vijayan the next day and closed a profitable derivative deal, grabbing a good amount of spotlight in the dealing room. The last salesperson for Universal Finance had not been able to break into the account despite trying for many years.

The schmucks managed to put up an impressive list of thirty senior clients for the offsite. Rekha looked at the list and exclaimed, 'I can't believe this, there is no woman on the list!'

Nitin defended it, 'That's a reflection of our client base. There are hardly any woman CFOs and treasurers in the corporate world. But you don't worry. Mr. Verma and Mr. David are bringing their spouses for the offsite.' He implied that it would be Rekha's duty to entertain their spouses and keep them in good humour. She was not happy but couldn't help it. What would she gain by spending time with the clients' spouses? But this was not happening for the first time. In fact, she would be the only woman from the bank as well.

The team spent the next four weeks working closely with Sapphire Events. It was a nightmare. The clients were too slow in providing their passports and other documents. Amit whinged to Rekha and Satya, 'It feels like I am inviting them to my daughter's wedding.'

'Not only that, they are desperate for free foreign travel but act as if they don't care. Just imagine, we have to leave next week and I am still running after Mr. Mittal for his passport. The travel agent has given up after the first round of follow-up,' Satya commiserated.

'The Sapphire guys are the least worried about client attendance. They have all our bosses on their side and will get paid, one way or the other. But if the clients don't turn up, Joe and Nitin will make our lives miserable.'

'Correct. I am travelling to Delhi this weekend to take the documents from Mr. Mittal and will board the plane with him. That's my key performance indicator this quarter. He is far too important a client to be left out.'

Rekha butted in, 'Can't you guys get some women clients please? At least the crowd will be a bit more balanced.' She was worried that an all-male entourage would be awkward for her to be in.

'I did call Ms. Prasad for the offsite but she politely refused.' Satya guffawed. Actually, her boss was coming for the event and must have told her to stay away.

Amit added, 'I also invited Ms. Chouhan but she declined as she works for a public sector company and their policy strictly prohibits her from accepting any favours.'

'These guys are the masters of hypocrisy. They will not accept anything on the record but I hear there is rampant corruption in these supposedly professional state-owned companies,' Rekha was now indignant.

She continued, 'You know our man Tiwari? He is Nitin's handyman for all public sector transactions. We are B-school educated idiots. They don't teach us how to crack public sector deals at IIMs.' Tiwari was a simple graduate but had spent a lot of time working with government departments and companies.

Satya added to the bitching, 'In fact, I was wondering the other day—whenever I get a large public sector request for bidding, Nitin calls Tiwari in and makes sure that he handles all client interactions.' Satya had quoted for a few transactions when Tiwari was away, but he could never win any. And as soon as Tiwari came into the picture, British Bank was able to win large bids.

Chapter 23

The offsite was christened the British Bank Global Markets Conference. Nobody could actually justify why the event needed to be held in Vienna. Air Austria operated only two flights to Vienna from India—one from Mumbai and the other from New Delhi. The clients were all booked in economy class as the bank didn't want to make it look like a luxurious holiday.

When Satya entered the plane, he could not help but notice that a few senior clients invited by Joe and Nitin were sitting in business class. It was already causing a commotion among the clients that were seated in economy. Mr. Vohra accosted Satya, 'How are you giving business class seats to some clients? We were told that there was only the economy option. I am going to opt out right now if not upgraded.' Others also joined him.

Satya stammered, 'Sir, give me a few minutes. Let me find out.' He went to Nitin and whispered in his ears. Nitin whispered something back. Satya came to the economy section and announced,

'Business class seats are available and you have the option to upgrade at your own cost. The cost of an upgrade one way is fifty thousand rupees.'

All the noise died down and people settled in their seats. The cost of an upgrade was more than the full cost of economy class seats. Mr. Vohra told his co-passenger, 'It is only an eight-hour flight, why bother with an upgrade?'

Satya and Amit were again feeling that they were hosting guests for a family wedding. However, the fun had just started. Amit whispered, 'I told you about Nitin's connection with Sapphire, right?'

'I can see it. Nitin, Joe and their select clients have been given the business class seats by Sapphire, even at the cost of making everybody else look inferior.'

The two flights arrived in Vienna at five in the morning. They stayed put in the arrival waiting hall because they were told that the airport opened at six and the staff for offloading the luggage were yet to arrive. Amit noticed this difference in quality of life—in India, late night to early morning was peak operational time for international airports.

At the hotel, the Sapphire representative briefed the group, 'You have a couple of hours to freshen up. We meet for breakfast at nine and the Global Markets conference starts at ten in the Salzburg Ballroom.' The short conference was the bitter pill everyone had to swallow before the actual sightseeing and fun began. The person continued, 'We hope to wrap up the conference by three, including a lunch break. For you, we have specially arranged an Indian buffet lunch using our influence here.'

This was pure hogwash as Indian food was available at most tourist destinations in Europe due to the large influx of Indian tourists and their rather inflexible taste. But Sapphire portrayed it as a big achievement. The person continued, 'We take a tea break after the conference and leave for the evening tour of the city at four sharp. As you know, it is chilly outside, so please do carry woollens and jackets with you.'

The conference room was decorated with white lilies, the tables set with mineral water bottles, notepads and wireless mikes. Nitin, Joe and the schmucks were waiting at the entrance in their formal best.

Nitin had invited a couple of speakers from the economics research team in London. They were amazed that clients from India had travelled to Vienna to listen to speakers from London about markets in New York and Tokyo. This was a truly global event. One of the speakers, the chief economist, was curious to learn about India. He asked Amit, 'So, what's the background of these clients, I mean what are the companies they represent?'

Amit was drowsy because he hadn't slept during the flight. He just wanted to get the clients seated and start snoring in his seat. He reluctantly answered, 'They are mainly from IT, auto, steel and power companies.'

The hall started filling slowly and they kicked off the conference with Joe's opening comments. The chief economist presented a succinct update about the world's macroeconomic conditions and the bank's expectations of growth in next few years. The next speaker was the foreign exchange strategist who gave his views on which way the currency rate will move. The common theme emerging from the talks was the increasing amount of risk-taking in financial markets. The vote was divided over when the boom will turn into bust. Mr. Narayan whispered to Mr. Gupta sitting next to him, 'These people sound so ominous.'

'The economists have been crying wolf for the last couple of years, but nothing has happened,' replied Mr. Gupta. The experienced clients knew better than to trust those numbers. To everyone's relief, the conference got over in time.

The tour covered the historic city's streets as it was late for most indoor venues. The party admired the monumental architecture while enjoying the crisp winter air. The coach moved slowly through the baroque and neoclassical buildings while a guide ranted away in a thick Austrian accent. By eight, most people were hungry. One client asked the Sapphire person, 'So, what's for dinner?'

'It's continental food, sir. We have also included some of the specialities of this area like Goulash and Weiner Schnitzel.' The client rolled his eyes, '*Hain*? What's that?'

'Sir, these are meat-based dishes. We also have vegetarian options but they are simple dishes with no spices.'

The dinner venue was a rustic heritage bungalow that had been converted into a sprawling restaurant. Rekha was admiring the place when she overheard Ms. Vohra, 'I cannot eat this grass and boiled meat combination. We are missing our chicken biryani.'

Mr. Narayanan, a Tamil Brahmin, joined in, 'The vegetarian food is equally ugly. The veg rice is sprinkled with prawns; can you believe it?'

'Looks like we will have to go hungry tonight.'

Most of the people were making faces at the food on the menu. Since it was pre-ordered and this was Europe, last-minute changes were not possible. The restaurant staff couldn't be less bothered about whether people liked the food or not. They served course after course in a cold manner and wanted to get it over with.

Rekha didn't find it strange because she had seen Indian tourists behave like this before. However, she was still unable to digest the fact that it had been hardly twelve hours in the city and they had already been stuffed with spicy Indian food for lunch. Why were they so averse to anything new? Satya and Amit, as usual, bore the brunt of client anger. They were made to feel as if they had invited guests home and didn't give them proper food.

After dinner, the Sapphire representative made the usual announcements. They would leave for another sightseeing tour next morning at 8 am. The coach was heading back to the hotel. Whoever wanted to explore the city nightlife could use public transport or cabs. Nitin, Joe and their select clients had already sneaked out in a stretch limousine. Before leaving, Nitin took Satya aside and stuffed a fat bunch of 50-euro notes in his hand, 'This is for you and Amit to take care of clients tonight. I don't want to hear any complaints tomorrow.'

The coach left for the hotel with a few clients who were very tired or had come with their spouses. Rekha accompanied them. Amit and Satya divided the remaining clients into two groups and hired two small vans. They planned to spend the night on Gurtel Road in Vienna that was famous for its nightclubs and strip joints.

One group settled for a nude show. As they entered the arena, it looked flashy, with golden metal lining on the walls. The seats were arranged in a semicircle around the stage, grouped in clusters of eight. They grabbed the front seats, just next to the stage. The plush seats with crimson red upholstery, coupled with dim lighting, made them feel like they were in the den of a high-profile mafia don.

The show started with a preamble in Austrian that no one understood. Champagne was on the house. Mr. Gupta was already tipsy but that didn't stop him from gulping down the free bubbly. After a few glasses, his bladder was almost bursting. He contained it with great difficulty for the fear of missing some action in the show. When the pressure became unbearable, he got up to move towards the loo. As it was dark, he stumbled and fell at the edge of the low stage. While the nude dancers continued unfazed, the Indian group was surrounded by hefty bouncers who thought that someone from this crowd was trying to get up on stage.

The bouncers understood the situation after a few minutes but still caused enough humiliation to the group. As soon as Mr. Gupta came back to his senses, the group headed out and searched for the evening's next attraction.

Slowly, the seasoned players separated from the group and proceeded towards the individual dens for some private adult entertainment. Amit and Satya were quick to hand out the 50-

euro notes to people on the pretence that they might not be carrying foreign currency. Satya also disappeared into the crowd to explore his options and Amit was left behind on the street. He found himself wondering whether to dive headlong into the world of reckless passion or hold onto himself. As he debated this in his mind, he pictured Anu's face and quietly left for the hotel in a cab.

Chapter 24

The next morning, the coach was at the hotel entrance at 8 am. Satya was a bit tense and told Nitin, 'Just five people out of forty have reported. What do we do?' Nitin just smiled and asked the coach driver to return at 9 am.

The three got down to calling the clients' rooms. As expected, most had not even woken up despite the wakeup calls by the hotel staff. People slowly started gathering in the lobby around quarter to nine and they had to literally drag a few out of their rooms.

First stop in the tour was the Hofburg, the official residence of every Austrian ruler since 1275 AD. The guide told them before entry, 'We will explore the areas open for public and admire its multi-faceted architecture from Gothic to Renaissance, Baroque to Rococo and a little bit of Classicism.' People put on their earphones that wirelessly connected to the guide's mike. It was a long and exhausting tour as the Hofburg is a city within a city. The guide took them to the Imperial Apartments, the Sisi Museum and the

Silver Collection. Mr. Vijayan complained to Amit, 'I don't have much stamina left after seeing this place. I would much rather sit in the coach for the rest of the day.'

Amit whispered to Rekha, 'Why has he come here if he can't walk a couple of kilometres?'

Next, they visited St. Stephen's Cathedral and stopped for photos at multiple sites like the Belvedere Palace and Prater Park. The sightseeing ended by four, leaving time for people to shop and relax. After the previous day's experience, Sapphire had organised Indian cuisine for dinner. Stuffing themselves with butter paneer, aloo gobhi, dal makhani, tandoori chicken and mutton biryani, the bankers and the clients felt as if they were in heaven.

Over dinner, Mr. Vijayan joked with Nitin, 'Your boys are better than prostitutes. Even a prostitute charges a client after providing the service but your guys charge beforehand.' He was referring to the deal that he was made to close before the offsite. Nitin didn't like the joke and walked away unamused. He didn't want to betray any knowledge of such a deal but he made a mental note to reward Amit for this smart move.

Meanwhile, many in the party were drunk beyond their capacity. Amit shared his fears with his comrades, Satya and Rekha, 'I am scared they may create a scene.'

'Me too. In Europe, it may be difficult to condone a ruckus in a public place. They better behave themselves.' Again, the party split into three groups: the privileged ones left with Nitin and Joe for a secret place under the guidance of a Sapphire agent, the second batch headed to the hotel with Rekha, the third and most difficult to manage crowd headed for nightclubs with Satya and Amit. The fat bunch of 50-euro notes was still to be finished.

The offsite was a very successful event by any standard. Sapphire had pulled through once again and lived up to the high standards of service. While waiting for the return flight at Vienna airport, Satya told Amit, 'What a blatant show of discrimination.'

'Why, what happened now?'

'Sapphire didn't stop at only business tickets for Nitin and his cronies, they provided bigger suites to them at the hotel. While all of the lesser mortals were travelling by the coach, they got limousines.'

'It isn't right but what can we do, yaar? We just need to follow the instructions.'

The clients were visibly happier on the return flight, though they were still trying not to show this. There were no major complaints and what happened in Vienna, stayed in Vienna.

Chapter 25

Rekha went to the nearby cafe with her mother and sat in a secluded corner. She wanted to discuss her situation in peace. That day when they had locked themselves in the kitchen, Neeraj had kept banging on the door. Rekha had called the police and requested urgent help. Surprisingly, the police were quick to arrive.

They forced open the main door and found Neeraj sprawled outside the kitchen. There was a small puddle of blood around him. He had accidently cut himself up with a broken beer bottle. After multiple assurances by the police officer, the mother and daughter opened the kitchen door. The police took Neeraj away to the police station and later left him with a stern warning, which had no effect on him.

She told Asha, 'Mamma, I have decided. I am calling off this marriage and filing for divorce.' Her mother let out a deep sigh. She knew that it was not an easy decision but there was no choice.

Rekha had forgiven Neeraj on a number of occasions but he

was not willing to mend his ways. She couldn't understand how a promising young professional like Neeraj had gone awry. Even after deep introspection, she could not find fault with herself.

'Mamma, please stay with me for a few months, I don't feel safe in the house after what happened the other day.' She had nightmares of Neeraj trying to strangle her with a cushion even though she slept in a different room, bolted from inside.

'Beta, I can stay for some time but I don't see the situation improving soon. How long will I stay here to protect you? Can't you work with him to solve the problem?' Asha was still hopeful.

Rekha cringed, 'Mamma, how can you even think of a solution? This man is so hopeless.'

'I know, Rekha, that you have tried your best to make this marriage work. I was only thinking if you could try once more,' Asha added, but feared a strong reaction.

'He has abused and cheated on me, and still you want me to bow down? I have run out of patience. I want a divorce,' Rekha knew her mother wouldn't like this but it was time that she accepted her decision.

'Hai rabba, I never thought my own daughter would go through a divorce. There has been no divorce in our family.' Asha was now shaking.

'Don't annoy me with your family history. I know your brother has been estranged from his wife for ten years. It's better to get divorced and move on. I have made up my mind, whether you and dad like it or not.'

'But what will people say, beta?' Asha knew that Rekha had done everything possible to adjust with Neeraj and that it was not her fault. Still, the mother in her was struggling to get over the social stigma attached to divorce.

'Let people go to hell, I need to get my life back on track. I agree, I committed this mistake and now I will correct it before it gets too late.'

'If you have decided, we will stand with you. Haven't we always supported you?' Asha was gradually reconciling herself to her daughter's fate. 'So, come stay with me till I work through this,' Rekha returned to the original point.

But Asha was not comfortable facing Neeraj every day. She said, 'Why don't you move to another place to get away from this miserable experience?'

Rekha had considered this but her lawyer had advised her against it. She replied, 'If I move out, Neeraj will portray me as the villain in the divorce proceedings and may make it dirty.'

Finally, Asha relented and agreed to stay with her till the matter was settled by the court. Now, Asha was thinking ahead, 'What are your plans after this? Do you plan to marry again?' *Our society is not kind to single women.*

'Oof Mamma, I can't believe this. A few moments ago, you were finding it hard to digest my divorce and now you are thinking about my second marriage.'

As they drove back to her apartment, she couldn't help thinking what it was about marriage that appealed to Indian parents so much. *Their only aim in life seems to be getting their children married and pushing them to have babies. Had I followed their advice, I would have been a mother of two by now and in a much bigger problem.*

She was happy to see that Neeraj was not at home. He had started spending more nights away from home now that his secret was out. She planned to serve the divorce notice within a week. As a self-respecting and working woman, she didn't want any alimony from Neeraj but wanted to divide the common property equally. She needed a solid case for that too. Neeraj and his lawyer would not shy away from painting her as characterless or worse to swing the case in their favour.

Chapter 26

The year 2007 had gone extremely well for the British Bank Global Markets in India and the risky bets had multiplied in the process. Looking forward to a great 2008, Rakesh realised that the majority of the bank's income would be coming from the Markets division. As the CEO, he wanted the whole team on his side just to be politically secure. He called Jenny and gave some quick orders, 'Jenny, please draft a short note for the Global Markets team to be invited to my place for dinner. They need to be invited with spouses; no kids please. You have my usual invite, just modify that and show it to me once before sending it.'

Jenny was surprised by this gesture from the CEO. *That's the money speaking. He never bothered to entertain the Markets guys before. Now, he is inviting the whole department, including the junior schmucks. It will be good fun to watch.* She was expected to be at the party to take care of administrative stuff.

Rakesh selected a Friday night for the party so people could drink as much as they wanted. His wife, Sophie, was always game for such events at home. She recognised the importance of these parties for her husband's career and she wanted to play her role in ensuring that the multimillion-dollar bonus cheques kept coming in year after year. She wore a black Ralph Lauren evening dress that she had picked up from London the previous summer. She was in her early fifties but retained the charisma of her youth.

It was 8:30 already and no one had turned up. Rakesh and Sophie were ready to receive the guests. Jenny was alert. She had come alone because her role was more of an assistant than a guest. Though Rakesh had politely invited her husband, she had decided it was not appropriate for her to bring him.

The doorbell rang and Vicky and his wife, Mala walked in with a large bouquet of exotic flowers. There was a round of cheek-to-cheek air kissing between Vicky and Sophie. Rakesh repeated the same formality with Mala. The ladies hugged each other as if they were long-lost friends and cries of joy erupted. Mala complimented Sophie, 'Look at you! Seems like you lost a lot of weight.' Sophie shrugged, 'Who, me? Not really, I have always been like this. Rather, you look thinner to me.'

Vicky had instructed Mala to flatter the boss' wife but it had backfired. Mala tried to salvage the situation, 'Very nice dress, yaa! Where did you pick it up from?'

'Oh, Rakesh got it for me from Paris last month,' Sophie quickly made this up to show that their love was still alive and kicking. Mala felt a deep pain in her heart as Vicky had stopped getting her gifts long back.

Joe came in with his wife. Nitin strolled in alone around nine and Rakesh greeted him, 'Hey Nitin, welcome. Where's Vani?'

'Oh, Vani is busy with the kids. Our younger one got a fever this morning.' Rakesh knew that it was a poor excuse as all of them had a bevy of maids and servants who were more than capable of taking care of a sick child but he smiled, 'Oh poor thing, I can understand. Come on, let's get a drink.'

Nitin never took his wife to an office event. He didn't mix personal and business matters. Given his playboy reputation and frequent escapades with female colleagues, he was insecure about his wife meeting anyone from work. One malicious piece of information and his marriage would be on the rocks.

Slowly, the living room of the five thousand square feet home filled up. Satya and Amit had come in with Kakoli and Anu respectively. Their eyes dazzled at the grandeur of the CEO's home. It added more fire to their ambitions—it was worth doing whatever it took to reach such stature in life.

Rekha arrived late. There was no question of bringing the rogue Neeraj to such an event. He was a drunkard and if he lost it after a few drinks here, Rekha's career might suffer irreparable damage. Rakesh had invited Azhar and Samir from banking as this was an excellent opportunity for informal networking among all business heads. Though he understood the dog-eat-dog culture of British Bank, he still liked to see a certain level of warmth among his senior team members.

As the evening went on, there appeared a stark division of class. The junior guys were talking to each other in one part of the room, concentrating on expensive single malts and exotic wines. The seniors were in another part, exchanging jokes, talking about their high-society topics.

In fact, the division was established when Kakoli and Anu had come in. Sophie and Mala just exchanged a polite 'Hi' and kept to themselves. There was no air-kissing. They also didn't like their husbands talking to these pretty young things. The husbands, aware of the consequences, stayed away from them. Anu spoke to Kakoli, 'This party feels a little weird to me. The ambience, food and drinks are great but I am still sweating in the AC. I am not at ease.'

'Satya prepped me well in advance. He told me to politely smile at everyone and not to spill any personal information. People tend to draw a lot of inferences and judge everyone quickly.'

'I wish Amit had told me the same, I would have been prepared. But I am glad you came. We can keep each other company,' sighed Anu.

'Look there,' whispered Kakoli, 'It looks like a royal courtroom to me. Rakesh and Sophie are sitting like royals. I am surprised by the way Nitin is kneeling in front of Rakesh's sofa and talking to him, looking more like a courtier in a king's court.'

'It's actually a lot worse. One of his knees is on the ground and the other in the air at 90 degrees, in a lunging position,' and they started giggling, trying hard not to make it obvious. If they had any idea about the amount of money at stake, they would have played by the rules of the game. They had not tasted the large booty yet.

'Hey, Nitin seems to have started a trend. Now Vicky and Mala are kneeling and talking to Rakesh and Sophie. It's becoming more and more a brazen show of sycophancy. We need to coax our husbands to do the same. Otherwise, they may lose out.'

The girls walked toward the bar where Rekha, Satya and Amit were gossiping, ostensibly about some office stuff. Kakoli whispered in Satya's ears, 'Can't you see, all your seniors are sucking up to Rakesh and Sophie so openly. Will you just keep gulping down whiskey or make good use of this time?'

'I can't do that, Kakoli. You can see very well we are not welcome in that part of the room.'

'Nothing like that. We have not driven 30 kilometres to south Mumbai just for a few drinks. You better make use of this time. This is my warning, otherwise you will have it from me!' Satya could not ignore his wife's stern threat. He knew the consequences. *I will be haunted for ages for not following her crucial advice.*

Anu also convinced Amit and the troupe advanced towards the royal couple and their subjects. Slowly wading through the crowd,

Satya managed to find an opening and bent forward to strike a conversation with Rakesh, while Kakoli did the same with Sophie. She was cursing Satya for not kneeling as her back was aching because of the bending.

'Hi ma'am, it's a great party. We are having a lot of fun. Thanks for organizing everything so well,' Kakoli complimented Sophie.

'Oh yes, these things happen with experience. Rakesh and I are born socialites, we have such parties every other day,' Sophie didn't give any credit to Jenny for the work that went in; the office tricks were handy at home as well.

As soon as they finished, Amit and Anu approached to pay their obeisance. Amit was a better courtier as he kneeled down, and Anu followed suit. Rakesh was warmer than his wife and asked them, 'Hope you are having a good time. Let me know if you need anything.'

'We are perfectly fine, sir. Your staff and arrangements are very nice,' Anu shouted, trying to make herself heard over the music.

'Party is on till late, drink well,' Sophie smirked, which actually meant 'Finish soon and get going!'

Nitin, Samir and Azhar again surrounded Rakesh, making sure that the schmucks didn't stick around him for too long. Sophie went to oversee the dinner arrangements and the other ladies followed her, as if she needed their help in addition to Jenny and the numerous waiters. Nitin told Rakesh, 'This new deal is going to be the game changer for us. I will need your help a little later to push it with the head office.' He was trying hard to cover up for the debacle earlier. The memory of getting screwed by Alex and Samir was still fresh in his mind.

'Nitin, anything for you, my man. Just keep the deals coming,' assured Rakesh.

Azhar, not wanting to be left behind, jumped in, 'In fact, Nitin, I was telling Rakesh about the same deal before you came in. Let's get this done soon.'

Ah, this asshole is already trying to steal credit for my deal. I need to stop sharing information with him. He rebuffed Azhar, 'But most of the work has already been done by us, so far we haven't needed your help.'

Rakesh sensed that an inter-departmental feud might spoil his party. He quickly changed the topic and asked Joe, 'What's the news from our trading boys? We have given them a good amount of risk limits, when will they start showing some revenue?' Joe understood that Rakesh was taking a jab at the lagging trading revenue. He looked around for the head of trading, Vicky. He couldn't believe that Vicky was smoking a cigar with his wife on the sprawling, sea-facing balcony while the CEO was screwing his happiness.

He signalled Vicky to join them. As soon as he came, Joe redirected the question to him.

'Rakesh is curious when your trading team will start delivering the results you have been promising for long?' he laughed, trying to lighten his comment.

Vicky thought of an intelligent response quickly, 'Yes Rakesh, it's true that we had some headwinds on the currency trading front because of the central bank intervention last month. First, they let the dollar fall for a long time and, as soon as we were lulled into building a large short position, they intervened through agent banks to reverse its direction and we made a huge loss. Our rates traders have done well and captured the whole move in interest rates. They positioned long bonds before the RBI started cutting interest rates owing to low inflation. I am hopeful that we will deliver strong numbers by mid-year.' He had delivered a long, defensive monologue and Rakesh seemed happy with it. Vicky called for a double neat Cardhu to regain his composure.

Nitin had spoken briefly with Anu and Kakoli and soon after their introduction to Nitin, their husbands whisked them away. Amit and Satya didn't want any meaningful interaction between their wives and their immediate boss. Inadvertently, Nitin would make some derogatory comment about them to disparage them in front of their wives. The wives would think that they were equally foolish at work as at home. In addition, they had briefed the ladies about his flirtatious nature and had insisted that they should not talk to him much.

The strategy worked. In the other corner, Anu and Kakoli had grouped again. Kakoli spoke, 'Samir and his wife, Amrita are the most balanced of the lot. They managed to move around and interact equally with the whole crowd. I don't know if Samir has the same career compulsions as the others.'

Anu agreed, 'Yes, even I noticed that. His wife is the friendliest among all the senior wives.'

'She gave me a few tips on holding my wine glass, in a friendly and inoffensive manner. I wonder why they don't have more of such people in British Bank.'

Kakoli was getting worried about Satya's drinking. She asked Anu, 'Does Amit also drink every day? And how much does he drink?'

'Amit drinks about once a week. He likes to have a drink with me on the weekend. Otherwise, he has a couple of small drinks only on important events or for social reasons. Why do you ask?'

'Satya drinks almost every day and he ends up having three or more large drinks. It is extremely worrying as he insists on driving after drinking.' Kakoli had forced Satya to hire a driver after his drunk-driving episode.

'Yes, that's too risky. I have prohibited Amit to touch the wheel if he even touches a liquor bottle.'

Kakoli let out a sigh, 'I haven't had any such luck controlling Satya's drinking habit. He used to justify this as a professional requirement for a long time but now his social drinking has developed into a drinking problem.'

People had started leaving. Kakoli noticed that only Amit, Satya and Rekha were still drinking and gossiping at the bar. All the others had left. Rakesh passed by the bar, 'Guys, the bar is open till you can drink. Don't call it a night yet.' He increased the volume of the music. Sophie was hanging around but was making her displeasure apparent.

Anu said, 'Kakoli, we need to ask our husbands to wind up fast. It doesn't look nice that we are the only ones still here.' Kakoli whispered something to Satya in Bangla and Anu did the same to Amit.

A few feet away, Sophie whispered to Rakesh, 'At least these girls have some sense and are not going mad over free drinks.' Rakesh pretended not to hear.

Satya said to Kakoli sternly, 'What's the problem with you? Whenever I am having a good time with my friends, you don't like it!'

'I am only asking you to leave this place. If you want, all of us can hit a bar somewhere else but it's a bit odd to hang around here,' Kakoli made her point despite being snubbed in public.

'I think she has a point, Satya. Let's leave now,' Amit said, indicating that he was still sober. Though he had matched Satya in drinking time, his alcohol consumption was a lot lower. He remembered the four golden D's of alcohol—Dilution, Duration, Diet and (no) Driving. Ignore any of these and you are headed for trouble.

Chapter 27

There was a different kind of buzz in the office in the first week of February, 2008. Rekha walked in and took her seat beside the other two, who were already whispering to each other. She looked at them curiously. Amit reminded her that this was the day every banker waits for. It was the compensation day or the day when bonus letters were handed out to employees. Expectations were sky-high because it had been a great year for the bank globally and in India.

Joe told Nitin, 'I want to be a part of all the comp discussions today. Let me know when you receive the letters from HR and we will have a pre-meeting to discuss what to communicate to each team member.'

Nitin agreed. *I know why he wants to be a part of the meetings. It will tell the employee that he also played a role in deciding the comp numbers and that they better be a good slave to him.*

Amit was the first one to be called to the far conference room that was hidden from the rest of the office. A mix of tension, excitement and expectation was apparent on his face. He entered the room and saw Joe and Nitin sitting on the other side of the table, looking grimly at a sheet of paper. It didn't look too promising.

Joe took the lead, 'Amit, as you are aware, the year has been great for the bank globally but India has had a few headwinds. We suffered some trading losses and higher than expected costs. Hence, our cost to income ratio isn't looking too good and the bonus amounts for the department have been moderated accordingly. I will let Nitin speak more about your performance and comp.'

'Amit, on the whole you did well but our standards of performance are high,' Nitin started. Amit could see it coming—the low bonus and no promotion.

Nitin continued, 'So, I have tried to be accommodating and, given the bonus pool constraints, we have managed an amount that should make you happy.' He handed over the sheet of paper to him.

Amit was devastated. His bonus was 30 percent lower than what he had expected. He had built up this expectation by talking to many colleagues in Mumbai in other offices. Even though Nitin and Joe tried managing expectations across the department, everyone knew that those statements had little meaning. At the end of the day, they needed to get paid well.

But Amit also knew that he could not throw a fit. Though the number was low vis-à-vis his expectations, it was still a healthy pay packet. He could use it to pay a substantial part of his home loan. He also wanted to start the new year on a positive note. If he upset Joe and Nitin with his antics, they may slash his bonus very badly next year. So, he looked at the sheet for a minute and glanced at them with an inexpressive face. Joe and Nitin studied his face for any emotion he might betray, but there was none.

Nitin concluded, 'So, you have any comments?'

'I am a bit disappointed as the bonus is way below my expectation.

I will still accept it given the constraints you talked about but why you didn't promote me this year. I meet all the criteria.'

Nitin, relieved, told him, 'Promotions have been rationed very strictly this year. Unless you rank in the top five percent globally, there is no promotion. Same with increments in fixed salary. I will see what can be done next year, just keep up the good work.'

Amit nodded, quickly got up and walked out. His mind was overflowing with thoughts. *To hell with next year. There are too many variables that may change over a year. Nitin may leave, I may leave or the market may not be good. I will tackle next year when it comes but now it's time to intensify my job search.*

Amit had started dreaming about working at Lehman Brothers, a major American investment bank. It was every financial whiz-kid's aspiration. He had already received a call from a head-hunter who claimed to have the mandate to hire for them. Lehman Brothers was about to make an entry into the Indian market. *If I don't capitalise on the market boom now, these bastards will keep exploiting me forever. I mean, which employer doesn't increase your salary two years in a row?*

When he left, Nitin and Joe smiled at each other. One done, two more to go. Joe laughed, 'That was easy. The schmuck didn't know what hit him. The trick to decide the bonus number is to pay just enough to keep them from revolting. You don't need to pay them all at the top end. This is what I told you when the numbers were being finalised.'

'Yes boss, it actually works. I am calling Satya next.'

Satya was sitting attentive, straight-backed and ready to march. He tried to glean if Amit was happy or sad, but couldn't make out. His phone rang and he understood his time had come.

Joe gave his customary global speech and handed over the discussion to Nitin. Nitin started with a grim look, 'Satya, you have been an important member of the team and have tried to contribute, but your performance has fallen well short of our expectations. In addition to the issues that Joe talked about, keeping your revenue numbers in mind, we are giving you this.' He handed over the sheet of paper to Satya.

Satya was not expecting a promotion and he had some idea that his bonus amount would be bad. But his heart kept telling him that it would be a good amount nevertheless as the bonus pool was really big this year.

He looked at his compensation sheet and his face turned red at the token amount. He burst out, 'What the hell is this? I have worked hard for the entire year and produced a reasonably good performance. You have rated me low on subjective parameters and I challenge that.'

'Satya, it's not unfair at all, we pay according to performance and in line with the internal benchmarks.' Nitin gave him the senior management mumbo jumbo to shut him up. But Satya was not in a mood to give up, 'I don't care, I need the bonus revised to at least double of what it is. I want to speak to the global head of Markets and the head of HR.'

This one was not going down well. The management used the bonus as a tacit indication of whether the employee was wanted in the team or not. They would have been happy to get rid of Satya but didn't want to create a scene at work. Complaints to senior management at the head office also tarnished Joe's and Nitin's image as people managers.

Meanwhile, Satya was becoming more insolent. Joe played the mediator and told him, 'Just give us some time and we will get back to you.' Satya tried his best to look like his normal self and came back to this seat. He didn't want others to rejoice in his moment of disgrace.

Joe scratched his head. He knew that nothing could be done to change Satya's numbers but he wanted the situation to be managed amicably. They quickly called the regional manager in Singapore and the local HR head and apprised them of the situation. The advice from the top was to escort the employee out of the office in case he created any more drama. The pros and cons had already been weighed before the numbers were cast in stone and they were prepared to lose him. They decided to have the second discussion with Satya at the end of the day. He would get some time to reconcile with the outcome and would be relatively calmer.

Rekha was next. Joe started his speech, 'Rekha, you have been a great addition to the team and we are glad to have hired you. This year has been quite tough for us owing to cost pressures, though we have done well on the revenue front.'

The first part of the speech was the opposite of what Rekha expected. *Why is he giving a defensive twist to this? Have they failed to promote me or is the bonus too low?*

Joe continued, 'In this context, the bank has decided to differentiate between the top performers and the mediocre employees. I am happy to share that you have been identified as one of the top performers. Now, I will let Nitin get down to specifics.'

Nitin was eagerly awaiting his turn and exclaimed, 'Congratulations, Rekha! You have been promoted to Vice-President. Your new salary and bonus numbers are here.'

Rekha was bubbling with joy and took the paper with trembling hands. She was ecstatic, 'Thanks a lot, Joe and Nitin. Joining British Bank and your team was the right decision for me. Thanks a lot again for your support.'

Joe warned her, 'We are happy for you, Rekha. But do bear in mind that the bonus, increment numbers and the ratings vary a lot across the team. We strongly discourage you from sharing any information with your colleagues. The news of your promotion will spread later but for now behave as normal and keep your joy to yourself.'

Nitin added, 'I will second that. I don't want any comparisons and complaints of unfair treatment by other team members.'

Rekha replied in the affirmative and thanked them again.

After many years in the industry, she was used to these processes. Earlier, Nitin had leaked the news of her promotion to her. He did it to ensure that Rekha knew he was single-handedly responsible for her promotion. This was a routine practice followed by managers to keep a tight grip on the favoured team members. They never knew whose support may be needed in a difficult situation.

Rekha was back at her desk with an expressionless face. She was having a rough time managing the divorce case and this good news was a welcome change. Was all the hard work and sweat worth it? Right now, it looked like it was, though she didn't have anyone to celebrate it with. As soon as she caught Amit looking at her, she tried extra hard not to betray any happiness.

Nitin called Satya and informed him that his case had been referred to the regional management. 'We will get back to you later, but for now, the bonus amount stays where it is.' Satya was relatively sober by now. He expressed his displeasure but avoided taking any rash decision.

Chapter 28

The next Friday, Satya met up with his college buddies at the new hip joint that had opened in the distant suburb of Vashi. Though he had to drive a long way through the town and suburbs, even crossing the Vashi creek bridge, he didn't mind it as this place was close to many of his friends' offices who were in the IT and BPO industries. He was looking forward to a relaxed evening and was the first to arrive.

Modelled on the theme of the movie *Matrix*, the interiors were a mix of black and emerald green. The door, the walls and all the tables were black, bathed in the green light. He was soaking in the refreshingly different ambience when he stopped in his tracks. In a corner, he saw Nitin hugging and kissing Rekha all over. However, since the bar was completely empty, there was no way he could have turned back without being noticed by them.

He stood frozen in his spot. *Even though it is a spicy piece of news to talk about, I don't want to take credit for breaking this out.*

It would have been so much better to hear it from someone else and then have some fun. Nitin and Rekha quickly disentangled and got up. While Rekha sneaked out without even looking at him, Nitin was more professional. He stopped in front of Satya, shook his hands and talked as if nothing had happened, 'Hey man, you here in Vashi? All well?'

Satya politely responded, 'Yeah, I am just meeting some friends over drinks.'

Nitin winked, 'Just remember, good friends are the ones who keep each other's secrets,' and he walked out. What friendship was he referring to? Nitin had always treated him like a schmuck and he would remain one forever. Then it dawned on Satya that Nitin was referring to his drunken driving episode. He was so frustrated at this thought that his evening was ruined. If the news of their cosy encounter broke out, Nitin would hold him responsible. In turn, Nitin would not shy away from informing the management about his police case. He was cursing himself for having this uncanny knack for landing in such losing situations.

What the heck? What was done was done. He ordered a double black without waiting for the others to arrive. He gulped the large drink, felt the heat flow down his throat and drowned his irritation in it.

As Nitin walked up to Rekha, she exploded, 'What now? Tomorrow, the whole office will be whispering about us. This bastard has probably started texting everyone frantically already.'

Nitin was cool. 'Hey baby, calm down. I have him by his balls. If he creates any trouble for us, I will hit him where it hurts the most. You don't need to worry. I have already settled the matter with him. Let's go to our real rendezvous place.'

She didn't understand. 'What are you saying? How is this possible?'

'You don't need to know anything more than what I told you.

Do you think I would not be worried if there was any threat from him?'

Rekha had been getting closer to Nitin despite not wanting to. It was complicated. She was in the middle of a divorce case with Neeraj and Nitin seemed like a nice man for emotional support. She had snubbed his early attempts to get cosy with her but he was persistent.

One day, a few months back, when they were sitting at a cafe after a client meeting, Nitin had grabbed her hand. Rekha had protested but he hadn't let go. 'I think I told you already the other day,' he answered when she asked him what he was doing. She had also developed feelings for him and it all came out that day. They had been going out regularly after that.

Nitin ensured that these outings were at obscure places. He was experienced at managing extra-marital affairs, unlike Neeraj, who was a drunkard and habitual womaniser, and terrible at it. She remembered having a couple of drinks with Nitin during their first such rendezvous. Nitin had asked her, 'Why don't we spend some time in the deluxe suite at the Modern Hotel? I can stay out all night tonight.' *And I am sure nobody is waiting for you either.*

Rekha regretted that she had shared her domestic situation with him. She felt that Nitin was zeroing in on her aggressively, but somewhere her personal situation had affected her emotional state and she couldn't say no. After all, Neeraj had been doing all this and worse for many years behind her back. She said, 'Okay, I will come but you will have to let me go whenever I want.' Nitin knew that he had to make her comfortable if he had to have his way. He answered, 'Of course, you can leave any time you want to.'

Nitin was already checked into the hotel and she walked in as his guest. The room was spacious, furnished with a large king-size bed and a sitting arrangement on the side. 'Make yourself comfortable, Rekha,' Nitin smiled and slipped into the washroom. She looked around and decided to sit on the long sofa. The purple velvet upholstery shimmered in the soft lighting.

'Would you like some wine or whiskey? The mini-bar is well stocked,' Nitin offered. While she was still making up her mind, Nitin took out a wine bottle for himself and that made the decision easier for her. Nitin knew that Rekha was feeling a bit hesitant and that a couple of drinks would help to get into the mood. In such situations, alcohol made up for what was lacking in courage.

Nitin poured some wine in the glasses, handed one to Rekha, said 'Cheers!' and looked straight into her eyes. He could sense that she desired him but needed to feel a bit more at home. He decided to go slow and gently sat beside her. She was the first to speak, after a pause that seemed too long. 'I'm feeling relaxed after a long time. The last few months have been very taxing for me.'

'I can understand, it's not easy. Now that you are not answerable to anyone, you can start afresh. Just chill and take your time to decide the future. Let me know if I can help in any way,' Nitin moved a bit closer and placed his arm on her back, gently caressing it.

Rekha, already inebriated and emotionally weak, felt a rush at the manly touch and craved more of it. She leaned towards him and fell into his embrace. They kissed like long-lost lovers and then continued drinking. Finally, Rekha let herself go in his arms and they spent the whole night wearing nothing but the white cotton sheets of the hotel room.

She hadn't felt this good in many years. As she got dressed the next morning, Nitin asked, 'Why can't you stay for the day? It's Saturday and my wife is at her parents' place.' 'I think I should go now. I need to go home, get some rest and clear my head.' All of this was happening too fast for her to digest.

Nitin kept his word, 'Sure, I promised that you can leave when you want. I just want to make sure that you are fine. Are you having second thoughts?'

'Not really, Nitin. I am a grown-up, independent woman. More so now. I'm good but let's agree that this relationship has no strings attached.' This was music to Nitin's ears. He remembered his last fling with the gorgeous gym trainer who ended up taking the affair too seriously. As soon as he had realised that the girl was weaving long-term plans, he ditched not only the girl but also the gym membership. It was a small price to pay.

He assured Rekha, 'Yes, no strings attached. What happens between us, stays between us.' Rekha was relieved too and quickly left the hotel, keeping her head down and hoping she wouldn't bump into anyone she knew.

Chapter 29

Satya tried to follow up with Nitin on the discussion, rather the argument, that had happened on bonus day. 'Nitin, you told me that the bonus issue was referred to senior management. Any update on it? It has been over a week now.'

'Look Satya, these issues are not limited to only you in the bank. There are a large number of employees who feel that they have been unfairly compensated. Many of them end up creating some noise. Although Joe and I referred your case to the regional management in Singapore, I haven't ever seen bonus numbers getting revised. If you still want to push your luck, feel free to call them yourself,' Nitin sounded rather stern.

Satya got the message loud and clear. They had played a fast one by calming him down and giving him tacit hopes of a resolution. But now that the event was a week old, he could not create the same amount of disturbance in the system. He realised that he was screwed and the only solution would be to look patiently for a job.

Lehman Brothers had just started the hiring process for multiple positions. Satya's interview was scheduled for the following week.

Meanwhile, Amit and Rekha had also been contacted by the same head-hunter and both had shown a keen interest in taking the discussion further. They knew that these kinds of opportunities came along only once in a while. All three were salivating at the prospect of tripling their salary in one swift move. Nitin was also being tapped by a senior partner in the same head-hunting firm. They wanted to poach the whole team from a successful bank.

The pain of hiring people one by one the old-fashioned way was too much and the time, too little. It was important that hiring was done quickly while the market was still hot. There was no point getting stuck with an expensive staff if the market busted.

The day of the interview had arrived. Satya adjusted his tie in the washroom of the Oberoi Business Centre at Nariman Point. There was no denying the importance of power-dressing and grooming. He had invested in a 120-count woollen bespoke suit and branded Italian leather shoes. The suit was stitched by one of the best tailors in town and fit him impeccably. A navy blue fabric coupled with a dark tan belt and matching shoes was a lethal combination. He had gotten a haircut the previous evening and had clipped his nails before bed.

He was tense. His heart was thumping and he could feel the sides of his temples throbbing. *I need this offer so I can slap my resignation in Nitin's face and walk out of that wretched place.* He tried to recall all that he had learned from his previous interviews. *Just be calm and composed. You are a seasoned professional and nobody expects you to know everything. If you know the answer, say it or get out of the situation by giving it a humorous twist.*

He took a deep breath and greeted the middle-aged Caucasian male sitting inside the room. He shook the person's hand firmly, recalling what his ex-boss always said, 'An energetic greeting and a firm handshake are the best moves to make a great start.'

The gentleman answered with greater vigour, 'Hey, morning mate! How are you today? I am Gary, Senior Managing Director for Asia Fixed Income Markets at Lehman.' Gary looked really fit, his chest straining against the tailored shirt. He sported an orange Ferragamo tie and his jacket hung on the suit-stand. His hair was gelled and spiked from the front while the hair behind was neatly trimmed and combed. In short, he looked like he had walked right down from Wall Street.

Satya saw two empty coffee cups on the table. One cup had a dark red lipstick stain. *Did Rekha also come here to try her luck?* He forgot that other banks were in this as well. Generally, people are more scared of competition they know. But it also meant that he couldn't quote arbitrary numbers while trying to impress Gary.

'Satya, right? I was told that is your short name. See, I am here on a quick trip and obviously interviewing many candidates. We have two positions in sales, one senior and the other mid-level. We are considering you for the mid-level position.'

What the hell? I think this girl, Jyoti, from the head-hunting firm didn't market me properly. Satya tried to focus on what was being said. He nodded.

'Since time is short, I will not go through the motions of asking you about yourself, your family and the weather in Mumbai. Let's get straight to the point. We have done our due diligence and we know which clients you cover and what revenue you contribute. Just tell me, what will be your strategy to get a new entrant like Lehman into the league of existing big boys in India?'

Great, half the problem was over. At least he was convinced that Satya was the right guy for the job. Satya just had to convince him that he was the best. He had to be as close to the truth about his current business but could really stretch his imagination when it came to future possibility. He made some outrageous commitments and ended his statement with confidence, 'Gary, with all these initiatives that I have detailed, I am confident that we will be among the top three players in India in the next three years.'

For most of the interview, Gary was juggling his three phones and a Blackberry, half-listening to what Satya was saying. At the end, Gary looked visibly pleased and shook his hand with the same energy as at the beginning. The interview ended. The bank had deep pockets and the Indian market looked very lucrative, so he didn't want to waste time on mundane matters like compensation. The offer would be too hard to reject, in any case.

Satya's fears had been true. Rekha had interviewed just before him. However, her interview had been more lukewarm. She was experienced in structuring but the new job at Lehman required client-facing experience. For structuring, they could use their expertise in Singapore or Hong Kong. Still it was important to interview Rekha to cross-check the facts and figures quoted by the salespersons from British Bank.

Amit's interview was in the afternoon. Amit was cursing himself for giving in to the temptation of eating the Punjabi lunch he carried from home. The parathas and the paneer were taking their toll—he couldn't stop yawning on his way to the Oberoi. He told Nitin he had to take care of some urgent personal work. Nitin knew these tactics but didn't want to spoil the fun, and granted half a day off to Amit.

Amit was 20 minutes early and headed straight to the washroom to check his hair, tie and the shoe-shine. He had stuck to a more conservative black tailored suit and a light blue double-cuff shirt with cufflinks. He spat out the mouth-freshening gum into a tissue paper and threw it in the bin. He completed the grooming with some light cologne. Satisfied that all was in order, he walked quickly to the coffee shop and asked for a large black coffee to go. A few sips of coffee and he was beginning to come back to his senses. He carried the coffee towards the assigned meeting room and took a few deep breaths before gently knocking on the door.

Gary spoke from inside, 'Come in.' He greeted him with enthusiasm, 'Hey Amit, this is Gary. Pleased to meet you!'

'Pleased to meet you too,' he tried to match Gary's energy level. *How on earth are these guys able to talk with such energy all the time? Our meetings are mostly dull and people are either half-dead or yawning during important meetings.* That was a big cultural difference he had noticed while on his overseas trips. He understood that looking and sounding energetic was the most important attribute any hiring manager looked for.

His interview lasted ten minutes and was along the same lines as Satya's. Only, his future projections of the business were more realistic. As Amit came out of the meeting room, he felt that he had done well and a lot of credit went to the black coffee he had had.

Unknown to the candidates, Gary had shortlisted Satya and Amit as his top choices. Since Amit was more measured in his promises, Gary kept him in second position behind Satya. This was a hallmark of such interviews in a heated market. Whoever boasted more had more of a chance of getting the job. The hiring managers accepted the boasting as gospel and didn't want to know the logic behind those promises. Gary just wanted to make the offers and wrap up the hiring fast.

Chapter 30

The phone rang at ten in the night and Kakoli brought it to Satya. It was Dan, the senior partner from the head-hunting firm that was managing the search for Gary, 'Hey Satya, good time?'

What kind of absurd question is this? In India, any time is a good time to call people on the mobile. In the US or Europe, it may not be. 'Yes Dan, tell me.'

'Gary was pleased to meet you and he would like to make an offer. Lehman Brothers will offer you a 50 percent increment over your current fixed pay and guarantee a bonus at hundred percent of the fixed salary for one year.'

'Okay, go on,' Satya's response was measured even though he was ecstatic.

'We know the situation in the market and hence, Lehman has made a great offer at the outset with no haggling or negotiation.'

Satya knew the seriousness of the situation. Even though the offer seemed too good to be true, he was a true sales professional and he could gauge that there was plenty of room for negotiation. He kept the joy of getting the offer hidden from Dan. He also had to keep his screwed-up situation at his current job under wraps. Anybody else in his place would have said yes immediately without pushing his luck further.

But he answered in a flat voice, 'Dan, thanks for this but I need to give it due consideration. I would be more inclined to accept your offer if the fixed salary is double my current salary and they pay a guaranteed bonus for two years.'

Dan could hardly believe this. In his long head-hunting career, he hadn't heard of any candidate bargaining over such a great offer. He had been advised by a colleague that Indians are master negotiators and that he should keep some buffer for that.

He tried another pressure tactic, 'Satya, I think you are demanding too much. I can certainly go back to Gary but I am not sure how he will react. There is a reasonable chance that he may offer this to the next guy on the shortlist. Do you still want me to try?'

If Satya had learnt one thing from Nitin, it was the ability to get the best deal from the other party. *You need to be prepared to walk away from a good deal in order to get a great deal.* He replied firmly, 'Yes, Dan.'

The line disconnected. While Kakoli was trying to make small talk, he was immersed in his thoughts. *I am rotting away in my current job and I should not undersell myself just to land up in another shit hole. The other place will not be the oasis that it appears to be. It will be similar, if not worse, in job pressure and stress. It's a new set-up and I will need to work extra hard to get clients and get the systems and processes in place. I may be unhappy with my current situation, but British Bank is a well-oiled machine that needs low marginal effort to run.*

He was half-asleep when the phone rang again. For a moment, he was caught between two worlds but he quickly came to his senses and answered the phone. It was Dan, 'Congratulations, Gary has agreed to your demands and they would like to make you the offer. Do you accept it?'

Satya couldn't tell if he was still dreaming. He answered, 'Yes, sure. I will take it. What are the next steps?'

'Gary will need to put up your offer letter for internal approvals as they seldom offer such lucrative terms to candidates. However, given the huge potential of this market and your capabilities, Gary is confident that he will get the approvals. The offer letter should be ready for signing in a couple of days.'

'Okay, that sounds fine.'

'Goodnight.'

But his sleep had vanished. Kakoli could tell something good had happened. He hugged her and broke the news, 'I have got an amazing job offer!'

Kakoli was immensely happy. 'We need to celebrate! Let me get the chocolate brownies from the fridge.' Both of them had a sweet tooth. They had a brownie each and hugged each other again.

Satya said, 'Our life is going to change forever.' As Kakoli settled down for the night, she recalled that Satya had said the same thing when he got the offer from British Bank four years ago. *But our life has hardly changed. In fact, the quality of life has gone down considerably in terms of time spent together. The only things that have gone up are the amount of alcohol Satya drinks and the money in our bank account.*

At his house, Amit was tossing and turning anxiously in bed. He told Anu, 'My interview went so well. I thought Gary would hug me and hire me right there. But there has been no call or anything.'

Anu was more composed, 'Amit, you were interviewed just a few hours ago. Isn't it too early to expect any call from them?'

'Maybe you're right. But I have heard that these guys are in a hurry to hire.' *Let me wait for a few days. I will not call Dan because it will show my desperation and will adversely affect any subsequent offer.*

He was right. If he called, Dan would immediately inform Gary that Amit was the more desperate of the lot and, if all other things were equal, they could hire him cheap. Even though Dan's commission was linked to the salary offered to the candidate, he would still want to close the hiring at a lower level to ensure that Gary was not using any other head-hunters for the same task. Competition was everywhere. Among banks, among candidates and among head-hunters.

Chapter 31

The morning brought its usual freshness and people had just started trickling into the office. However, Satya had barely managed to drag himself to work. He had a terrible hangover. He popped a couple of disprins and had a large black coffee and felt a little better. *Let me get to the work that's pending. I need to be diligent till I get the offer letter, or Joe and Nitin may get suspicious.*

Satya's hangovers never made him consider reducing or giving up drinking. He was still young, in his early thirties. In fact, he and his friends ridiculed people like Samir who maintained a healthy lifestyle. It was hard for him to imagine what he would do if he didn't drink at office parties or with his other friends.

After a couple of drinks, his reality got blurry. Even though he was interacting with people, he was there mostly to enjoy the spinning sensation in his head and to ogle the gorgeous babes hanging around the bar. Undoubtedly, he had developed a few very close friendships over drinks but the alcohol was his crutch. If he didn't drink, he would feel completely out of place. The hangover or the threat to his health was not a significant concern.

In the seat next to him, Amit was anxiously punching his keyboard. It was apparent that his mind was elsewhere. While typing some client deal proposal, he was thinking hard about the probable offer from Lehman Brothers. He needed it badly. He was having trouble keeping his hands off the mobile phone. Any follow up with Dan could cause a lot of damage. *If Gary really liked me, he would call me. If he didn't like me then he will not call even if I follow up. I need to control myself.*

'Here is the next deal outline for you to work on. Could you work out an innovative structure by the evening and then we'll talk?' Nitin handed Rekha a bunch of printouts.

She started reading but she hoped it wasn't a ploy for another night out with her. Nitin had been quite demanding in office even after their fling had picked up. *But I have got paid well and got promoted ahead of others, so I don't mind giving my best at work. This interview with Lehman Brothers was a good opportunity to take a shot at bettering my salary. If they give me an offer and I take it, Joe and Nitin will feel cheated. But I have to look at my financial goals and not at their emotions. There are no friends here.*

In the adjacent conference room, Joe was catching up with Nitin, 'So, how have you managed Satya's post-bonus hysterics?'

'Boss, you are a veteran, I am just learning from you. I told him that we have referred the matter to regional senior management in Singapore while I just sat on it. It has been over a week now and he has followed up only once with me rather timidly.'

'Looks like he has run out of steam. Why pay more when he has nowhere to go?' Joe chuckled.

Amit saw them share jokes and whispered to Satya, 'These bastards are having a good time after pocketing some hefty bonuses at our expense.' Satya only nodded. He didn't want to reveal his disastrous bonus outcome. The risk of being made fun of by the rest of the team was too high. Inside, he was still seething.

Just then, a couple of young boys and a girl, all dressed in crisp white shirts and formal suits, walked into the dealing room. They were accompanied by the head of HR, Sonia. She gathered the room's attention and announced, 'I am here to introduce Dev, Om and Nikita. They will be with us for the next two months as part of our summer internship program. We have selected them from the country's top B-schools and will be assigning them to some of you. Please give them challenging projects so they can utilise their time well here.'

All eyes were on the young female summer intern. Joe, Nitin, Vicky, everyone was gawking at her as if they had never seen anything like her their entire life. Understandably, because most of them were IIT and IIM graduates who had spent their high testosterone years in desert-like conditions when it came to females. Their studies, grades and jobs left them very little time to indulge in luxuries like dating. In addition to time, the inability to behave normally with members of the opposite sex was a real hindrance. Any refreshing female company, even for two months, was more than welcome.

Nikita was assigned to Joe. Dev and Om were assigned to Alex and Samir respectively. Joe was quick to offload the responsibility to Nitin for day-to-day supervision. Nitin called for a meeting with Nikita and Amit. He started the discussion, 'Amit, this is Nikita from IIM Kolkata. I have decided to give her the project of finding out the correlation between foreign exchange rates and interest rates. It will be your job to guide her in the project and I will do weekly review meetings.'

Amit had no choice but to accept. Nitin left after his initial guidance. Amit asked Nikita, 'So, what do you know about foreign exchange rates and interest rates? Do you know how to use Reuters or Bloomberg terminals?'

Nikita just stared at him with her large black eyes. The eye makeup was great though, complete with artificial eye lashes and eye liner. After a two-minute silence, in which Amit mourned his summer trainee's lack of knowledge, he said, 'I get it. You need to start fresh. We have eight weeks and if we plan well, we can complete the project.'

'Sure, Amit. Actually, we don't have elective courses in the first year but I am willing to put in the hard work.'

Amit was relieved that the trainee had the intention to learn. 'Here are a couple of books to read. Please make a list of your doubts and you can solve them with any of us. I will slot a separate time to train you on Reuters and Bloomberg so that you can start collecting data.'

Nikita felt a lot better after this guidance. But after reading a few pages, the list of her doubts was longer than the text she had read. She hesitantly approached Rekha to resolve the doubts. Rekha was abrupt, 'Don't even think about disturbing me till seven.'

Satya, at the adjacent desk, was overjoyed that Nikita would be forced to approach him. He had all the time in the world for such a sweet summer intern. As soon as she did, he asked her to join him in the meeting room and patiently resolved all her doubts for the next hour.

Chapter 32

Finally, the offer letter from Lehman Brothers reached Dan's office. He rang Satya, 'Hey mate, your offer letter is here. Why don't you drop by in the evening and formally accept the offer?'

Satya was ecstatic, 'Oh sure, I will, Dan.'

Dan greeted him with the same enthusiasm that Gary had shown—a firm handshake and a loud outburst, 'Here you go. There are two copies of the offer letter. Even though the letter is 15 pages long, much of it is legal crap. The things that matter are on pages 6 and 7. Just read those and sign one copy as a token of your acceptance.'

Again, Satya was ready. 'Look Dan, I will appreciate it if you give both the copies to me. I would like to read the letter properly at home and then sign the other copy for you.' Dan understood that he was dealing with an experienced person and that the usual pressure tactics wouldn't work. He smiled, 'I understand, please do that.' He knew that Satya wanted to screen it for any malicious fine print.

Satya drove straight home and shared the good news with Kakoli. She was happy, 'So, when do you join them?'

'You innocent girl, these things don't work in such a simple manner. Let me sit peacefully and read this letter in detail, then I will decide the next course of action.'

He changed quickly and made himself a large drink, memories of his morning hangover now distant and forgotten. Kakoli countered, 'Why do you need to drink to read this paper?'

'You don't understand, today is a big day for us and we need to celebrate.'

'Of course, and you know only one way to celebrate.' Satya didn't want to prolong the argument and ruin his mood so he began reading every line with concentration.

The offer letter looked more like a pre-nuptial agreement—it talked more about separation than staying together. Still, it was a great offer and there were no hidden traps. He remembered British Bank had inserted an innocuous clause, thus retaining the flexibility to pay his sign-on bonus in bank shares. And they used the clause to pay him shares that would vest over the next five years. His dream of making a large down payment on his dream home with the sign-on bonus was shattered.

Noticing no unfavourable clauses, he called up Dan, 'I am happy to accept the offer. I will drop the signed copy at your office tomorrow.' He cut the call and relaxed in the armchair with his drink. Kakoli had prepared fish-fingers to participate in the celebration as she didn't drink at all.

Chapter 33

The summer interns made it a point to get together every day for lunch in the small makeshift canteen the bank had managed to put together. Most seniors had their lunch at the desk or in the meeting rooms. There was no concept of socializing informally over lunch without worrying about rank and department.

Dev was cribbing about his project guide as usual, 'Alex has still not briefed me about my project. Whenever I ask him, he tells me to read his clients' credit files. How does he expect me to make any sense of the credit files? I am an engineer and have done only one basic course in accounting in my MBA so far.'

Om was relaxed, 'Guys, my guide, Samir, is far too chilled out. The first day I met him, he gave me a long lecture on the importance of maintaining my health and well being. Can you believe it? He actually gave me a CD to meditate to at my hostel. I wanted to tell him that meditation and jogging will not get me the pre-placement offer from the bank.'

'Looks like my seniors are expecting a lot from me. My project has been so systematic so far that I am afraid I might not meet their expectations. Nitin has given me an interesting project and instructed his team members to keep guiding me every day,' Nikita was happy and nervous at the same time.

Dev and Om exchanged glances but didn't say anything. It was the same story at college. The professors were always eager to resolve the doubts raised by good-looking female twenty-somethings. But the same professors rebuked them when they asked questions. They had reconciled themselves to this fact of life. There was no difference between the frustrated middle-aged profs and these pot-bellied bankers.

Nikita was the first to finish lunch, 'See ya, I need to get back to sit with Amit.' She rushed out without waiting for a reply. Dev sighed, 'Oh God, why didn't you give me what you gave her?'

'Don't worry man, you will also turn into one of those deprived men in due course,' Om counselled.

Nikita was surprised that Nitin himself came to the meeting instead of Amit. After talking a bit about the project, he asked her, 'Are you on your own in the city? I mean, how did you arrange for a place to stay?'

'I was lucky to find a place in Wilson College's girls hostel. It's a great location, right on Marine Drive and there are plenty of cool hangouts close by.'

'Yup, that's good. Why don't you join me for a drink this evening... if you're free, that is?' he added as an afterthought.

Nikita was surprised. *He is asking me out. What should I do? I can't piss off such a senior guy. That will surely kill all my chances of a pre-placement offer.*

She agreed to go out but added, 'Yeah, I can come along but I need to reach the hostel before ten or they will complain to my local guardian—my uncle who lives in Andheri.'

'Oh, don't you worry. You will be safely back before ten.'

Nitin then sent in Amit for the actual project discussion. He was sure that Nikita would not talk about his offer with anyone. He had tasted success with interns before and was emboldened by that. In the worst case, nothing happened.

But Nitin didn't want to leave the office with her. He called Nikita at four in the afternoon and told her, 'I need to step out for a client meeting and will see you directly at Hotel Marine Plaza.'

'Sure, Nitin,' she said, feeling nervous. She didn't know what the evening had in store for her but she was comforted by the fact that the location was not secluded.

Chapter 34

Nitin was so enamoured by Nikita that he found himself taking unreasonable risks. He knew that if he had called her to the far suburban joints, she would have declined. Marine Plaza, a vintage boutique hotel, was located close to the business district in south Mumbai. Meeting her there was fraught with danger as any of his acquaintances could spot him. While he was still weighing these thoughts, it was time for the rendezvous.

He reached Geoffrey's, the bar at Marine Plaza, ten minutes before the appointed time and tipped the waiter a crisp five hundred rupee note. The waiter judged him to be a high-profile guest and obliged by offering a table in a corner, away from most people. It was early in the evening but a couple of old patrons were already sitting on the high stools at the bar. The brass lining and pipes running across the furniture gave this bar a unique classic English look. It was frequented by people who enjoyed the old-world charm of south Mumbai, while the younger crowd hung out in Lower Parel.

Nikita was on time and the waiter escorted her to Nitin's table. She had come straight from work and looked like a well-dressed professional in her formal dark grey jacket and knee-length skirt. Her height was accentuated by pencil heels. The corner was dimly lit by medieval lanterns made of multi-coloured stained glass. It was a round table surrounded by a semi-circular maroon leather upholstered sofa and a couple of antique chairs. She sat diagonally opposite Nitin on a chair. She looked good in office but here she looked awesome. The extra effort she put in to get ready was visible.

'Hi Nitin.'

'Hey Nikita, you look stunning!' he stood up to receive her, dropping the first hint of things to come later in the evening. Nikita was used to handling flirts at college but it was different with a senior colleague.

'What can I offer you to drink?'

Nikita was not entirely comfortable. 'A sweet lime soda.'

'What? Give me a break. How do you hope to succeed in the corporate world without alcohol? Don't tell me you don't drink.' After all, she was young, receiving a healthy stipend from a global bank and out to enjoy life in the megacity. He made Nikita's non-alcoholic choice feel like a crime. Under pressure, Nikita changed her order to a small Smirnoff vodka with orange juice. She still wanted to make it look like a mild drink. Nitin motioned to the waiter, who had been standing at a distance but with all his attention directed to their table, in the hopes of receiving heftier tips.

'A Grey Goose vodka with orange juice for the lady and a Lagavulin 16 years, large, on the rocks please.'

Nikita admired the finesse with which Nitin ordered the drinks. He had changed her choice of mass-market Smirnoff vodka to the premium Grey Goose and had chosen an expensive single malt for himself. The drinks arrived, they toasted and Nitin sipped his whiskey without taking his eyes off her. Meanwhile, she kept her glass down. Nitin chided her, 'Hey, you never keep the glass down without taking a sip after saying 'Cheers!' And look into the other person's eyes when taking the first sip.'

What? Look into his eyes? He is definitely up to something.

Nikita was trying hard to convince herself that it was a normal meeting. She nodded and quickly tried to undo her mistake by sipping the drink while looking at him. In her nervousness, she drank half the glass instead of the customary sip, but felt better immediately as the warmth of the vodka filled her up.

She has come out with me for a drink, she must be available. Nitin was becoming bolder in his thoughts. In his experience, if a girl didn't object to the first few attempts at flirting and she also accepted a quasi-date invitation, he was likely to succeed. But for now, he was enjoying his drink and enjoying looking at her. Conscious of being checked out continuously by a well-built and handsome senior, Nikita also began enjoying his company. But she was sure she would not let him progress further—she would draw the line if things started getting out of control.

Nitin, a veteran, kept the conversation casual with movies and books and steered clear of personal topics. 'So, how is your training going?'

'Very well, Nitin. I am happy with my project and the guidance that you are providing.'

'Would you like to get a pre-placement offer?'

'Yes, who wouldn't?'

'Well if the person is interested in it and also likes the workings of a global bank, only then may they want to join as a full-time employee.'

'I am interested and have liked the work profile so far, especially on the sales side.'

Nitin, sure of her interest in the job, played his cards, 'That's great, Nikita. But you know, it is difficult for the bank to gauge the quality of work in just two months. HR needs a very strong recommendation from one of the senior managers to extend a pre-placement offer to any summer intern.'

He continued, 'In your case, only I can give that recommendation. Your conduct and work is good but I still don't have any incentive to recommend your name.' Now, he winked suggestively.

She was expecting this from Nitin. *I have a very short time to make up my mind. The first option is to politely excuse myself from the conversation and go back to the hostel. That would mean saying goodbye to the full-time job at British Bank. The other option is to play along. It will increase my chances of the pre-placement offer and avoid the madness of campus placements in the final year of MBA. The pressure of studies, grades and projects would ease off considerably.*

She decided to take a chance with him, 'What do you think I can do to increase my chances of a strong recommendation?'

'I am glad you are thinking hard about your career. You just need to come with me for a trip to Karjat—only a few hours away. My friend has a small bungalow there. He lives abroad and I supervise that property.'

'Hmm.'

'We will stay overnight on a weekend, have a good time and come back early the next day. Nobody will know anything.' *I like to talk straight, girl. Take it or leave it.*

Now, Nikita really had to take a decision fast. She was a couple of drinks down and was feeling less nervous about the whole thing. Nitin seemed like a seasoned and safe man. He didn't waste any time making unwanted overtures and came straight to the point.

Nikita again weighed the pros and cons. *I wouldn't feel comfortable going to a secluded place with a fellow student or a boyfriend. But Nitin is a respectable person and I don't expect any surprises beyond the explicit understanding we have.* She gave in to the temptation of an easy job offer, 'Are you sure you can pull it through for me?'

'Oh yes, one hundred percent. I have a free hand from Joe on these matters. If you make me happy, I will return the favour. It's a deal.'

'Hmm, sounds fine.'

'Great, we will leave Friday night and come back Saturday morning. You can tell your hostel warden that you will be staying at your local guardian's place like you do every weekend.'

She merely smiled. They quickly finished their drinks and left Marine Plaza separately.

Chapter 35

Satya entered the office with a strong sense of purpose. He read his offer letter once more in a secluded meeting room and called Dan, 'I am going to pull the trigger now. There's no going back after this, right?'

'Right mate, go ahead and all the best.'

Satya approached Nitin at his desk with great confidence. He had not been so sure of himself in ages. The offer letter for him was a certificate of excellence and made him feel a foot taller. 'Nitin, can I have a word with you?'

'Yes,' said Nitin, and accompanied him into the meeting room. Nitin had an inkling that this conversation was going to be different. Normally, Satya hid behind his desk and spoke to Nitin and Joe only when he cracked a big deal or when eye contact was inevitable.

They didn't sit down. Nitin asked him, 'Tell me, what's the matter?'

'Actually err… Nitin, I want to put in my papers.'

Nitin's first reaction was of surprise. He knew that the market was hot and that several banks were on the prowl, but he hadn't expected this schmuck to be the first one off the block. He maintained a stoic face and responded, 'I see, which bank is it? What level and salary are they offering you?'

Satya knew that Nitin had no right to ask such questions. Still, Satya didn't want to spoil his relationship, whatever that relationship was. So he politely evaded the questions. 'Nitin, I am not in a position to discuss any details. Rest assured, all details hold up and the opportunity is great from a financial and career perspective.' This was the modus operandi. The resigning employee didn't show his cards and this was his time in the sun to enjoy some long-needed attention.

Nitin decided not to ask any more questions because it would insult him further if Satya didn't answer. He gave some quick advice, 'Okay Satya, I will convey this to Joe and to other senior managers. Meanwhile, just stay put at your desk and don't do anything stupid. Also, remember that this industry is small and one should avoid burning bridges.' The last bit was a terse warning to not say anything against Nitin and Joe in his exit interview. Satya got the message in no uncertain terms.

Nitin called Joe and informed him. Joe asked him to arrange a conference call with the Asia Head of Sales, Martin, as soon as possible. On the call, Martin asked about Nitin's opinion of Satya. Nitin was direct, 'I don't consider him the top talent in Markets but he is good for the job. I think we shouldn't really go out of our way to retain him if he has made up his mind.'

Joe added, 'I agree with Nitin, he is an average employee and I will not worry about losing him.'

Martin, though younger, was sharper and understood the practical side of the matter well, 'With due respect, gentlemen, I don't agree with your assessment. Here in Singapore, I can see that the Indian market is booming more than in any other country.'

Martin continued, 'I will ask you not to let your ego obfuscate your assessment. Rather, think from a replacement cost perspective. Losing a salesperson also means that valuable client data and information goes out.'

Joe got the hint and changed his stance, sycophant that he was, 'Martin, you are right. I don't think we will be able to replace him at the same cost. My estimate is at least double the fixed salary and two years of guaranteed bonus.'

'Yes, I agree with both of you. In fact, our business plan calls for hiring more salespersons and Satya's departure may make it more expensive, if not tougher, to hire from the market,' Nitin added quickly, feeling left out.

'In that case, I will ask both of you to woo Satya and do everything possible to keep him. You have my approval to better his offer. That will be all from me,' Martin jumped off the call. Nitin admired this trait in Martin—he thought on his feet and took the right decision.

But Joe and Nitin were annoyed with the situation. Now, it was their turn to flatter Satya. Joe reminded Nitin, 'If your name gets proposed for promotion, you will need to show some achievement on the people front, in addition to revenue. This is your chance.' He implied that he would not participate in this demeaning process and left it to Nitin.

Nitin needed some time alone to think and strategise. He went to a small conference room in the basement and put on the 'do not disturb' sign. Having thought about it for half an hour, he felt better and more in control of the situation. He asked his secretary to send Satya to this obscure conference room. Holding prolonged discussions in another meeting room would raise suspicion across the floor. The challenge was twofold. One, he obviously had to court Satya and two, the mission was to be kept a secret.

Satya knocked on the door and went in. The equation was markedly different today and Satya was enjoying every bit of it. Nitin opened the discussion, 'I talked to the seniors about your decision. I have proposed and others have agreed that we value you as a team member. We would be sad to see you go. Let me know what I can do to make you happy and stay with us.'

Satya was shocked. He had not imagined such a scenario. His past treatment in this organisation had indicated that submitting the resignation and walking out would be a cakewalk. *Now, I am in a bargaining position. This is so rare and I must make use of it.*

He stated calmly, 'Nitin, when I decided to put in my papers, I was sure that I wanted to move on. Even now, I don't see any reason to stay.'

Nitin could see the greed in his eyes and his stance softening. He made his move without giving Satya much time. 'We are willing to match or even better the offer in all parameters.'

Satya leaned forward a bit and Nitin knew that he was interested in a counter-offer.

'Look, I will encourage you to give it serious thought if you are thinking of moving to a new entrant in the market. You never know whether they will be able to find their feet in India. I have seen many such flamboyant names come to India and make a splash with high salaries and higher promises. In 1997, there was Peregrine, which came in with much fanfare but flailed equally fast, leaving dozens of bankers jobless.'

Satya was all ears. *Whatever Nitin is saying makes sense.* His stance was softening rapidly and it was visible in his body language. Instead of sitting straight in his chair, he was bending forward, indicating that he was inclined to bite Nitin's bait.

Nitin emulated Jorge's management speak, 'Although I advise people to use their silver bullets carefully, this is one rare instance to use your silver bullet.'

He really has a point here. Satya was strategizing about what to settle for.

'I will leave you with one last thought—a known devil is better than an unknown one. Whatever your offer is, I will better it by ten percent and match all other conditions. I will promote you to VP, you have my word. Think over it and let me know by the evening. Meanwhile, behave as usual and keep it to yourself,' Nitin had virtually closed the deal.

'Sure, I will let you know by tomorrow morning, if that's okay with you,' Satya bargained for a little more time. Nitin nodded and they returned to their seats pretending nothing had transpired.

Satya and Kakoli couldn't sleep that night. They hadn't ever imagined that they would face such a sweet problem. However, a decision had to be made. Dan was calling Satya through the day to make sure he remained committed to Lehman Brothers' offer. Satya told him that he had tendered his resignation and was awaiting the release formalities. Dan reminded him of the promises made to Gary and the risk of ruining his name in the market if he backed out.

By the time the sun rose, Satya had made up his mind. *I need to maximise my own interest and I will take the counter-offer from Nitin. But I don't want to sign on the dotted line so easily.* He wanted to test what more was possible.

As expected, Nitin called him to the hidden meeting room first thing in the morning, 'So, young man, hope you got some good news for me.'

He has been behaving so well since yesterday; hope he doesn't go back to his old ways after I accept his offer. Satya smiled, 'Your offer looks good but I have some concerns. Will you be putting all the promises on paper? How do I feel confident that the bank will not be vindictive towards me after this episode? Which level of senior management is committing this?'

'These are valid questions. All the new conditions of your employment will be given to you in writing. About the rest, you have to trust us. You just pack your bags for London and spend a week there. I will set up a meeting with Jorge for you. He is now the Global Head of Sales and will reinforce our commitments for your comfort. Take Kakoli with you as it is more like a holiday,' Nitin winked. He knew he had won the final round. Now, his own promotion was on track. He and Joe would push for a comprehensive salary revision for themselves in light of the new offer received by this schmuck.

'One last thing, Satya. You need to give a copy of your offer letter to HR for verification and we will get your new offer drafted soon. We need this to document the rationale for your increment and promotion.'

Satya walked out of the room feeling like a king. He quickly called Kakoli to convey the good news and asked her to prepare for the holiday. Meanwhile, he had missed three calls from Dan. Satya didn't know how to handle Dan. He wanted to keep him on hold till he got the counter-offer letter from HR. He called Dan and told him that all was well and his exit formalities were proceeding well. Dan, an experienced poacher, didn't believe a word of it and contacted his own sources in British Bank.

Chapter 36

Satya and Kakoli were admiring the business class seats inside the new British Airways Boeing 777. They had so much space to themselves and the seats could recline to 180 degrees. Kakoli turned on the in-built massager. Each passenger had a cabin with a large screen for entertainment. The new upholstery shone and one could still smell the new leather. Their tickets had been paid for by British Bank and it was a golden opportunity to travel business class for free as a couple.

The air hostess greeted them with a glass of Dom Perignon champagne, which Satya gulped impatiently, hoping to get another before the flight took off. Kakoli settled for watermelon juice. The luxury of fresh juice in a plane was enough to give Kakoli a high. She still didn't understand how the bank had financed her ticket. It was actually Nitin's plan. He got Sapphire to buy the ticket for Kakoli. They would adjust the amount in another bill which would be approved by Nitin.

Satya took out his new offer letter and read it again with Kakoli, hardly able to believe the quick and positive turn of events. Really, luck had played a big role in this. But it was also true that Satya had always dreamt of improving his situation. He had made it a practice to remind himself of his dreams and goals in a positive manner.

In London, he gazed at the mammoth stone building that housed the British Bank headquarters. Situated in the old business district in central London, it was made of stone blocks that had light carvings, unlike the modern glass structures. It was not very tall but was a few hundred feet wide. When he entered the Markets dealing floor, he was immediately lost—it was so huge that there was no way he could locate Jorge's office himself. There were rows and rows of traders sitting in front of innumerable screens. Once in a while, someone shouted in excitement or frustration but the sound was muffled due to the vast expanse of the floor. Security told him to call Jorge's assistant from the reception. She came ten minutes later to receive him.

She could tell that Satya was overawed at the size of the dealing floor. She casually mentioned that it was larger than a football field and that there was an equally large area on the floor below occupied by the same department. It was the culmination of 30 years of breakneck expansion in financial markets. It was also the dream of youngsters looking to make a mark in the world of high finance.

Jorge welcomed Satya with open arms in his expansive office. The office was furnished with expensive colonial furniture—mahogany lined with plush genuine leather. Legend had it that the mahogany table in Jorge's office cost the bank fifty thousand pounds, roughly fifty lakh rupees.

'How are you, bro?' howled Jorge in his energetic baritone.

Satya recalled Jorge's lukewarm greeting to him during his visit to India—the contrast was almost comical. But Vicky had told him that seniors like Jorge only salute a rising star and that he was lucky to be seeing him.

He decided to have fun while the going was good, 'Hi Jorge, I am very well. How have you been? You remember we met while you were in India?'

'How can I forget? You kept me company, drinking till the very end. I trust you reached home safely and didn't suffer a hangover?'

Painful memories of the stay in the filthy police station and the bouts of vomiting came flashing before his eyes but he maintained a happy front, 'Oh, not at all. I am used to such drinking episodes, being in sales. I am honoured to meet you, Jorge. I am carrying a two-page business plan for what I intend to do in my new senior role.' Satya tried to give the conversation an official twist.

'Hey man, just forget it. You treat this trip like a holiday and call me any time you want. Here's my number.'

'Thanks a lot for this gesture, Jorge.'

'Satya, the bank has faith in your capabilities and for the next few years you should just keep your head down and perform well.' Jorge continued his motivational tirade but Satya had already tuned him out. *Keeping my head down means stop looking for another job for a few years. Not an unfair demand considering they are courting me with such sweet deals. Kakoli and I shall build a great life together with so much more money coming our way.* He left the office a changed soul. There was something about Jorge—his charisma, his energy and his motivational way of speaking could make a hero out of anyone.

Satya and Kakoli spent the next five days roaming around the streets and museums of London and Paris. It was like a paid honeymoon. For Kakoli, it was a welcome break and she hoped it would help their relationship. *I just pray that Satya won't revert to his workaholic and alcoholic way of life once we return. I want a happy life with Satya, even if the money is less.*

Chapter 37

Nitin fixed the outstation rendezvous at Karjat for the next Friday. He wanted to execute his plan before Nikita changed her mind. He had found that girls were fickle and could not make up their mind about anything. They wouldn't be sure about an action even after it had been done, whereas he did what he wanted without looking back.

He instructed Nikita to meet him at the parking lot of Mahalaxmi Racecourse at half past seven. She showed up on time and he was relieved that there was no last-minute change of heart. *Ambition can really push people.* They proceeded to Karjat in his shiny new Audi Q5. Once in the car, Nikita felt safe in his company. They reached the place in a couple of hours.

The bungalow was compact, with two bedrooms on the first floor and the kitchen and a large living room on the lower level. The caretaker opened the door for them and told Nitin, 'Sir, fresh food has been prepared and the fridge has cold water and ice. I have stocked the grocery as you instructed. If you need anything else, please call me.' He stayed not too far away with his wife and two children.

Nikita could tell that Nitin was a regular at the bungalow. Nitin tipped the caretaker a thousand rupees and bolted the door from inside. There was an awkward silence for a few minutes. Nitin poured himself a large whiskey and asked her, 'What do you prefer? I have vodka and red wine as well.'

'Which red wine?' Nikita tried small talk.

'Oh, it's Sula. It's produced in Nashik, pretty close by.'

'Okay, then let me get a taste of the local wine, but give me a little bit only.' She didn't want to get sloshed with hard drinks and lose control of the situation.

They all start small, then the mood picks up! 'Sure, make yourself comfortable,' he said, handing her the wine glass. He sat next to her on the long velvet sofa. The dark brown colour hid the dirt and stains, making it easier to maintain. They kept their glasses on the wood top centre table.

She said, 'Is that why Nashik is called the wine capital of India?'

Nitin took off his shoes and stretched his feet on the table. 'The soil in this area is good for producing wine grade grapes. The area has six large vineyards, each producing its own wine.' He was inching closer to her.

'I heard they produce champagne as well?'

'They do produce sparkling wine but you cannot call it champagne! That name can be used only by the sparkling wine producers in the Champagne region of France. Some more wine for you?' Her glass was already empty and he proceeded to fill it without waiting for a reply.

He now sat with his arm around her and tried to sense her comfort. He wanted to move slowly so as not to cause Nikita to panic. They had an understanding before going to the venue but he had been in a tricky situation earlier where the girl backed out at the last moment.

Not facing any perceptible resistance, he gently planted a kiss on her ear lobes. A sharp sensation ran down her spine and she recoiled a bit. He retracted and concentrated on his drink before making the next move. 'This place is so relaxing, with clean air and greenery all around. You can actually see the stars from the roof,' he said. Nikita looked much more at ease now, the soft music in the background helped soothe her.

'I really like watching the night sky studded with billions of tiny lights. In cities, they are drowned by the night light thrown up by us. What a pity!' she replied.

'We could go to the roof now,' and he led her up the stairs. Looking up, she exclaimed, 'Wow, it's so cool out here.'

As they finished their drinks looking at the galaxy, he placed his arm around her petite waist. This time she was much more receptive and responded softly. Then, he held her hand and led her to the bedroom. The caretaker had done a good job preparing the room, spraying a good quality lemongrass freshener and covering the bed with a clean crisp white sheet.

They drove back from Karjat early the next morning. Nikita was half asleep. Understandably, because she got very little sleep all night. Nitin had been in great form and had no intention of sleeping.

Karjat's undulating landscape was passing by fast. Nitin concentrated on driving while Nikita alternated between dozing off and feeling guilty about what had happened.

Nitin dropped her at the taxi stand at Worli Naka and zipped away after a brief goodbye. Nikita felt an emotional vacuum and felt used. Again, she went through the rationalisations and felt marginally better. Before they parted ways, she told Nitin, 'Make sure I get the offer.' Nitin assured her that the offer was hers and she could relax for the rest of summer training and the MBA.

Chapter 38

Dan kept following up with Satya for an update. 'When are they releasing you, mate?'

'I will get back to you, Dan.' Satya didn't give him any details and stopped taking his calls after a couple of days. Dan got the message and stopped calling him. *Not only is he taking up a counter-offer but he is refusing to admit it. This kind of behaviour can get one blacklisted. He should at least have the decency to answer my calls and tell me the truth.* He felt that the quality of being upfront was missing in the east. The culture here did not encourage frank communication and a lot of things were left unsaid. After confirming the facts with his contact in British Bank, Dan called Gary, 'The bird has flown away. Shall we activate Plan B?'

'What kind of shit is this? Why can't people keep their word?' Gary was livid.

Dan was surprised at this sudden morality. *This is a routine occurrence. When I brokered a deal for Gary to get hired at Merrill*

Lynch, he stayed back at Lehman Brothers after getting a better counter-offer. However, hypocrisy was another hallmark of the educated and high-flying people.

He kept quiet, leaving the ball in Gary's court. He didn't want to take any responsibility for Satya's actions. Handling such undue pressure was easy for him because he made it a point to not own responsibility for something outside his control. It eased off the stress considerably and was good for his health in the long run.

Gary paused for a few long seconds and blurted his instructions, 'Okay, go ahead and talk to the next dude. I have even forgotten his name.'

Dan reminded him, 'It's Amit. I will go ahead and make him an offer with the terms we gave Satya initially.' Gary cut the line abruptly, showing his displeasure.

The phone rang as Amit was walking to his car that was parked in the open circular parking at Kala Ghoda. It was the call he had been waiting for. The last two weeks had felt like two decades. He answered, 'Hey Dan!'

The excitement in his voice told Dan that he could expect a positive response. Dan gave him the good news, 'Hey Amit, hope it's the right time to catch you. Gary would like to extend an offer to you from Lehman Brothers.'

Amit was ecstatic and controlled himself with great difficulty. But he could not mask his happiness, 'Wow, that's great news, Dan. Give me the details.'

Dan gave him the terms. Amit knew there was always room to bargain and he demanded, 'Can't you guys do something better?' But the delight in his voice gave him away and Dan was firm, 'Look mate, this is a great offer and it is on the table for the next five minutes. Take it or leave it. I need to call Gary with a confirmation soon.'

Amit, not wanting to jeopardise this golden chance, agreed on the spot. Dan asked him to wait for the written offer letter and the next steps.

Amit had a hunch that he was not the first choice but he didn't care as long as he got the offer. The initial offer itself was too good. As soon as he got the letter from Lehman Brothers, he approached Nitin, 'Nitin, can I have a word with you?'

Nitin didn't like the confidence with which Amit spoke. He went to the meeting room with Amit, who said, 'I am putting in my papers today.'

That's the second one in two weeks. Taken aback, Nitin said, 'We have been taking good care of you, what makes you do this?'

Amit was surprised that even after such lowly treatment, the management felt they cared for the people. But it was too late to make any complaints and he just wanted a smooth exit. He said, 'Thanks, Nitin, but it has got nothing to do with British Bank. It's a better role and better career prospects.'

'Can we work out something for you here?' Nitin tried to cast his net.

'No, no, I have made up my mind.' Nitin had no choice. He said, 'Since you seem to be decided, we will relieve you as per the terms of your employment.'

'Nitin, could you relieve me earlier than the contractual notice period of three months?'

'I see that you are eager to start your new innings but I need to ask you to proceed on gardening leave.' Gardening leave was the glorified Wall Street term for the notice period.

'But—,' Amit tried to negotiate.

'No ifs and buts. In sensitive and customer-facing roles, we insist on gardening leave. You sit at home for three months and we will pay your full salary.' Though it was a welcome break for any banker, and sometimes saved people from burning out, Amit wasn't happy with the outcome.

Chapter 39

The judge walked into the courtroom and everybody stood up as a mark of respect. Rekha and Neeraj's divorce case was up for hearing. Their parents had put up a lot of drama before the actual divorce case began.

Rekha still remembered the first meeting with Neeraj's parents after she announced her decision to get divorced. His mom was hysterical, 'You shameless woman, I always knew that you wanted to ruin my poor son's life! You never intended to stay with him for long. My innocent child, what will happen to him now? Oh God, please help us.' She cried and shouted at the same time. Her eyes bloodshot, she added, 'This girl has brought poor omens to our family. I had asked for the horoscopes to be matched before the marriage but nobody listened to me.'

'If you guys wanted me to stay with your son, why didn't you ever correct him? First, he was only interested in drinking and now he is sleeping with a new woman every day,' retorted Rekha.

Neeraj's father was adding fuel to the fire, 'Listen, all these discussions are useless now. Our poor son has been driven to this point by this irresponsible girl. She only focused on her job and had no time for her husband. Hey bhagwan, what happened to the old family values of Indian women?'

Now, it was Rekha's mom's turn to jump in, 'Hai rabba, I can't believe that you are protecting your wretched son. He has not taken care of my daughter. I brought her up to be educated and responsible. She is so talented and earns more than he does. What was she supposed to do? Leave her job and be dependent on him, so that he could exploit her forever? You guys needed a maid not a daughter-in-law.'

During their courtship, Rekha remembered how categorical Neeraj had been, 'I want my wife to have at least an MBA and a nice job. It is difficult to live a proper life on a single salary these days.'

After their marriage, Rekha understood the situation. They wanted a second source of income, a well-trained housewife and a sexy siren, all in one. The mud-slinging match lasted for a couple of hours and it was apparent that no reconciliation was possible. Both parties deputed lawyers to draft a divorce deed with mutual consent. Since both were earning well and there were no kids, it was a simple case.

Their friends advised them to make it clean because such an event can scar one for life. Rekha didn't stake any claim other than the common property, which was taken against a huge loan any way. Neeraj didn't need to pay alimony as she was earning well. The judge had given them six months to work out any differences but they didn't intend to. The families stood by their respective offspring; six months passed quickly and here they were in court.

The judge, a portly man with grey hair, took his seat and the assistant read out the case with a brief history. He asked Neeraj to come to the witness box and asked, 'Are you sure you want to go ahead with the divorce?'

Neeraj answered, 'Yes, sir.'

Next, he posed the same question to Rekha and she replied in the affirmative as well.

The judge pronounced them divorced and they were free. Rekha felt a bit emotional and hugged her mother. She shed a few tears—of regret and relief. Regret for the wrong decision with Neeraj and relief at getting out of it rather quickly, while she still had time to rebuild her life. She felt light as she walked out the door. Asha also felt like crying but maintained a strong front in public. She was sad that her daughter's marriage hadn't worked out and now Rekha would have to live with the divorcee tag. Rekha's repeated assurances that she didn't really mind it didn't help her parents get over the social pressure.

Neeraj was defiant as he led his parents out of the court. His mother was talking loudly in the corridor, 'What do these people think? I will find a prettier girl for my son. I will show them.' His father followed the mother and son in a huff.

Rekha gathered herself and asked her mother to go to the new flat that she had rented closer to her office. She wanted to spend some time alone and went to a coffee shop close by. After adjusting her makeup and ensuring that nobody could tell she had cried, she ordered her favourite americano and settled into a seat in the corner. Everybody at work had found out that she was getting divorced and she needed to strengthen herself to face the social stigma. Though misplaced, the stigma was there nonetheless.

Chapter 40

Amit's gardening leave started in the last week of February, 2008 and he decided to relish each day of the three-month holiday. He travelled with Anu to Kashmir, Ladakh and Bali. It was a carefree holiday and reminded them what life could be if they had all the time in the world. Obviously, they seldom got a chance to enjoy like this while the salary was coming in.

Anu snuggled up in Amit's arms in the Singapore Airlines flight back to Mumbai but he was lost in his thoughts. Finally, he said to Anu, 'Baby, I have taken this very attractive and exciting job offer but I am not feeling confident that I will be able to set up this business from scratch for Lehman Brothers. They have high expectations from me.'

'Look Amit, they have given you a fabulous offer. You must have some talent for sure.'

'You are not getting it. There is a big gambling game going on in the world. And all the gamblers know that they may be thrown out naked at any time. That's causing the fear.'

'That's very cryptic.'

The world markets were in a bullish phase. All the large central banks like the US Fed and the European Central Bank wanted to keep the markets vibrant and growing in the belief that it was an indicator of economic prosperity. However, it was the other way round. If the world prospers by producing and consuming more goods and services, the markets go up as a reflection of this prosperity. But in this case, the markets were getting pushed up without much growth in demand.

Amit concluded, 'The bull market can collapse any time, Anu.'

'How does this worry you?'

'The investors are leveraging big time and playing large hands in the big bad world of derivatives.' He explained that these hi-tech financial instruments allowed people to borrow multiples of their own money and invest in markets in search of quick profits. This leverage magnified the profits but could wipe out the investments if the price moved against the bet.

'But everyone seems to be making money,' Anu quipped.

'Yeah, this has been working well for many years starting in 2002, after the burst of the dotcom bubble. The painful memories of the dotcom bust of 2001 are still fresh in the minds of central bankers... like Ben Bernanke of US Federal Reserve.'

'Understood, but how is this bad?'

'Thanks to poor supervision of the financial sector, bogus loans are given to those with poor credit quality across the US.' Amit described the situation. These loans were called sub-prime loans and fetched high interest rates for the lending banks. Since it made housing available to poor people, the politicians played it as a social revolution—finally, the poor were able to realise the American dream. The banks converted large bunches of these loans into derivatives and sold them to large institutions like insurance companies and pension funds in the US. The rating agencies like S&P and Moody's played along and rated these derivative instruments at the highest possible AAA credit rating.

'I get it, but this seems to be a US issue. How are we affected?'

'This trend of blind investing and reckless risk-taking has spread to foreign exchange markets and it is causing the boom in the derivatives market in India.' Amit knew that the Indian market was also sitting on a ticking time bomb.

'Oh, that's why Lehman Brothers is so bullish in India!'

'Yes, let's hope the party goes on a little longer so we can retire comfortably.'

'It will, baby. Don't worry.' Anu said this just to cool him down. She didn't like the idea of discussing work in the middle of his gardening leave. At the same time, she understood that it was important to encourage Amit in his professional life. After she had taken the backseat in her career, Amit needed to do well and earn more than enough while the going was good.

She reiterated her confidence in him, 'I am sure you will do very well, Amit. It is just the fear of the unknown that's bothering you. Remember when you joined British Bank from ICICI Bank, you were equally anxious? You wondered every night whether you would be able to adjust to the high-pressure atmosphere and survive the hire-n-fire culture.'

'You are right. Thanks for being my pillar of support.'

The plane's cabin lights came on and the airline crew started making landing announcements. They would land in 30 minutes. It was a smooth flight; little did Amit know that some turbulence awaited him after landing in Mumbai.

As soon as he switched on his phone while waiting at immigration, he saw several messages from his friends and colleagues asking him to call them. It was past midnight so he decided to call Kunal, his bachelor friend, 'Oye Kunal, what's up? I just saw your message after reaching Mumbai.'

He had woken Kunal by his call and had to listen to Kunal curse him for the first few minutes. Then, he came to the point, 'Dude, you are in deep shit. Bear Stearns went belly up yesterday. It was going to go bankrupt but the US Treasury Secretary, Hank Paulson, brokered a deal and got it acquired by J. P. Morgan at a price of two dollars a share.'

'What the fuck? I can't believe it man. Bear Stearns' share price was about 150 dollars last year.'

'Yeah, its share price had already fallen to 60 dollars last week and after the rumours of its financial troubles started building up, it crashed to 30. Over the weekend, the rumours became so strong that all major business news channels were forecasting its demise on Monday. Then, Paulson convinced Jamie Dimon, the CEO of J. P. Morgan to buy it at two dollars.'

'Boss, I am screwed. Let me follow the news online. See ya, bye.'

Anu was overhearing the whole episode but she could not make the connection between what was happening with Bear Stearns and Amit's career at Lehman Brothers. She did not know that Bear Sterns was another mammoth US-based investment bank, in the league of Merrill Lynch and Lehman Brothers.

Chapter 41

17 March, 2008.

The Monday after Bear Stearns' crash and subsequent take-over—or rescue—by J. P. Morgan was one of the wildest days in the world financial markets. All the greed and blind risk-taking had come back to haunt the investors and corporates. The global financial crisis, the biggest crash in history after the great depression of 1929, had officially started.

Satya, sitting in his imported German swivel chair, was comparing the situation to his favourite scene in one of the National Geographic documentaries. When a herd of zebras approaches a river to drink water, they are extremely cautious. They move inch by inch towards the riverbank, keeping a watch for crocodiles lurking underwater. Slowly, one by one, they start drinking water. They don't drink water continuously, they just take one sip and again look around for danger.

Then the thirst takes over, the sips become longer. Cool water hits their dry throats and refreshes them. More zebras start pushing to try to come to the front to drink the sweet water. Worries about the lurking crocodiles are relegated. They actually start believing that there are no crocodiles in the water. Maybe this time it's different. Let's have more water, take deeper sips.

As the zebras start relishing the water and become comfortable in their spot, the crocodiles strike in one swift motion. Before the zebras know it, it's over. The crocodiles grab an animal each by the neck and drag them deep into the water. Only a few zebras fall prey but a majority of the herd quenches its thirst. This is where the similarity ends between the natural world and the world of finance. Here, only a few smart ones are able to escape and a majority of investors suffers a fate that scars them for life.

There was tremendous commotion on the dealing floor—the Indian markets had just opened. Numbers were flashing on the screen but they were meaningless. There were no actual prices in the market, whether in currencies or in bonds. Shares were hitting the lower circuit and trading had seized like an engine without lubricating oil. The liquidity or the sea of money that had kept the markets on a roll had suddenly dried up, leaving investors with loss-making positions. The crocodiles had surfaced and the zebras had nowhere to run to.

Today, Satya didn't have any clients to call. In fact, clients were frantically calling them to ask for the bank's view on the whole episode. They wanted to know what was going to happen in the next few months. Little did they know that the bank's highly educated and well-paid economists and professionals had no clue which way the market would move in a normal scenario, let alone in such uncertain conditions.

For decades, banks, financial advisors and fund managers have been putting on the charade that they are capable of predicting the financial markets. In the ten years of his career, Satya had keenly observed these so-called experts speak on the business news channels and had read their elaborate reports. These programs and reports were useful if one wanted to digest a lot of information and see historic trends but were useless in telling the future.

Still, every year the top universities produced a crop of people who believed that they could predict where the market would be headed. Very few had the right mix of intellect, instinct and ability to play the markets profitably. Most finance professionals thrive on finding a person or client who is willing to take a risk. They just pocket the fees from them for providing the risk-taking instrument.

The world of high finance was focused on getting more and more zebras to the water and killing a majority of them in the process, leaving a few crocodiles very fat. The next batch of zebras think that their time will be different but the crocodiles know the game all along.

'What's happening to the Japanese Yen and Swiss Franc deals I did with you last month?' shouted a customer. The Japanese Yen and Swiss Franc had moved as much in one day as they hadn't moved in the last decade and a half. The historic lack of movement had lulled the banks and their clients into a false sense of security, and they had piled massive positions in supposedly innocuous risk-free and profit producing derivatives. These worked well as long the exchange rate of one currency against the other was stable. But the markets were so rattled by the Bear Stearns event that exchange rates had been terrifyingly dislocated.

'Sir, the deal is in a loss today but don't worry, the market will stabilise and I am sure your losses will reduce in some time. Today is not the day to cut your losses; in fact, it is the worst possible time,' Satya calmed his client. He knew very well that the stability after an earthquake doesn't rebuild fallen buildings.

Traders were throwing a fit and cursing brokers. Vicky, who was caught in a bad position in Indian Government bonds, spoke to his favourite broker, 'You bastard, you always chase me with prices through the day. Today, you can't make a price even for ten million dollars?' He banged the dealer phone so forcefully that it shattered. Traders made such huge amounts of money that banks granted them the luxury of breaking expensive phones and abusing on recorded lines. They were too valuable to lose over such mundane matters.

One client requested Rekha to ask the trading desk for an opinion on the Indian Rupee. She asked Roshan, the spot trader, 'Hey, what do you feel on the rupee today?'

Roshan was smarting from the losses and shouted across the floor, 'Ask that asshole to buzz off. These fuckers don't have anything else to do other than calling the banks, sucking our brains.' Rekha understood that he was not going to share any view. Actually, he didn't have one. And language used on the dealing floors was quite filthy even usually; such occasions simply brought out the best.

Luckily, Rekha had pressed the mute button on the call. She politely responded after unmuting, 'Sir, we think it will be very choppy today. RBI should intervene if it gets too bad.'

The client was barely satisfied with her non-committal reply. Today, at least, nobody pretended to know everything.

Chapter 42

After her divorce, Rekha had moved to the rented place close to her office. She wanted to focus on reducing the commute and getting her life back in order. No sooner had the dust settled than her mother started hinting that she should think about getting married again. One evening Asha called her, 'So, what did you think about the marriage proposal I forwarded last week?'

Rekha had just returned from work and was stressed out and annoyed. She barked, 'What about the proposal, mamma? Do you even realise what I have gone through? I beg you to give me some time. Once I reconcile myself to the situation, I will decide what to do next.'

Her mother got the message and quietly cut the phone before starting to cry in solitude. She remembered her Guru's advice, 'You need to be like animals when it comes to raising children. Let go of them at the right time and you will be happy. Hold on to them longer than required and you will only face unhappiness.'

So easy to say but impossible to do for most Indian parents whose lives revolved around their kids. Most dreamt of witnessing their grandchildren's marriage also, if the grim reaper permitted.

Rekha wanted to make a fresh start but was finding it hard to think peacefully with the distractions at work and at home. She decided to take a few days off to compose herself. She switched off the phone and instructed the maid not to come until further notice.

She sat in the living room with a cup of coffee and stared at the wall in front of her. Her thoughts let go like untethered horses. Wild at first, they slowly subsided. She felt her mind become clearer just like muddy water when left undisturbed. She didn't know how long she sat like that; she shut her eyes, not to fall asleep but to dive deeper within.

When she opened them, it was dark outside. Feeling fresh and light, she realised that ultimately, she was looking for happiness. She wanted to be peaceful and joyful. Her life revolved around her health and well-being, relationships, financial strength and social duties. It dawned on her that she needed to take care of each of these aspects if she had any chance of achieving peace and happiness. She took out a fresh designer notebook and started writing what she actually wanted from life. Whether she called them dreams or goals or objectives, she needed to write them down. It turned out to be a long list of things by the time she was done.

She wrote that she wanted to keep herself away from the usual lifestyle diseases and maintain the health indicators in their prescribed range. She wanted to have a better relationship with her parents and also wished to find a good partner soon. She needed to balance her savings and expenditures and consult experts for her investments to secure her future financially. Her conscience also coaxed her to do some social work and she decided to devote a couple of hours every week to it. Her writing continued well past midnight—she was overflowing with energy and excitement. This process gave her a clarity that she had not experienced in a long time. As she closed her eyes to think more, gradually sleep took over. After a long time, she slept without setting an alarm.

Waking up naturally, after a deep and peaceful sleep, Rekha felt as fresh as a daisy. She was determined not to lose the sense of purpose she had found the previous evening. Even though she was terribly hungry, she decided to have a light breakfast and continue the soul searching. She got down to jotting what she needed to do to achieve these newly formed goals. By the end of the exercise, she had filled quite a few pages of the notebook. She named it the diary of her life and vowed to keep it close at all times.

Continuing the introspection, she also realised the value of looking young and glamorous and was not happy about the flab developing on her sides. She was disappointed with herself as she considered her figure. Even at a young age and with a beautiful face, she had started looking middle-aged due to her weight. She sensed that this was her last chance to get back in shape. She vowed to take her health in her hands; it was screaming for attention. Her fitness and health were essential for her to be in good spirits and to run the corporate race well.

So far, all her resolutions had broken down after a couple of months of effort. She had usually blamed her mother, Neeraj, people at work and her friends. But this time it was different. She understood that she alone was in control of what she did with her life.

Chapter 43

The buzz in the dealing room had decreased considerably after the recent blow-up. Nitin had hired a salesperson from Axis Bank, an Indian bank, as Amit's replacement. The markets were still in turmoil but all parties concerned, the bankers and the clients, wanted to believe that things would normalise soon and it would be business as usual.

Satya was in charge of training his new colleague, Kumar. Though experienced, Kumar needed to be taught the systems at British Bank—sophisticated ones that could price complex derivatives, book transactions and send settlement instructions worldwide. The risk in the trading books was evaluated and detailed reports were sent to senior management every day. It allowed the CEOs and other senior bankers to sleep peacefully, anticipating fatter bonus cheques year after year. However, despite receiving detailed reports, the managements of most banks chose to ignore the risks in favour of greed.

Kumar was astonished at the scale of operations at his new workplace. Indian banks were bigger in terms of client base and lending operations but the foreign banks had a disproportionate share of the markets or the treasury business. This part of the business called for quantitative and technological sophistication. Umpteen rocket scientists and mathematics wizards were recruited by the banks to borrow this sophistication from the tech space.

'And that's how you book a cross currency swap with embedded options into the system,' Satya ended day one of the tutorial. Kumar woke up with a start. He was prone to getting lost in his own world while listening to important lectures in college. He was sure that he would pick up things along the way and nodded as if he understood everything.

Nitin walked in and asked Satya, 'How is it going with Kumar? You don't have much time to bring him to speed. I want him to start talking to clients next week.'

Satya was honest, 'All going well, boss. Things are slow these days. Not many clients are interested in speculative and risky derivative transactions. I guess we have some more time to train Kumar.'

Nitin was furious, 'Look man, we don't run this place on complacency. If clients are not interested, it is your job to make them interested. Remember, this year's targets were set when the market was still looking bright. I am sure this Bear Stearns shit will be a blip on the radar and the appetite for risk will rekindle. Don't lose focus and be ready for the kill.'

'Yes, boss. I didn't mean that we will not try,' Satya said meekly. After negotiating his counter-offer and meeting Jorge in London, he had experienced a high but it had drained away quickly after he settled in the job again. He realised that the confidence gained through external rewards was temporary at best. He needed a more permanent confidence building mechanism.

The markets were trying to settle down after the Bear Stearns collapse but the monster of financial doom was out in the open and could not be ignored. Joe met up with Vicky. 'Now that there is some semblance of peace, we should think about our business. Let me call Nitin and we can strategise.'

Vicky agreed. Nitin joined them in the meeting room looking visibly shaken. Vicky joked, 'Looks like your next prey is not getting caught!'

Any other time, Nitin would have tolerated his joke but not now. He shouted, 'Mind your own business. Your life is simple. You traders have no work to do.' His angst was justified because the management had instructed the traders not to run any positions, cut down all risk and sit tight. For sales, it was not that simple.

Joe tried to contain the fight, 'Yes, I agree Nitin, that's why we called you to discuss the strategy for the remainder of the year. What kind of issues are you facing?'

'All our clients are neck deep in long-term derivative trades. As the market volatility has reached unprecedented levels, their deals are running into huge losses. The clients are nervous and asking us to give them a way out.'

'Way out? These deals belong to the clients. They have been reaping gains for many years and now that the tide has turned, they want a way out?'

'So far, none of the clients have disowned the transactions but if things continue like this for a few more months, their losses will far exceed all the gains of the previous years.'

Joe turned to Vicky, 'What do you feel? How are the markets going to pan out?'

Vicky tried to summarise what he had observed in his research and the media in the last month or so. 'They are discovering tremendous problems in the US financial system. Total losses are being pegged between one to three trillion US dollars.'

He continued, 'All the sub-prime derivatives so far rated as AAA have been downgraded to junk status. Due to this, all the banks and funds holding such paper had to immediately write them off and take on huge losses.'

Many smart banks like Goldman Sachs had gotten rid of such toxic investments well in time, but the greedier ones had been caught holding a large pile. They had been bought with cheaply borrowed money and it was now exploding in their face. Their lenders were demanding the money back. Joe said, 'So, we will know who has survived only after the smoke clears after a year or so.'

But Nitin wanted some practical guidance, 'How do we contain the clients' anxiety? What do we tell them? If we paint this gory picture, they are going to run away from the loss-making deals. How do we handle credit officers? They have suddenly woken up and are making our lives hell.'

Joe had some ideas, 'There is no need to cause panic among clients. We should try to restructure some of the deals. This is also a money-making opportunity.' They strategised about how to cancel the deals with small losses and ask the clients to pay up. Meanwhile, Joe would chat with the regional head of credit to keep her dogs under control.

Joe's offer of help was a pleasant surprise for Nitin. 'But if the situation worsens, there will be nowhere to run for cover,' Nitin concluded.

The sales team under Nitin was working overtime. Poor Kumar never got to see the adrenaline pumping race of derivatives but was employed to clean up the rubble after the crash.

Chapter 44

The summer interns had finished their projects and had submitted their reports to HR. They had to present their projects to the senior management before they were done. The three senior guides were also part of the panel. Nikita's presentation was the best in both structure and content. Nitin heaved a sigh of relief. His task of getting her an offer was taken care of.

After the interns left, the panel had a quick discussion to decide the top summer intern. Joe took the lead, 'I think Nikita's work is the best and our traders can actually use her report for new insights.'

Alex had neglected his intern, Dev throughout the summer and his project report was therefore hopeless. Samir supported Om, 'I agree. But I think Om's project also turned out nicely. His communication and analytical skills will make him an asset to our bank.'

But Nikita was the unanimous top performer. They documented the outcome and recommended a pre-placement offer for Nikita and Om was recommended as a back-up in case Nikita decided not to accept the offer.

The panel's recommendation was recorded in HR's system and would be used at the year's end to churn out pre-placement offers depending on vacancies in various departments.

After their weekend escapade, Nitin had taken an extra interest in Nikita's project. He also pushed his three schmucks to go out of their way to help her. He knew that in this professional set-up, blatantly backing a poor quality intern would not achieve the desired objective. Now, he could relax and keep his end of the bargain.

Many years ago, he had failed to keep a similar promise and the girl had called him multiple times to protest. He had made flimsy excuses and offered his help to get her placed in another bank. She had threatened to complain to HR but developed cold feet when it came to taking action. She stopped calling him after a couple of months and he was emboldened by that experience to regularly exploit the opportunities around him.

Chapter 45

Amit was supposed to join Lehman Brothers in May, 2008. He called Gary one day as he was getting impatient, 'Hi Gary, can I have a minute of your time?'

'Yes you can, but be quick. I have to juggle multiple calls and meetings thanks to the ongoing turmoil,' Gary was curt. Amit knew after the interview that this was part of Gary's personality—turmoil or not, Gary wanted to process five things at once.

'Sure. I want to know if Lehman Brothers is in good shape. I am joining you in a month and there are rumours about the firm in the market and media.'

Gary made an irritated sound. 'We are doing very well. Dick Fuld, our global CEO has assured all stakeholders that we are going to weather the storm. My personal advice to you—this market is not for the faint-hearted. It is not always spring. I am sure you will join us on the appointed day but be prepared for winter.' Amit was barely assuaged by this. He was counting hours and days because he knew the situation could worsen at short notice. The firm he was supposed to join might just vanish from the face of the earth. He shared his worries with Anu.

Anu just wanted him to calm down. 'Don't worry, Amit. Enjoy the remainder of the gardening leave. Anyway, these things are not in your hands. Remember our plan of meditating and exercising together?'

'In such a tense situation, I can't think of doing anything. Let me join the new job peacefully, then I might start these things.'

Anu was infuriated, 'This pattern is familiar. When you are doing your job, you don't have time. When you are on leave, you spend time worrying. If you take care of your mental and physical well-being, you will be able to face these situations better. What's the guarantee that things will be smooth once you join? The outside world is always going to be in turmoil. You can only create peace inside.'

Amit lost it, 'I came to you for some solace and here you are, lecturing me. Why don't you understand my state of mind? I have the responsibility of earning money for both of us. We will be out on the streets, if anything unfortunate happens.'

Anu tried to cool it. 'Baby, that's why I am supporting you in this difficult time. Sorry if it sounded like a lecture. You take your time and decide how you want to handle it.'

She usually had some time to spare after her work and could easily take up high school tuitions to generate additional income—a back-up in case Amit's job blew up. They had also saved up money for the loan instalments for a couple of years. She had faith that they would be able to tide over a difficult phase together.

Fortunately, Amit joined Lehman Brothers without any hiccups. He reported for work at the swanky office building, CeeJay House in Worli, and couldn't believe the lavishness. His new office looked no less than a seven-star hotel; in comparison, British Bank's office looked like a highway motel.

Adarsh was his boss at Lehman's India office. He greeted Amit, 'Good to see you, Amit. You can call me Adi. I am glad you joined.'

'Thanks, Adi.'

'This is your desk and all your systems are set up. It's a small dealing room now and it will be our job to make it grow fast. Unfortunately, you don't have much time to settle down. Get cracking right away!' They ordered the in-house butler to bring him some Columbian gourmet coffee.

Amit was surprised. Lehman was making the rounds as a potential bankruptcy candidate but its aggressiveness seemed intact. He replied energetically, 'Yes, Adi. I will do my best!' He wanted to start fresh, building an enthusiastic and aggressive image from the beginning. Otherwise, he ran the risk of joining the ranks of the schmucks in the new firm.

He started dialling his clients' numbers frantically. The first on the list was Universal Finance. Mr. Vijayan recognised him instantly, 'Aah Amit, you moved to Lehman Brothers? I tried your number many times but could not get through.'

'Actually, sir, I was travelling overseas for a month. Tell me, how can I help you?'

'You remember that deal? The one you made me do in a hurry just before the offsite in Vienna. British Bank is telling me that it has run into huge losses. Please help me get out of that deal, otherwise my management will fire me.'

Old deeds were coming back to haunt him. But, in an instant, he spotted an opportunity here. He replied, 'Yes, sir, I remember. But please understand that this turn of events is a once in a lifetime affair. The probability of loss was very small when we did the deal but unfortunately it has materialised.'

Mr. Vijayan was angry, 'What do you mean by once in a lifetime? This kind of deal is sufficient to kill me in one blow. You have to do something! British Bank is acting funny and asking us to deposit money as collateral to cover the losses, even though we are not contractually obliged to do it.'

'Sir, can I suggest a new deal for you? We will increase the leverage in your old deal and you will get funding to cover the losses for the next two years,' Amit's eyes were shining with the anticipation of a large deal in his first few days at Lehman Brothers. He continued, 'Since we don't yet have a banking license in India, we will route this transaction through an Indian bank. The Indian banks cannot devise such sophisticated structures themselves, hence we will supply it to an Indian bank of your choice and you can take it from them. You don't need to pay anything.' Financial alchemists were back to creating money out of thin air while all parties chose to ignore the threat of bigger losses.

Mr. Vijayan discussed the new structure and agreed, assuming that it will help him manage the losses on the old transaction. All banks on the street were getting back to brisk business by offering such restructuring of old transactions that were running into losses. The clients could not believe this financial wizardry but accepted it nonetheless.

As soon as the deal was done, an ecstatic Amit called Gary to inform him. Gary exclaimed, 'Very well done, mate!' But in his excitement, Amit forgot to inform Adi. At 11 that night, he got a call from Adi, 'What do you think of yourself? I am happy you did your first deal and made some money but you can't call my boss without keeping me in the loop. Don't try to bring in the dirty politics of British Bank here, understood?'

Amit was acutely embarrassed. He apologised, 'I am very sorry, Adi. You had stepped out for a meeting and I forgot to inform you. Rest assured, it was not intentional.' He had shot himself in the foot within the first week of starting the new job. Adi was a good-natured person and was not at all insecure about his position. He had been deputed by the global management from New York to take command at the India office. He needed to set the rules.

Chapter 46

The week of 8 September, 2008 started like any other week. Amit was winding up work on Monday and CNBC was on in the background. Suddenly, he noticed Lehman Brothers flash on the screen and he turned up the volume. It was live coverage from New York and the anchor was hysterical, 'We learn from credible sources that Lehman Brothers is facing severe liquidity problems. We believe Lehman is holding billions of dollars' worth of sub-prime assets. Most banks are refusing to lend money to Lehman for its balance sheet funding.'

Not only were the assets on Lehman's balance sheet junk, they were also financed through cheap borrowing. Other banks, so far, only looked at Lehman's good credit rating and lent it money without worrying. Since the rumours of Lehman holding junk assets were picking up every day, many banks started cutting their lending to Lehman as a prudent step for their own protection. This was a perfect example of a self-fulfilling prophecy—the media hyped the news initially, the banks got worried and cut some funding, the media got more hyper and the banks cut even more lending. Undoubtedly, Lehman had junk assets on its balance sheet but the safety net of funding could have kept the bank running.

Amit and Adi brushed aside this development as there had been similar instances before. There had been internal discussions that the US government, through its central bank, will ultimately step in to save them like they saved Bear Stearns. Lehman was too big to let fail.

By Wednesday, the noise had grown louder. Major financial channels and newspapers were pronouncing Lehman Brothers dead. The only question was—when would Hank Paulson step in and save the collapsing giant?

And it was imperative that Lehman Brothers be saved because Lehman was inextricably intertwined with several other large financial institutions. If it failed, it would destroy many other large firms—like a large ocean vessel sinking, it would take down with it any ships and boats in its vicinity.

At the close of the world markets on Friday—12 September, 2008—Lehman was taking its last breaths. The US government decided to stay away and make an example out of Lehman. The government feared that if they saved Lehman, popular opinion would turn against the government and it would be accused of wasting tax-payers' money to save the greedy crooks at Wall Street. However, what the government didn't realise or perhaps didn't want to realise was that the eventual cost of Lehman going down could be way more than the money spent on saving it.

A section of the government believed that the bankers pocketed large bonuses for taking risks and, now that the risks were exploding, the bankers needed to pay for them with their own jobs. There were also theories that Hank Paulson was an ex-Goldman Sachs executive and wanted to see Lehman go down due to historic rivalry. Many shrewd hedge funds were positioned in a way to make huge gains if the prices of junk assets fell more and Lehman's collapse would surely send the prices of these assets even lower.

On Monday, 15 September 2008, Lehman CEO Richard 'Dick' Fuld called a press conference and announced that they had filed for Chapter 11 Bankruptcy. It was the largest bankruptcy in US history, with assets of 639 billion dollars at stake.

Dick Fuld calmly walked out of the press conference, headed to his suite, changed into gym wear and hit the treadmill. Sure enough, a disgruntled employee, pumping iron in the gym, punched him in the face. Although the gym episode was not broadcast on TV, Amit and Adi sat in their office, shocked. It was over. The dreams of thousands of financial wizards and 158 years of history were wiped clean in a matter of seconds. Amit walked out of the office and sat in his car, and started crying uncontrollably. He called his wife, 'Anu... Anu –,' he was hyperventilating.

Anu was worried, 'Hello Amit, what happened? Are you hurt? Where are you? Shall I call the police?' He took a few minutes to be able to speak coherently, 'Anu, it's all over. We are doomed, my firm went bankrupt just now.'

Anu was relieved. Things could have been a lot worse. If something happened to Amit, what would she do? However, having learnt from experience, she decided not to offer any unwarranted advice and limited the chat to empathizing with him, 'It's really unfortunate, Amit. I am very sad to hear this. Will you be able to drive? Please leave the car at work and hire a cab.'

Amit had recovered, 'No no, I am okay. I will drive carefully. Let's talk when I reach home.'

Amit reached home in an hour. Anu hugged him and asked him to freshen up while she prepared tea. On TV, they watched the live telecast of employees carrying their belongings out of Lehman's headquarters in New York. Many were crying, others were agitated. There was nothing anyone could do.

'When I got this job, I thought our luck had turned. But now I am left hanging without a job. I don't know what to do. How will this whole thing pan out?'

Anu kept nodding her head. *This too shall pass.* She was not well-informed about these matters, but was stronger internally and ready to face any calamity.

Chapter 47

A week after Lehman crumbled, there was an eerie silence in the Markets dealing rooms at British Bank and Lehman India.

A worried Mr. Vijayan called Amit, 'I am very scared Amit, what is happening?'

Amit was also tense but tried to pacify him, 'Sir, this week is seeing a flurry of activity in New York. The US government has finally swung into action.' Maybe they had been waiting for one large event to take corrective action. That way, they could justify that the crisis could snowball and affect the average US citizen. With official intervention, Merrill Lynch was sold to Bank of America, AIG was bailed out by the government at a cost of 180 billion dollars and Goldman Sachs and Morgan Stanley were converted into bank holding companies and were forced to accept government help.

Mr Vijayan exulted, 'Oh, that looks positive! But what's the impact on India?'

'Sir, while India is a distant spectator, many companies like yours are directly impacted due to their derivative positions. The Indian stock market is crashing and the currency is collapsing like that of all other emerging markets. The money that had flowed in during the golden years of 2004–2007 is now trying to rush out faster, choking all outlets.'

Mr. Vijayan's excitement was short-lived, 'Amit, I am even more worried now. What will happen to my job? Can you explain the new deal we did last month after you joined Lehman? It doesn't seem to be giving me any respite. British Bank is demanding more every day.'

'Sir, I am at the office but Lehman has ceased operations for all purposes. I am not authorised to speak to you but let me still explain. The new deal actually increased the risk in the hope that the market will recover soon. But with the worsening crisis, the new deal has also run into deep losses. You better speak to the Indian bank through which we dealt with you. We don't have anything to do with your company.'

Mr. Vijayan was having trouble breathing. 'How will I explain this mess to my company board?' *The greed for a few thousand dollars and the foreign trip is costing me millions now.* 'Listen Amit, can you at least help me make a detailed note for my company's board of directors?'

'Sorry, sir, I am not authorised to do anything till I hear from our new management,' Amit said.

A few days later, Amit opened *The Economic Times* to find that Universal Finance had fired its CFO, Mr. Vijayan, for financial misconduct and for indulging in unauthorised foreign exchange transactions. They had also filed a case against British Bank and the Indian bank through which Lehman Brothers had dealt with Universal Finance. Amit sank deeper in his chair. There were seven missed calls from Mr. Vijayan.

The strategy of restructuring the deals had backfired. All hopes of a quick recovery were dashed while the clients sunk deeper. Many clients were contemplating legal proceedings and had flatly refused to pay the losses on these deals. Many companies fired their CFOs and treasurers on the charge that the deals were not authorised and they were not aware of the transactions. Lawyers were preparing for booming business and battle lines were being drawn between banks and the companies.

Meanwhile, there was some positive news for Amit. Adi informed him that Nomura Investment Bank had agreed to acquire Lehman Brothers in Asia and had guaranteed employment to most employees on their original terms.

Adi told him, 'This is great news and our financial issues are taken care of for another year. However, from a career perspective, it makes sense to be on the lookout and move to a more established firm.' At that point, Amit didn't care much about the long-term career perspective, he just wanted a respite from the ongoing doom. Reaching home, early in the evening, he exclaimed, 'Anu, I have some good news!'

'I am so relieved to see you happy, what's the news?'

'Nomura has taken over my firm in India and has guaranteed my employment for one year.'

'Wow baby, this calls for a celebration!'

'Yes baby, our finances are back in order. You were such an anchor in this difficult time. Thanks, I love you,' and he hugged Anu.

Chapter 48

December, 2008.

Normally, at this time of the year, bankers were busy making holiday plans and dreaming about the upcoming bonus cheques. It was also usually the time to scout the market for investment opportunities. But this year was different. Most bankers were hiding under the table for fear of getting fired.

The buzz was that a list of staff to be fired had been prepared at British Bank and the separation letters would be handed out any time now. Satya was preparing to leave work a bit early as he had a severe stomach ache. But when he informed Nitin, Nitin asked him to hang around for some time because he was going into a meeting with Kumar.

The glass conference room was occupied by Joe, Nitin and Sonia, the head of HR. Kumar's line rang and he picked up. Nitin was on the other side, 'Hey Kumar, why don't you drop by the conference room for a quick chat?'

Satya could sense something was wrong. The business head and HR was an ominous combination for a meeting, but he kept his thoughts to himself.

Kumar entered the room with a smile. Nitin began, 'Kumar, you have been a recent hire to the team. You are aware of the global developments and their impact on Indian business.

What are they getting at?

'In light of this situation, the bank has decided that today is your last day at work.' Sonia took over, 'This is your separation letter. Please sign this copy and give it to me as an acknowledgement.'

Kumar had come from a traditional bank and was not used to such stuff. He had not even seen anyone getting fired around him and didn't know how to react. Trying to hold himself together, he whimpered, 'Please give me a day's time to read this.'

Joe chimed in, 'You have been with us for only six months, still we have worked out a generous separation package for you. If you don't sign this right now, I am not sure if we will be able to offer the same to you. In line with global procedure, I need to report your acceptance to the London office before close of business today.'

Kumar was helpless. Instead of getting nothing, he decided to escape with whatever little he was offered. He signed on the dotted line. Sonia told him, 'Please hand over your ID and the corporate credit card to me right now. If you have a company laptop at home, please deposit it by tomorrow. You will not be able to log into the laptop or the bank computer as your login ID was disabled ten minutes ago.'

Kumar collected his copy and walked out of the door without looking back. The security person standing outside escorted him to the main gate. All his personal belongings would be gathered from his desk and sent to his home.

Satya was watching with mixed emotions. He didn't expect any danger for himself—it was not possible to fire more than one in the three-member team. Besides, the cost of firing him would have been much higher for the bank as he had contractual payments due over the next couple of years thanks to the renegotiation earlier in the year. He thanked his stars he hadn't joined Lehman Brothers.

Vicky had just returned to his desk after the evening tea. He tried logging in but could not. He called the IT helpdesk and requested them to reset his password and he had just put the phone down when Joe called him to the conference room. Vicky knew that some separations were scheduled but he was not aware of any name from his team. He figured a last-minute inclusion meant he may be asked to let one of his traders go. He confidently walked into the room where Joe and Sonia were looking at some papers.

'Yes, tell me.'

Sonia took the lead this time, 'Vicky, the bank has decided that today is your last working day here. This is your severance letter. Please sign a copy and you are free to leave. You know the rest of the formalities.'

Vicky felt a surge of emotion. It was a classic case of the hunter becoming the hunted. He hadn't expected to get fired in his wildest dreams. Nevertheless, he signed the paper quickly—the severance package was as per the bank's policy—and darted out of the office before anyone could question him.

Joe had strategically chosen the two people to be fired. Kumar was a new resource and could be fired cheaply. Besides, he needed the more senior salespersons to handle tricky client situations in the next few months. Vicky was an expensive resource and, as the head of trading, was a threat to Joe. *In case I don't fire Vicky and there is another round of staff cuts, the bank could get rid of me. By firing Vicky and taking direct charge of the trading team, I will cement my position as a revenue producing manager.*

There were eliminations in corporate banking, transaction banking and operations too. The people who survived heaved a sigh of relief as the next round of firing was a few months away.

Chapter 49

Nikita's phone rang around midnight. It was her school friend, Joy, who was doing his MBA from IIM Kolkata. Joy was excited, 'Hi Nikita, I have managed to get a pre-placement offer (PPO) from British Bank. I remember you told me you were also expecting a PPO from them. So, I thought I would share the good news and congratulate you.'

Nikita was happy—her dream of getting a PPO was inching closer. She replied, 'Congrats, Joy! I haven't heard anything from them yet. Maybe my letter is delayed in transit.'

'Oh, I understand, good luck.'

Nikita could barely wait for the morning. She was sure that the administrative office had received her letter and she just needed to collect it from them. She skipped her second lecture and went to the office but the clerk told her, 'We haven't received any letter from British Bank. Why don't you call their HR department?

Nikita called her contact in the HR department, 'Hi, this is Nikita. I did my summer internship this year with your bank.'

'Yes, how can I help?'

'I understand that PPOs have been sent out. Could you confirm if my name is on the list?'

The person on the other side replied, 'I can't see your name on the list.'

Nikita couldn't believe it, 'Could you tell me how many PPOs have been given this year?'

'Sorry, Nikita. That is confidential information.'

Nikita panicked and decided to call Nitin, 'Hey Nitin, this is Nikita. Remember?'

'Hi Nikita, how can I forget you? Tell me, what's up?'

'I understand that PPOs have been sent out but my name isn't on the list. Could you look into this and let me know soon?' Nitin was confident that she would be receiving the PPO. He told her to relax, 'Just chill. I will speak to HR and get back to you.' Nikita was starting to get really worried but she didn't have a choice—she had to wait for one more day.

Nitin called Sonia, 'Remember, we had recommended this summer intern, Nikita, for a PPO after the summer internship? Has she been given a PPO yet?'

'Oh, I forgot to update you, Nitin. Since there has been severe pressure for headcount reduction, the bank has decided to offer only one PPO to an exceptional trainee. This guy trained in our Singapore office and has been selected on personal recommendation of the CEO there.'

Nitin's face turned pale. His mind went through every moment of his escapade with Nikita. Although he had faced similar situations before, he knew that she was more assertive and aggressive. He got down to the task of devising a strategy to tackle her.

He called her the next evening. Nikita was bubbling with

excitement, 'Hi Nitin, thanks for calling. Did you manage to check? How could they miss my name? It has to be there, right?'

Nitin put up a confident front. 'Actually Nikita, the global financial crisis has taken a toll on placements this year. The bank is not even participating in final placements and there is a freeze on hiring. In fact, just last week, we fired Kumar and Vicky.'

Nikita was wild, 'Then how come my friend Joy got an offer?'

'He is an exceptional performer and the only pre-placement offer in British Bank. Please understand, I will try and make it up to you.'

'Make it up? You had your fun and now you want to throw me away like a used condom? You don't know who I am. I am not afraid to screw your life if you don't get me a PPO.'

'Nikita, I know senior management in many foreign banks. I will get you placed in one of those. Just give me a couple of months' time.'

'You have a week's time. And I won't settle for a second-grade bank. I need an offer from the likes of Bank of America, J. P. Morgan, Deutsche Bank or Barclays. By next Monday, if you don't arrange this, you will know that I mean business.'

For the first time in his career, Nitin was truly frightened. He frantically started calling his contacts across various banks to get Nikita placed. The response was the same. Every bank was in firing mode.

Chapter 50

Joe saw Aden, the CEO of Sapphire, enter the lobby at Taj Land's End in Bandra. The lobby was grand with a high ceiling and a vast expanse interrupted only by a few huge square pillars of polished red marble with brass inlay. Joe and Aden walked towards each other on the expensive Persian rug in the open coffee shop. They shook hands and hugged each other.

'Long day?' enquired Aden.

'Yes, without much work, the day feels really long,' Joe chuckled.

'We are not seeing any more business from British Bank. What's happening, Joe?'

'Listen my friend, you should know this. You are an old hand in this industry.'

'What do you mean? Things are still looking good.'

'I can understand your exasperation. Each of us sees our business in isolation but we are part of the grand economic circus. If one link breaks down in the economic chain, the whole chain falls apart. Once broken, it takes its own sweet time to repair,' Joe was trying to be cryptic.

Aden wasn't convinced.

'Look man, the economy works in a circle. When corporates do well, banks do well. Banks distribute business to service providers in IT, real estate and others, like you. Actually, the cycle starts with the consumer on the street. If consumers feel good, they spend more and that pushes the corporate earnings up, leading banks to lend more,' Joe tried to explain.

Aden was irritated, 'Oh boy, come to the point.'

'This time the economic chain has broken from the banks' end. Other links are going to take a hit one by one. Since you are one of the service providers to us, your business is bound to take a beating. My advice would be to concentrate more on recession-proof sectors like weddings.'

'You are right, Joe. People spend on weddings even in recessions. In fact, my team is already working on this. Anyway, I called you here to fulfil my promise.' Joe's eyes twinkled as Aden handed him an envelope, 'This is a small token of our gratitude for giving us the contract for your Vienna offsite.'

Joe slipped the envelope inside his jacket's pocket. Aden continued, 'It is a week-long trip for you to Seychelles. Everything has been taken care of and Pooja from Sapphire will keep you company,' he gave Joe a knowing look.

'Oh, I have seen Pooja at your events. Nice choice. Thanks for this.' Joe was drooling.

'Just keep the business flowing, man. Even in a recession, I am sure you can find ways to organise events.' The meeting concluded with Joe agreeing to do whatever was possible.

Chapter 51

The job search for Nikita proved futile; not surprising when the financial world was crumbling and even seniors had nowhere to go to. Who would hire a fresher? Nitin couldn't gather the courage to give Nikita the bad news. Secretly, he was hoping that she would let it pass after making a small fuss, like his earlier preys. Sure enough, the phone rang after ten days, 'Nitin, this is Nikita. I hope you have some good news for me.'

Nitin fumbled for words, 'Look, I am working on it. Give me few more days. My friend at Citibank has told me he could work out something in retail banking as that is the only area they may look to hire.'

'I am not willing to work in retail banking. Your time is up. Next time we see each other will be either in front of the bank's HR head or in court. You have messed with the wrong person this time.'

It was chilly in the office but Nitin was sweating profusely. He could feel his temples throbbing. As he pulled his chair to sit down, he ended up literally falling into the chair. He tried to regain his composure as there were people around. Rekha asked him, 'Nitin, are you okay? You look hassled, can I get you something?'

'No no, thanks. I will be fine.' He stared at the screens without really noticing what was happening in the market.

There was some noise and one of the traders started abusing loudly. It was Roshan. A client had hit him for a few million dollars, which was peanuts for any routine transaction. But the loss of liquidity meant that the Indian rupee was fluctuating wildly. Before Roshan could cover his position, the price moved so much that he lost a few thousand dollars just like that. In this environment, simply coming to work meant losing money.

After Kumar had been fired, Rekha had moved into a full-time sales role. She was talking to a client who said, 'When I did this deal, Amit told me that I will make a two-million-dollar gain. Can you tell me what's the position now?'

'Sir, actually you are sitting on a loss of eight million dollars,' she hated breaking the bad news but was getting used to it.

'What? How is that possible?'

'Sir, the potential gain was two million dollars but since the market moved against you, the loss is eight million dollars and could increase in the future if you don't cut it now and pay us.'

'I have emails from your bank guaranteeing the profit. Let me dig them out and send them to your global bosses in London and Singapore. After all, they should know how you treat your clients in India,' the client slammed the phone before Rekha could explain to him that this was the scene in pretty much every country.

Ten minutes later, the client's email popped into Rekha's mailbox. Rekha frantically called Nitin, who was recovering from the other shock, 'This client has sent an email demanding a gain of two million dollars on a transaction that has lost eight million dollars. He has marked the mail to Rakesh, Jorge and Martin. He has also attached an email sent by Amar.'

'What nonsense? We do not guarantee clients any profits. Forward the client's email to Joe, Compliance, Legal and me. The timing could not be worse—bonus discussions are about to start,' Nitin was nonchalant.

Rekha was surprised at both Nitin's dismissal of the client's complaint and his continuing effort to maximise his bonus even in the midst of all the firing and mayhem. *I have still much to learn. Nitin is so focused on money and just wants to put the complaint into a bureaucratic loop.*

Nitin was lost in his own thoughts. *Thank God for small mercies—this email was sent by Amar with a copy to Amit only. I can feign complete ignorance about this matter. It pays to get the dirty work done by schmucks. Let me worry about Nikita.*

Suddenly, Rakesh walked in. He was fuming. 'Who authorised Amar to send this kind of an email to the client? I build senior-level relationships with great effort and you guys ruin everything. This is a serious complaint and someone will pay for this.' He was furious that the matter had gone out of the country, to the global management, without his knowledge. His prospects of an overseas posting were seriously hampered by the spate of client complaints and impending lawsuits.

Rekha remembered that Rakesh had taken full credit for this deal on the day it had happened, just about a year ago.

Chapter 52

Sonia was relaxing in her office after her year-end vacation. This December had proved especially hectic for HR as they had to execute a round of staff cuts. There were indications that more headcount reductions were being planned. The phone rang and disturbed her peace. A female voice said, 'Hello, I am calling from Supreme Court Senior Advocate Shyam Kumar's office. Can I speak with Ms. Sonia from the HR department at British Bank?'

Sonia straightened up in her chair upon hearing such heavy names, 'Yes, this is Sonia. Please go ahead.'

'Advocate Shyam Kumar would like to send a legal notice to your office. Please confirm your address that I have with me.' Sonia confirmed the address and asked, 'What is this about? I don't remember any case that warrants a notice.'

'Ma'am, you will receive it by tomorrow. You can read it yourself.'

The notice arrived, sent by the advocate on Nikita's behalf. Shocked, Sonia called Rakesh immediately. Rakesh was out for a cosy lunch with his wife, Sophie and he promised to call her as soon as he returned.

'Sonia, what's so urgent that you disturbed me during my important lunch meeting?' Rakesh demanded once he was back in the office.

'Look at this notice served by the legal heavyweight Shyam Kumar. It accuses Nitin of sexually exploiting the summer intern, Nikita.'

'What does it say?'

'Nitin promised her a pre-placement offer and demanded sexual favours in return. Advocate Shyam Kumar is a politically well-connected lawyer and we need to take this seriously,' Sonia summarised the situation for Rakesh.

'Oh my god! That's a grave allegation. Please get Shyam Kumar on the line immediately.'

Jenny got Shyam Kumar on the phone and Rakesh was at his polite best. He began in his pseudo-American baritone, 'Sir, we are in receipt of a legal notice from you regarding Nikita's complaint. I would like to assure you that British Bank takes these matters very seriously. We will institute an official inquiry and will take the sternest action possible.'

Advocate Kumar was cold. 'I don't care what you do in the bank. You need to compensate my client suitably otherwise, I can assure you, this case will be taken to the UK Supreme Court, as you are headquartered in London.'

Rakesh wanted to buy some more time. 'Sir, please trust me. We will do everything we can You need to give us a month's time at least. We have duly acknowledged the notice already.'

'Whatever you do, British Bank needs to pay two million US dollars as compensation to my client,' Advocate Kumar got off the phone. Rakesh was worried that any adverse publicity due to this case would cost him his job. His role was to protect the bank from any regulatory and reputational risk. He didn't really care about Nitin losing his job or the bank paying a hefty compensation privately to Nikita.

He instructed Sonia, 'Please institute a task force for investigation right away. The team should consist of the members of the regional Prevention of Sexual Harassment (POSH) committee and the head of Legal. I want the investigation report within three weeks.'

Sonia rushed to her cabin to get cracking on the case. As soon as the task force met, it unanimously decided to ask Nitin to proceed on leave until further instructions. His presence in office, while the investigation was going on, could be seen negatively by outside investigators and regulators.

She called Nitin as soon as the call was over, 'Nitin, can you come to my office please?'

As he entered her office, he was surprised to see that Joe was also present. He smiled, 'So, is it my turn to get fired today? I thought the next round was a few months away.' Sonia and Joe didn't react to his joke. Sonia said flatly, 'Nitin, the bank is asking you to proceed on indefinite leave. We have received a complaint of sexual exploitation against you.'

Nitin stiffened and a few creases appeared on his brow, 'You can't ask me to go on leave without giving me details. Who has made the complaint and why is the bank believing it blindly?'

Sonia brushed him aside, 'I cannot share any details with you as of now. You will receive your salary while you are away. Further action will be decided after the investigation report is reviewed by the management. Any more questions?'

Nitin finally understood that Nikita had carried out her threat, even though he hadn't taken it seriously. Like Kumar and Vicky, Nitin also disappeared from the office, though under different circumstances. This left Rekha and Satya in the driving seat as far as the sales team was concerned.

Vani was pleasantly surprised that Nitin had taken a few days off from work. She asked, 'What happened? You have taken this leave without planning.'

'It's the work. It was getting too much to handle and my blood pressure was shooting up. I got it checked and the doctor advised a few days of rest.'

'Oh, why didn't you share that with me? Don't you consider me a part of your life? Chalo, at least your health forced you to spend some time with us.' Vani and the kids were happy to see him around more than what they were used to.

'Do you mean I was not giving enough time and attention to you and the kids?' Nitin was irritated and took comfort in the offensive.

'No, no, it's not like that. I don't want to start a fight, let's enjoy this unscheduled holiday at home. Let me know what you would like to eat. I will cook it for you myself!' Vani tried to salvage the situation.

It was Nitin's usual style at home and so far he had gotten away with it, taking advantage of Vani's sweetness. He was hoping that the case would be buried and he wouldn't have to tell Vani anything. Meanwhile, he decided to take stock of his financial situation in this forced holiday. But when he saw his updated portfolio statement, his face crinkled. Nothing seemed to be going well. He called the broking house customer line, 'This is Nitin Sharma, can I speak to my stock advisor?'

'Sir, I am your new advisor. I have just joined from another firm.'

'What? My stock advisor changes every few months. Who do I hold accountable for my investments?'

'What's your query, sir?'

'The stock market index has crashed from a peak of twenty thousand to under ten thousand. I was expecting this portfolio also to be down about fifty percent. But I am aghast that I have lost ninety percent of my money.'

'Sir, I can see that only five out of your fifty shares are part of Sensex. The rest are all small and mid-cap shares. They have suffered the most in this crash.' This was a direct result of mindless trading in shares based on tips given by brokers. These shares, that did well because of organised noise and not because of earnings growth, had fallen like a house of cards.

As Nitin looked at the stocks he was left with, he could not identify more than five companies. He shouted at the broker, 'What are these companies? Can you take me through each of these and advise the future course of action?'

The new broker, in his innocence, admitted, 'Sir, we ourselves don't know about the businesses of the companies we recommend. Our research team sends a list of stocks to buy and sell, and we advise our clients accordingly.' Nitin understood that there was no hope that most of these share prices would ever come back to the dizzying highs of 2007. He was doomed; he had lost a lot of the money that he had earned in the good years.

Next, he looked at his real estate investments. He called his friend in the leading real estate advisory firm, 'Rajan, I have a couple of bookings in under-construction projects in the suburbs and in south Mumbai. Any idea what rates I'll get if I wanted to sell?'

'Are you joking, Nitin? I didn't expect this question from a well-informed finance professional like you,' Rajan laughed. 'The quick answer is you can't sell anything even if you want to, in the current situation. There are no buyers as most investors have lost a lot of money in the stock market. Genuine home buyers will now wait for a good three years at least, hoping for lower prices.'

'Can't you at least try to sell?'

'It is impossible to sell an under-construction property as the market is rife with rumours of many reputed builders being in trouble. They don't have money to pay interest on their loans, forget keeping the construction on. Many small builders have already deserted their projects and have gone underground.'

Nitin could feel the despair taking over. *When the going was good and the bonuses large, I invested in all the wrong places. I thought times will always be good and money will keep flowing. What will I tell Vani? I have taken my wife, family, job and money completely for granted. But, all is not lost, I will find a way out. I may not be in a position to inform Vani about all this but if I rebuild successfully, she may not even realise that this happened.*

Chapter 53

Amit was trying hard to pass his time at Nomura's plush office, which they had inherited from Lehman Brothers. It was difficult to be professionally satisfied in the current job—it was a dead end. Nomura had advised him that he was part of the retention pool, that is, he would not be fired for at least two years. Still, he was used to frantic activity at British Bank. He could only think of Samir for some guidance in this condition.

'Hi Amit, how are you, my friend? Long time,' Samir answered his phone with his usual boisterous laugh.

Amit wondered whether Samir was living in the same world and in the same industry. He couldn't think of anything to be happy about. He replied, 'I am okay, Samir. How are you? Can I take a few minutes of your time? I need your advice on some personal matters.'

Samir laughed again, 'Are you kidding me? There's no work and I have all the time in the world. Tell me, how can I help you?'

'Samir, I am getting bored at work. There is nothing to do and no value addition as a result. I fear that I will rot here if I don't move out quickly. What do you say? What areas should I try to look at?'

'Look my friend, you are like a well-fed polar bear and the winter is here. If you try to move around too much, you may get killed unnecessarily. You do what the polar bear does—hibernate. You have earned good money over the last few years. Nomura has agreed to retain you and that's a great outcome.'

Amit started to see the positive side, 'It makes sense, Samir. But in case I want to take pre-emptive action to safeguard my career, what are the options?'

'Look, at the cost of repetition, you should stay put. There are no safe banks out there. There are no jobs across industries out there. Maybe a year down the line, the market will start opening up. Think about the people who have been fired and are willing to join anywhere for lesser compensation. Which company has time to interview you and negotiate a salary package? They can readily hire any jobless banker today.'

'Can't I go for some higher degree in finance or an MBA from a top university in the US?'

Samir laughed again, 'It is an old formula where people go study during a downturn and by the time they come back, markets are up nicely—it is easier to get a more senior level job.' But Samir forecast that this downturn was unlike any since the great depression of 1929. If Amit went to study, he would forego a couple of years of salary and would also spend a bomb on tuition and other expenses. And, this time there was no guarantee that he would get a senior level job after completing his degree.

'Got it, Samir. What about managing my investments? My mutual funds are down, in line with the market. I have only one real estate investment that I can comfortably service for the next couple of years.'

'Well done—this is where most people falter. When they are

earning, they are careless about money. Hold on to your mutual fund investments and any blue chip stocks. They are bound to bounce back. I never dabble in frivolous trading. Investing in a real estate asset where you can comfortably pay the instalments is a good idea. Investing in multiple under-construction properties with the hope of making a quick profit and exiting is not. When the market crashes, real estate is the first asset that seizes up and it is impossible to sell. In short, you are well-positioned and no action is the best course of action for you.'

'I understand, Samir. Thanks a ton for your advice,' Amit said.

'Hope all's well with Anu. Bye and take care,' Samir hung up.

Amit had lost sight of all the good things he still had. He felt much better after talking to Samir.

Chapter 54

The investigating team summoned all the employees to take their feedback on Nitin. Satya was next for questioning.

'Satya, you have worked with Nitin for a few years now. Do you want to say anything about his attitude towards female colleagues?' Catrina, from the regional team, asked him point-blank.

This was his chance to take revenge. He was not worried about his own police case anymore because it was quite old and frivolous in comparison to the charges against Nitin. He carefully weighed his words, 'Umm... Nitin is a nice person. He is friendly with everyone irrespective of gender.'

'I am asking whether you noticed him being extra-friendly with any woman in the office or any other objectionable situation?' Catrina stuck to her line of questioning.

'Now that you mention it, I can recall one instance where I saw Rekha and Nitin getting intimate at a suburban bar.' He recounted the details of what he had seen.

'That's revealing indeed. Any other cases?'

'Otherwise, I thought he took personal interest in Nikita, the summer intern. I found it a bit unusual for a senior manager to spend so much time with a junior trainee.'

'I see, Satya. Thank you for your comments. Please understand that false allegations can get you in trouble. Do you confirm what you have just said? I will be taking this statement on record.'

'I do.'

They called Rekha in next. She confirmed what Satya had said but denied that their involvement proceeded any further than that. She also absolved Nitin of demanding any sexual favours in return for her promotion. Catrina was not fully satisfied with her explanation but didn't have any grounds to indict Nitin in Rekha's case. Still, this instance confirmed Nitin's inclination to flirt with female colleagues.

Sonia entered the room with Nitin's file and made a startling statement, 'I have gone through his records. Interestingly, there was a similar complaint over email by a management trainee, Ankita, three years ago.'

'Why was he not punished then?' Catrina asked.

'There was a short investigation after which the management acquitted Nitin of any wrongdoing and Ankita resigned. Catrina, we know that it's usual for companies to gloss over minor complaints, especially if the complainant is a junior and didn't pursue the case legally.'

'Unfortunate, but true.'

The committee summoned Nikita for an interview. Advocate Kumar sent a female lawyer with her to ensure that she was not unduly pressurised. For her comfort, she was interviewed only by the female members of the task force.

Catrina led the interrogation, 'Nikita, the charges levied by you are very serious. If true, they might severely damage Nitin's career. So, I need you to be truthful and precise in your answers.'

'I understand, ma'am. Please ask me whatever you want to know,' Nikita didn't have anything to hide. She got into the when, where and how of the exploitation. The minion lawyer sent by Advocate Kumar took copious notes through the meeting. They parted with the promise that appropriate action would be taken after verification of everything that was alleged.

The committee members then travelled to the farmhouse in Karjat. The caretaker was caught off guard by the smartly-dressed bankers in large SUVs. The presence of a white lady made him believe that it was a foreign police delegation. He spilled the beans without any resistance and begged with folded hands, 'Madam, I was only obeying the orders of Nitin sir. I hope nothing will happen to me. I am the sole breadwinner of my family, I cannot afford to fight a case or go to jail.'

They assured him that he was safe and left the place. Sonia joked on the way back, 'The poor caretaker doesn't know that British Bank is more afraid to go to court even though we can afford that.' Catrina looked stern. Such jokes were not taken lightly by the sentries of the bank.

Chapter 55

Satya had been unable to eat well for the last few days. Kakoli took him to the doctor and he was advised a full body check-up. While filling the questionnaire, Satya ticked 'moderate' for his alcohol consumption and Kakoli noticed this but kept quiet. After the tests were done and the report prepared, the doctor called them in for consultation. He said, 'You claim that your alcohol consumption is moderate. Can I clarify, how much is it, actually?'

'About a couple of pegs every alternate day,' Satya replied. Evidently, that was his perception of his own drinking.

'Even that is not moderate, it's on the higher side. I find it hard to believe though, looking at the condition of your liver.'

Now Kakoli had to intervene. 'Doctor, he drinks every day. When he drinks at home, he doesn't stop before three large pegs. I don't know how much he drinks outside the house.'

The doctor was alarmed. 'Your reports show that you are suffering from ulcers in your stomach and liver cirrhosis. This is associated with high alcohol consumption. I will prescribe some medicines and you have to completely stop consuming any kind of alcohol. If you are unable to control the urge to drink, that means you are addicted and we may have to send you for rehabilitation.'

Satya didn't expect such bitter news. On the way back, Kakoli was stern. 'Satya, no more playing with your life. Your health is bad and you lost money in the stock market. It is enough.' Satya nodded. He was almost crying.

Kakoli continued, 'I am still willing to support you, provided you follow the regime of diet and recovery that the doctor has prescribed. This is the only chance I am willing to give our marriage. I will also ask your parents to visit us and update them about what has been happening.'

Satya was now genuinely apologetic. He hugged Kakoli and wept like a baby. *What have I done? I was blinded by the high income and a rash profession. Both are under threat. Kakoli is still willing to give me a chance and I will not disappoint her this time.*

Tackling his traditional Bengali parents was a different and difficult matter. They were due to arrive in a few hours by the Howrah-Dadar Gitanjali Express. They had vehemently refused his offer of air travel because, for them, it was a waste of money. Satya and Kakoli arrived at the platform at Dadar station well in time to receive his parents.

As soon as his dad disembarked from the train, he started shouting at Satya, '*O boka loka*, you foolish man! You look completely wasted. Did I educate you so well for you to become an alcoholic?' He continued to shout in Bangla.

A small crowd started to gather around them—people are always interested in a spectacle. Satya was whispering, 'Baba, let's go home, we can talk there.' But he was also relieved that his father had not taken off his slippers to start beating him.

A police constable approached them, 'Any trouble here? Has this man harmed you?' He was asking his father and his mother answered, 'Nothing at all, we are meeting our son after a long time, hence his father is emotional. We were just leaving.'

Satya's father kept yelling all the way home. Kakoli and his mother failed to calm him down, he lectured Satya long enough to last a lifetime. Finally, he paused when he was offered a cup of tea at home and only after Kakoli repeatedly assured him that the situation would be under control going forward.

Chapter 56

Nitin appeared before the POSH committee. He flatly denied all accusations. Nevertheless, the committee was unanimous—there was irrefutable evidence of sexual exploitation. Nitin's character, which emerged in the testimony, and his history supported its decision. The committee submitted a report to British Bank's management.

Sonia invited Nitin for a meeting after the investigation report was finalised and accepted by the bank's management. She, Rakesh and Joe waited for him in the conference room while Catrina and Martin joined via phone from Singapore.

Catrina briefed everyone before Nitin arrived, 'I will speak as per the script given to me by legal. You guys don't need to say anything or react at all. Please refrain from offering sympathy or advice. This conversation needs to be carried out in an impersonal manner.'

Rakesh added, 'If the accused reacts wildly or threatens, I will ask him to leave the office. If he refuses to leave, we have security standing by. Understood?'

Everyone replied in the affirmative. Nitin made a quiet entry and smiled at everyone. They just nodded and Sonia asked him to take a seat. Nitin had a bad feeling about this.

Catrina began, 'Nitin, as you have been informed, there was a complaint of sexual exploitation against you. Upon investigation by the internal task force, you have been found guilty of sexual misconduct and of jeopardizing the bank's reputation. You are being relieved of your duties immediately. You are no longer an employee of British Bank.'

Nitin crumbled in his seat. His head hung low with shame, finally.

'Sonia will hand over a short separation agreement to you now. You can sign it in duplicate and hand a copy back to her,' Catrina finished.

Nitin took the papers from Sonia and tried hard to read them, but it was impossible to concentrate. His hands shook and his eyes were blurry with tears. He barely managed to speak, 'Can I take a couple of days to read this and return the signed copy?'

Catrina was all too familiar with such tactics. 'No, I am sorry, we don't have the luxury of time. The bank is letting you go without claiming any damages. You have to sign this right now, or the peaceful separation offer will expire.'

Nitin read whatever he could. He realised that he was losing more than what he expected. 'But all my unvested stocks are being taken away. You are paying me neither a notice period salary nor a bonus for this year. After all, I worked for the full year in 2008,' he whimpered.

Rakesh explained, 'Nitin, your separation is happening under extraordinary circumstances involving gross violation of the bank's policies and misconduct bordering on criminal offence. You should be thankful that the bank is not dragging you to court. We are also managing the complainant at our end, though we can't guarantee that she will not sue you directly. So, it's your call—you can sign this paper and walk free or we meet in court.'

Nitin knew that 'meeting in court' was an empty threat. Even so, in his judgement, ending his employment and moving on was the best option. He quickly signed the papers, collected his copy and left.

Joe, even though experienced, was stunned at the cold execution of the whole operation. Catrina spoke in a relieved tone, 'That will be all for today. I am glad Nitin chose the sensible way out. Hopefully, he will learn from his mistakes and make a fresh start. We are giving him a clean letter.'

Sonia wanted to speak but kept quiet. *Why should he be given a clean certificate? Serial offenders tend to continue until they receive severe punishment. I guess it is part of give and take. The bank doesn't want to squeeze Nitin too much and risk strong retaliation.*

Chapter 57

Rakesh was entrusted with the task of negotiating a settlement with Advocate Kumar. The bank didn't want this case to reach the media—a sexual exploitation lawsuit exposed to the public could spawn other complainants. He travelled to Delhi and arranged a meeting with the advocate in a private suite at the Taj Mansingh hotel.

'Sir, thanks for your time. I have come to personally apologise for the unfortunate events during Nikita's summer internship,' said Rakesh as he shook the advocate's hands.

Shyam Kumar stared back at him.

'As I told you, such behaviour is not condoned at our bank and we have fired Nitin, effective immediately.' Rakesh hoped that the quick punishment would calm him down.

'That's fine for your own protection, Rakeshji. But what about the compensation for my innocent client?'

'Our management accepts that we should pay some

compensation, but two million dollars is too high. We will not be able to get approvals for this amount even if we wanted to pay you that much. We are a listed company and the amounts paid as compensation need to stand the scrutiny of auditors and regulators. Please understand our situation. We are willing to offer a quarter million dollars,' Rakesh made his opening offer.

The advocate maintained a stern face. He made a counter-offer, 'If this case were to go to the UK, the compensation could run into tens of millions of dollars. However, to close it now, I may be able to accept one million dollars and not a penny less.'

The advocate knew that taking the case to the UK would be a challenge because the terms of summer training explicitly mentioned Indian jurisdiction. He also knew the Indian legal system and understood that the case could drag on for over a decade and the compensation would turn out to be only a few thousand dollars. But Kumar was exploiting the fact that foreign banks were extremely averse to bad publicity. He had told Nikita before entering the negotiations that any sum in the vicinity of half a million dollars would be a good outcome.

Rakesh was relieved that the negotiation was proceeding in the right direction. He had authorisation from the management to go up to one and a half million dollars. He said, 'Sir, if you insist, I can try for seven hundred thousand dollars. This offer is subject to confirmation from my management in Singapore. If you agree, I can make a quick call and take their approval.'

The advocate didn't want to push his luck further. The compensation amounted to three-and-a-half crores in Indian rupees. He didn't expect any Indian court to grant more than ten percent of that. Factoring in the additional pain and stigma for his client, he nodded and agreed. Rakesh excused himself and stepped out into the long corridor lined with portraits of Mughal emperors and called Catrina, 'They are willing to settle for seven hundred thousand dollars. Do we sign?'

Catrina was happy with the outcome, 'Sure, please sign before they change their mind.'

'Okay, please send me a confirmation over email.'

Rakesh completed the formalities without wasting any time. He had carried a settlement agreement with him. They quickly filled in the amounts and signed it right there. They parted on a solemn note but both were happy with the outcome. Rakesh touted this cost-saving to his boss and hoped that it would count in his favour as a positive contribution in an otherwise disastrous year. He was desperate to move to Singapore to enlarge his territory.

As the advocate entered his home, Nikita asked him, 'Dad, what happened?'

'I have helped you this time but don't do anything this stupid in your life again,' Shyam Kumar berated his daughter.

Chapter 58

Vani wondered why Nitin had been home for more than three weeks. She had asked him many times if all was well at work but the last time she asked, Nitin gave her a dirty look and kept silent.

Around noon, she was sipping her tea when the doorbell rang.

'Oh Nitin, you are back so soon! You went to work after three weeks and missed me so much that you returned before lunchtime?' Vani was in a jovial mood.

Nitin went straight to the sofa. He told her, 'Vani, I want to share some terrible news with you.'

'What happened? I hope you are fine.'

'Due to the severe downturn in the world financial markets, a lot of senior people have got fired across banks. The bank has asked me to leave. It happened three weeks ago but I was trying to work something out. I couldn't. I hope you'll understand.'

Vani was a well-educated and well-informed lady. She had been following the global financial crisis and the widespread job losses.

Like a good and supportive wife, she hugged him. 'Don't worry Nitin, I understand and I'm with you in this time of distress. We have had a great run at British Bank. I am sure we will tide over this difficult time together.'

Nitin was relieved. Vani bought the story and sympathised with him. *Since I have kept Vani completely isolated from my office crowd, there is no chance she will find out the real story. Now, I can concentrate on finding another job and rebuilding our finances.* He only had enough to meet expenses for a year or so because he had blown away a large part of his fat bonuses. Vani was blissfully unaware of their financial mess and thought they were in an enviable position. That's why she was not disturbed by the loss of his job.

They had a short afternoon nap. Later, Nitin told her, 'I am going out for coffee with a head-hunter to begin my job search.'

'Okay sure, I will wait for you to have dinner.' When he left, she decided to clean up his wardrobe as he didn't take any interest in organizing his belongings. Disorganised wardrobes gave her a headache and she put his in order periodically. As soon as she started removing his clothes, a bunch of papers fell out. Generally, she wasn't interested in reading Nitin's papers but the legal stamp caught her attention. She got more curious when she saw that it had been signed the same day. She read the entire document. When she reached the end, she fell on the bed, incapable of emotion.

Nitin returned just before dinner time expecting a sumptuous home-cooked meal. He saw Vani lying on the bed with the papers in her hands, her eyes swollen from hours of weeping. 'Oh, I see that you read the papers. I wanted to tell you but thought I would save you the trauma. There was a conspiracy at work to get me fired. Rakesh doesn't like me and connived with HR to take stern action on a frivolous complaint.'

Vani kept quiet. *I want to see to what depths he can fall.* She stared blankly at him and Nitin tried to hug her, 'I apologise for hiding this episode but believe me, there is no truth to the allegations.'

She pushed him away, 'I trusted you blindly and this is how you have paid me back. If you would have shared everything with me, I could still believe you. The fact that you tried to hide it is proof enough of your guilt. Just get lost!'

'Listen to me, Vani. These days, banks are trying to find excuses to get rid of people. There is no truth in this.'

'Just leave me alone tonight. I need to recover from this shock. I don't know what all you have been doing behind my back, taking advantage of my faith in you.'

Nitin went to sleep in the living room.

Chapter 59

Amit called his father after his job stabilised thanks to Nomura's take-over of Lehman Brothers. He tried to play the situation down, 'Papa pranam, how are you and mummy?'

'We are fine, beta. You tell me, what's new in Mumbai?'

'Papa, my bank, Lehman Brothers went bankrupt a few days back.'

'Oh, what's the meaning of bankrupt, Amit?' his father asked.

'It means that the bank doesn't have money to pay back their debt and they have officially declared it.'

'But I thought banks always gave money to other people. Why should the bank take on debt? They must be having their own money. You only told me that Lehman Brothers' size was over 600 billion dollars.'

'Banks have a small amount of their own money. They normally borrow about ten to fifteen times their own money and use it to make loans to other people. But my bank ended up borrowing hundred times its own money. At the same time, they made loans to unworthy people. That's why they went bankrupt.'

'Aha, I get it. But you boasted that your bank hired qualified professionals, with PhDs and MBAs. How could such people commit these mistakes?'

'Papa, these people work on many assumptions. They place more faith in their computer models than in actual humans. Most of them are also driven by greed. They look to maximise their earnings and, in that process, sometimes, some banks go under. The others are saved by the governments.'

'But in our relatively poor country, we haven't heard of banks failing.'

'That's because our market is under-developed. There are no complicated products for risk-taking in our market. RBI, our central bank, keeps a vigil on all risk-taking in the banking system. Any weak banks are merged with stronger banks before it gets too late.'

'So, that's why I never lost any of my money kept in fixed deposits. Thank God I live in an under-developed country.'

'It's not like that, Papa. These foreign banks are very big and they operate across hundreds of countries.'

'But what's the use of this sophistication and size? Their lenders are losing their money and their employees are out of jobs. I am not very well-informed but I'm sure the banks' shareholders also got ripped.'

Amit was losing patience, 'But Papa –'

'But what? Our banks are clearly better. Our neighbour, Ghosh babu served in Bank of India for 35 years and is leading a peaceful retired life.'

'But he didn't make a truckload of money. He lives a lower middle-class life.'

'At least he had a stable job his entire life. He gets a nice pension, which is enough to meet his meagre needs. You people earn a lot of money, learn new ways of spending that money and then want to earn more.'

'I cannot explain these things to you, Papa! You are still stuck in your backward world,' Amit snapped at his father and cut the call.

His father was still scratching his head, 'What did I say that Amit got so angry?'

Chapter 60

Late next morning, Nitin was snoring away on the couch in the living room while Vani frantically searched for the number of any of British Bank's employees on her phone. Finally, she found Gita's number—Nitin had given it to her as a back-up, in case he was unreachable when he travelled.

She dialled Gita and asked for the head of HR's name and number, which Gita promptly gave her. Next she called Sonia, 'Hi, can I speak to Sonia?'

'Speaking, how can I help you?' Sonia answered with a touch of irritation at receiving a call during breakfast.

Vani tried hard not to break down. 'This is Vani, Nitin's wife. I won't take up much of your time.'

Sonia forgot her irritation and started thinking about how to handle her questions. She said, 'Sure, I have a couple of minutes and then I need to leave for work.'

'Just tell me whether the accusations of sexual exploitation against Nitin are true or is he a victim of office politics, as he is claiming?'

Sonia thought about it for a minute. In her long career, she had learnt to be truthful as far as possible. She replied, 'This is the bank's internal matter and we do not share any information with non-employees. Since you are his spouse, as a personal gesture, I can tell you that a high-powered committee investigated the case and found him guilty. He is lucky that criminal charges have not been pressed against him as the bank tries to keep these things away from the media.'

Vani got her answer and started packing the children's bags, and hers. Her parents lived in the same city and she decided to move there with her kids till she taught Nitin a lesson. And she hadn't ruled out a divorce. She was almost out the door when Nitin woke up.

He jumped from the sofa, 'Vani, please don't leave like this. I can explain everything. Why don't you believe me?'

'You have lost my trust forever, Nitin. When I caught your crime last evening, you still tried to cover it up with a heap of lies. I have spoken to the people at your office already and they verified the facts.'

'These people will never tell you the truth, Vani.'

'If you are such a saint, why didn't you contest your firing? Why did you forego your stock options? You better prepare for one more legal battle. This time it will be with me.' Vani dashed out with their kids, aged five and eight.

Her parents were pleasantly surprised to see her with the children that morning. Though well-to-do, they were conservative people. Her mother said, 'So good to see you and the kids. Come in.'

As soon as her mother hugged her, Vani started crying. Her parents understood that all was not well. After she settled down, her father sent the kids out to the garden to play with their dog. He took Vani's hand in his and said, 'I can see that you are deeply hurt but don't take any decisions in a hurry. Let me call Nitin and have a proper conversation with him.'

Vani continued to sob, 'I don't want to talk to that cheat.'

'Vani, calm down. I am not asking you to compromise. Let's see if he is willing to confess his crime and ask for genuine forgiveness.'

Vani was in no mood to forgive Nitin even if he asked for it. With the proof of his infidelity, she was well-armed for a divorce case.

Her mother was more aggressive, 'We need to ask Nitin to come here and give a detailed explanation. Vani also needs to take stock of all the financial assets. Whenever I asked her to be informed about their joint wealth, she didn't take me seriously.'

Nitin called her father after an hour, 'Daddy, has Vani reached safely? She left in a hurry without giving me a chance to explain or apologise.'

Her father responded coldly, 'Even an apology may not be enough in this case. I suggest you let her cool down for a day or two and then come over to have a chat with us.'

'Actually, I wanted to come now but if you feel waiting is better, I will come day after.'

'Yes, and when you come, please bring details of all your assets like bank deposits and accounts, tax returns, shares, mutual funds, property investments and insurance policies. We need to take stock of both of your lives.'

Nitin's troubles were increasing by the hour. Now he would have to reveal the financial mess he had worked himself into.

They met two days later. Nitin and Vani sat diagonally opposite on the large marble dining table. Nitin placed his elbows on the cold white stone and leaned forward but Vani refused to even look at him. The children met their father briefly but were ushered out by their grandfather. He offered Nitin a cup of tea and the discussion started.

'So, what do you have to say about this episode?' Vani's mother asked.

Nitin knew that there was no point hiding the truth anymore. Vani had since spoken with more of his erstwhile colleagues and everyone had confirmed the story. He meekly submitted, 'I am very sorry for what happened. I made a mistake and I'm here to assure you that it will never happen again.'

Vani gave him a sarcastic smile, 'Just get lost. You don't deserve a second chance.'

Her father squeezed her hand to calm her down. 'We will come to that later. Show me the financial papers I asked you to bring.'

He was a retired chartered accountant, well-versed in financials. Nitin gave him the documents with trembling hands. It took her father a couple of hours to go through the documents. He made detailed notes and tabulated the data systematically. At the end of it, he took off his thick reading glasses and put one stem of the spectacles between his teeth. 'You are in deep trouble financially.'

Nitin didn't have anything to say.

Her father continued, 'You have lost heavily in the stock market. A large chunk of your money is tied up in properties that are unsaleable for the next few years. In fact, if you don't pay as per the builder's demand, they may forfeit what you have already paid. That leaves you guys with one flat and some cash to meet expenses for a few months.'

Vani wailed loudly upon hearing the financial report. 'This rascal has ruined my life. Not only was he sleeping around with women, he also blew away all the money that he had earned in his prime years.'

'I am sorry, Vani. I really am,' Nitin apologised profusely with tears in his eyes.

'I let him be free, thinking he was working for us. I gave up my career and invested in his by giving all my time and devotion to the family. To hell with him!' Vani yelled. 'I don't want to see his face. If he has any shame, he will not face me again. I want a divorce.'

This was too much for Nitin to handle. Although her parents were trying to pacify her, Vani was getting increasingly agitated. Nitin got up and left without saying another word, wiping his eyes on the sleeves of his shirt.

Chapter 61

Profits at the Mumbai branch of British Bank were drastically down that year, due to the lack of business, the write-off on the assets, trading losses and so on. All things that could have gone wrong had gone wrong—all at the same time. The pundits described it as a one in a billion chance event. Such events were referred to as the Black Swan in the world of financial markets. Nicholas Nassim Taleb had coined the term and written a famous book about it, which also proved that the millions of people who had read the book hadn't learnt anything from it.

Suddenly, the cost of operations in India was a sore point. The regional management sent in a team of investigators to look into the operating costs. After a comprehensive review of client entertainment, travel expenses and employee costs, the team zeroed in on a few suspicious points.

There was a general disregard for corporate expense policy. The first task of the team was to enforce the expense limit on all items.

They reported two of the largest expenses—the Global Markets offsite in Vienna and the brokerage paid by the bank to foreign exchange and bond brokers.

The brokerage was a legitimate expense. Traders depended on the brokers for efficient pricing and a fraction of the amount was paid as brokerage. This was standard market practice but what made the team suspicious was that a large fraction of the money was paid to a single broking house for the last several years. It turned out that Joe was pushing his traders to deal with this particular broker for all products. They decided to quiz the traders and they confirmed this. Roshan mentioned that Joe indirectly incentivised the traders who dealt with this particular broker.

Next, they audited the expenses incurred during the Vienna offsite. Many startling facts came to light. A few employees and clients had travelled business class and had stayed in presidential suites against company policy. Why did Joe and Nitin get extra favours? The team carried out an independent assessment of the costs of organizing such an event. They estimated costs to be 50 percent lower than what was paid to Sapphire Events. Who was responsible for approving these inflated bills?

Joe and Nitin. Nitin was already fired but Joe was hanging around. Joe was an extremely well-paid Managing Director; he didn't need to do these things to survive, but apparently he still did.

They decided to quiz Aden, the CEO of Sapphire and the head of the brokerage house that got the most business. Both were threatened with criminal cases against their firms on the charges of bribery and corruption. Under pressure, both admitted to providing financial and other favours to Joe. After the investigation, Joe was summarily fired from British Bank. Another unceremonious exit of an erstwhile star due to greed and unethical behaviour. Alas, Joe would have to chart out a new plan to get his Patek Philippe and BMW Z4.

Chapter 62

Jorge was surveying the vast dealing floor at the London headquarters of British Bank. The activity and noise had decreased markedly. Most of the employees walked with drooping shoulders and worried about the future all day. His thoughts were interrupted by a call from his secretary, 'Boss, Ram wants to see you.'

'Okay, send him in. How much time do I have?'

'Your next call is in 15 minutes. I will remind you if Ram doesn't leave by then.'

'Thanks Mary, you are wonderful.' Mary showed Ram into the glass-walled office and closed the door.

'How are you, mate? Anything urgent?' Jorge didn't waste any time. Bull market habits die hard.

'Not too well, Jorge. I was running the credit trading desk. After the global financial crisis, we have suffered a deep gash in the trading book. The credit default swaps and high-yield bonds are both untouchable for the next couple of years.'

'But why are you complaining? The bank has taken good care of you even in this difficult time!'

'I am thankful for that, Jorge. But how long will the bank keep me if I don't justify my existence? What's next for me? This question haunts me every moment,' Ram shared his fears. He was a career banker at British Bank and he knew that it worked on the principle of survival of the fittest. If he didn't reposition himself, the bank would push him out soon. Business crashing was no excuse. The smart bankers would either reinvent themselves or invent a new business opportunity to keep their jobs.

'Leave it to me. I have a call with our global head, I'll take it up with him. The position of Head of Markets in India has just opened up. Would you be keen to take it?' Jorge offered.

'What's the size of the India business?'

'We make about two hundred million dollars, top line in India, if that excites you.'

'Looks good, Jorge. I will be keen to take it.'

'Well then, see you at five in the evening.'

'Sure, thanks!' Ram left just in time for Jorge to jump onto the next call. Mary had already transferred the call to his cabin. *God! It pays to have an efficient secretary.*

Jorge knew that Ram was part of the inner circle because he personally monitored the careers of his superstars. The bank didn't worry about losing schmucks at a small branch office but the stars at the head office needed to be retained. Once the market revived, they could be brought back to manage the larger businesses. Ram's name was approved after a brief conversation.

Ram was elated. He called his wife, 'Pack your bags, we are moving to Mumbai. I have landed a plum role in India.'

'What the hell are you talking about? I cannot stay in that place. We have been living abroad for the last 15 years. How can you imagine that my child and I can live there now?' His wife's reaction was more drastic than he had expected.

'Baby, please understand. If I stay here, I will surely lose my job. This move is to save my career.'

'Then you please carry on. I am not going anywhere. Once things settle down here, you can come back.'

'What are you talking about? I will be gone for a few years. I can't miss my time with our little princess and with you.'

'I have told you my decision. Either you care about your career or us.'

Years of a million-dollar income have blinded her. She is not willing to see the reality. The writing is on the wall but how do I explain this to her? Ram was certain that he had to move. If he lost his job in London, he would be in deep trouble—leaving his family in London was the less unpleasant option.

On his flight to Mumbai, he watched a documentary on the annual migration of millions of wildebeest across African plains to greener pastures. Many lose their lives in the process but he felt justified in his decision. He had joined the migration of bankers from London and New York to Asia.

Chapter 63

As the sun went down, Mumbai's coastline was bathed in a rust red glow. Thousands of cars were lining up on the northbound lanes of posh Pedder Road, in the southern part of the city.

Nitin was walking along the road. After the confrontation at Vani's home, he was too disturbed to even consider calling a cab. His perfect life had come crumbling down. It seemed like yesterday that he was being showered with dollars by one of the most reputed banks in the world. He was using his charm and power to seduce young girls while, for the rest of the world, he had an ideal family life, a gorgeous wife and two cute little children. What more could one ask for?

He was lost in thought. *I probably overstepped a bit when it came to girls, but who doesn't do it? At least I wasn't hiring prostitutes. Vani is overreacting. Even if I lost money in the stock market, we still have a house of our own in this expensive city. We have enough to rebuild our lives.*

But Vani is also right. She trusted me wholeheartedly and I did break that trust. I should not have gotten carried away with money, power and lust. How do I save my family? What do I do? God help me!

Brakes screeched and interrupted his thoughts. A second later, the car hit Nitin and flung him a few meters away. A large crowd gathered around the fallen body and the traffic came to a standstill.

'Is this the Police Control Room?' a passer-by shouted hysterically into his mobile phone. 'There has been an accident on Pedder Road. A car hit a man and he is lying on the road. There is blood all around him.'

The voice on the other side was composed, as if nothing had happened. 'Did you note the number of the vehicle that hit him?'

'No, I just arrived at the scene. Please send an ambulance fast!'

'I don't have an ambulance nearby. I will message the closest patrol unit. Can you tell me the exact location?'

'Opposite the telephone exchange on Pedder Road, southbound lane.'

'Okay, give me a few minutes.'

A crowd was swelling around Nitin but nobody was willing to check if he was dead or alive. 'Call the police!' shouted someone. 'He is dead for sure,' said another. A few cars slid through the space between the body and the sidewalk, but none stopped to help or take the victim to a hospital.

A traffic police constable was the first to arrive. He examined Nitin—clothes soaked in blood, laboured breathing, no other signs of life. Meanwhile, a Mumbai Police van pulled up on the opposite side as it was impossible to approach the scene on the lane the accident had happened. It had taken them 30 minutes to reach; there was no concept of an emergency lane in a city where normal life unfolds like an emergency.

The police constable used his baton to turn the body over and threw some water on Nitin's face. The breathing had stopped by now. He took the wallet from the body's trouser pocket and pulled out a visiting card. The man was a bank official, though the bank's name looked alien to the constable. From the other pocket, he pulled out his mobile phone.

There was no chance of getting an ambulance without wasting another hour. The constable decided to put Nitin's mangled body in the van and took him to Jaslok Hospital, a few hundred meters from the accident spot.

The hospital staff shifted Nitin onto a stretcher and carried him into the trauma centre. The doctors immediately got down to assessing the damage. Vani's number was listed as the emergency contact in the mobile.

'Hello, is this Ms. Sharma?' spoke the inspector.

'Yes, this is,' Vani replied.

'Mr. Nitin Sharma has met with an accident on Pedder Road and he is in Jaslok Hospital right now. Please come to the hospital fast.'

It had been only an hour since the bitter confrontation and Vani was still in a foul mood. But her heart sank when she heard the news. She and her father rushed to the hospital, leaving her children with their grandmother.

'Doctor, I hope he will survive. What injuries has he suffered?' her father asked, while Vani sobbed in the background. She didn't know why she was feeling anything for Nitin after all he had done.

'He has suffered multiple fractures in his legs, the pelvic area and the ribcage. He has lost a lot of blood but the police managed to get him to the hospital within an hour of the accident and that's very good by our standards.'

The doctor continued, 'Fortunately, the impact was sideways and the brunt was borne by the pelvic bones. We are not expecting any lethal damage to his heart or other internal organs.'

The doctor asked Vani to sign a few forms. It was going to be a long night. The doctors would give their verdict only after the surgery. They got down to the task of putting all the bones in their place.

Her father called home, 'Listen, the accident is really bad. By God's grace Nitin is alive. They will operate and keep him in the ICU for a few days. We haven't been allowed to see him yet so we'll stay the night at the hospital. You don't worry about us. I will buy my medicines here and try to feed Vani something.'

'How is Vani? Is she still angry?'

'She has been crying a lot but it's too early to say whether it is general sympathy or forgiveness. I am giving her some space. We will figure it out later,' her father said.

They sat in the waiting area outside the operating room. The doctor emerged after a couple of hours with some papers and asked for Vani, 'We will have to carry out an extra procedure as the damage is more severe than what we assessed. I need your signature to approve that.'

Vani had no choice but to sign wherever the doctor asked. As the doctor re-entered the operating room, she slumped lifelessly on the bench. Nitin was shifted to the ICU at around four in the morning. According to the doctors, the surgery had been successful but they still had to wait for Nitin to regain consciousness to know for sure.

Chapter 64

At British Bank's Mumbai office, Sonia introduced Ram to Rekha, 'As you know, Ram is taking over as Head of Markets today. Please show him around.'

'I am so glad to meet you, Ram. I have heard so much about you and your legendary trading skills. Welcome to India,' Rekha knew that her career now depended on him. She had the skill of getting into any manager's good books. Joe and Nitin were history as far as British Bank was concerned.

Ram was measured in his response, 'Nice to meet you too, Rekha. Let's sit down later today. I need to get a grip on the business as soon as possible.'

'Sure, we can sit now, if you like.'

'Okay, why not?' Ram liked the earnest response and the urgent action. 'Why don't you start by telling me about the size of our business here, the kind of clients and the products that we deal in.'

'Our business is India is about two hundred million US dollars this year. The clients and products have been severely curtailed due to credit risk concerns and regulatory tightening after the derivatives' blow-out. Further, we are embroiled in multiple lawsuits with our erstwhile clients.'

Ram tried not to look shocked. *How is she managing to smile in such a situation?*

He soon realised that he had jumped from one sinking ship onto another. He also gauged that he had about a year to work something out in the Hong Kong or Singapore offices of British Bank. His wife was also more likely to move to the first world cities in the third world. Moving back to London or to another bank in this scenario was completely out of the question.

He decided to keep his new team on their toes while he searched for a suitable role within the system. He summoned Roshan, the senior-most trader on the floor after Vicky's departure.

'Hey Roshan, nice to meet you!' he tried to begin on a pleasant note.

'Hi Ram, great to meet you. I was told that you were running one of the largest trading books in London. What made you move to India?' Roshan showed his lack of people skills by discussing a touchy subject. He thought he could get away by just making money but he was mistaken. Ram didn't like the rather direct question and immediately ranked Roshan lower than Rekha in his mind.

'Actually, things were terrific in London and business was booming. Still, I wanted to do something new. I like to take up challenging assignments and that shows in my career graph,' Ram boasted.

Roshan knew Ram was fibbing. He had made money by reckless betting in credit markets till 2007 and had lost all of it, and more, when the day of reckoning had come. But he exclaimed, 'Of course, who wouldn't want to look at India when it comes to challenging assignments?'

Ram made a mental note to get rid of this asshole at the next available opportunity.

Chapter 65

Two weeks had passed since the fateful day when Vani's life, as she knew it, had ceased to exist. Nitin was recovering well and had been shifted from the ICU to a normal ward. Vani was spending time in the hospital caring for him but still didn't speak to him other than in monosyllables. She had experienced intense emotions for him after the accident but was still unable to pardon him for his faults.

Nitin, on the other hand, was observing Vani closely. When he regained consciousness, two days after the accident, he didn't expect Vani to be around. Still, hers was the first face he saw when his eyes opened. She was reclining on the couch next to his bed; her eyes shut tight due to exhaustion.

He moved his hand slowly to touch Vani's hand, which was holding on to the side rail. Vani pulled it away without opening her eyes. He couldn't figure out whether she did it in her sleep or deliberately. But he felt deep remorse. As he recovered slowly, he thanked his stars for being alive.

True, he had lost a lot but he was alive. His love for Vani had multiplied in these few days. One day, as she passed him the juice, he said, 'Vani, I am very sorry for whatever I have done. You have been a true support in my life and a major reason for whatever I could achieve in my career.'

Vani looked away, out of the window, into the deep blue Arabian Sea. She replied, 'Drink the juice and give me the glass. I am done taking care of you. I am going home today, never to come back.'

Nitin didn't want to give up easily as this was his last chance to salvage their marriage. 'I didn't value you and took you for granted. I thought you would be there for me irrespective of what I did. I searched for happiness outside our home when it was there inside, waiting for me. I feel like the biggest fool in the world.'

'I know, you will recover and start again on the same path. People like you never change.'

Nitin was crying uncontrollably, a release of all his anguish, pain and fear over the last month. The nurse rushed in thinking that the patient was in pain. She quickly realised that it was a family matter and left them alone.

'Please forgive me. I have been the biggest fool. I have been a terrible husband but please give me one last chance?'

Vani had softened to his overtures in the last few days. She wanted to see if he was sufficiently guilty and willing to mend his ways. His unconditional and agitated apology had given her some proof of his change. Still, it was too early to pardon him.

Nitin cried tears of remorse for the first time in his life. He realised that he was a bigger schmuck than the three schmucks under him at British Bank

Chapter 66

Satya's condition failed to improve even after a couple of months of treatment. He was forced to take a break from his job. The bank allowed him to proceed on leave, without pay, on medical grounds with the promise that he would be employed again, as and when deemed fit by the doctors.

With the recent loss of employees, some deliberately fired and others due to misconduct, the Markets team was getting seriously understaffed. Rekha emerged as the senior-most member of the sales team. Ram designated her Head of Sales and authorised her to recruit the new crop of schmucks.

Ram and Rekha interviewed scores of candidates as plenty were available in the market. They ended up hiring two mid-level managers who had been fired by other banks. The taint of getting fired, prevalent earlier, was now gone. It was understood that the firing had a lot more to do with external events than with the person's performance.

Rekha was not taking chances anymore with her career or her personal life. She took good care of herself and was looking to find an eligible bachelor soon.

Amit had taken Samir's advice and had stuck with Nomura till they kept him. After paying his contractual amounts, Nomura let him go. He proceeded to Berkeley for an advanced degree in Finance. He hoped that by the time he earned his degree, the market would bounce back and he would be absorbed at a senior level. But when Amit completed his degree, not many roles were available for quantitative finance and derivatives whiz-kids in the US. He returned to India and had to accept a junior role in a commercial bank. *Once a schmuck, always a schmuck.* He cursed his luck; he had taken this decision despite Samir's explicit advice against it.

Nitin moved to his in-laws' place after the doctors discharged him from the hospital. As he entered the house supported by a male attendant, he stopped and again apologised to Vani. 'Please forgive me, Vani. I am ashamed of what I did and am feeling too weak to live alone.'

Finally, Vani melted and said, 'Don't talk too much or you will hurt your stitches.'

'Should I take this as forgiveness?'

'I will get tea for both of us.' Having tea together meant that she had pardoned him. Her mother's eyes moistened. Nitin was finally relieved. He forgot all about the physical pain and felt immense happiness. Now, he could focus on rebuilding his life with Vani and the kids. He vowed never to take his blessings for granted.

Rakesh moved to Singapore as Asia CEO of British Bank. He did exceptionally well as he had managed to dodge all bullets during the crisis.

Samir also lost his banking job in 2009. He joined a large corporate as a consultant and later got an offer from a Chinese corporate bank and happily joined them. The foreign bank's compensation was way better than what he got paid as a consultant.

He had also managed to keep his life in order in the midst of all the mayhem. His colleagues had suffered on multiple fronts but he stood rock-solid, thanks to the emphasis on his well-being. He resolved to write a book to help everyone take charge of their happiness, success, health and life.

Epilogue

At the large global banks, even after the massive meltdown of 2008, senior bankers still hoped that the business would recover. They wanted to retain their valued employees and they feared that they would lose top talent if they didn't pay them bull market salaries. This illogical theory was propagated by managers who wanted to get paid themselves. In light of ensuing restrictions on bankers' bonuses, imposed by regulators in US and Europe, the banks hiked fixed compensation by as much as 60 to 80 percent. So, the bonuses fell but the overall compensation remained high.

Since the promised recovery in business never occurred, barring a dead cat bounce in 2010, it became increasingly difficult to maintain the overpaid employees. The indiscriminate firing resumed and still continues. The US government enacted the Dodd-Frank Act and Volcker's Rule, aimed to discipline large banks by severely limiting proprietary risk-taking, prescribing elaborate procedure for client dealings and increasing the cost of compliance manifold.

According to unconfirmed estimates, hundreds of thousands of bankers were fired by large global banks. The trend continues even now in 2019. In addition, the too-big-to-fail banks have paid a cumulative 251 billion US dollars in regulatory fines so far, to cover for their unethical practices during the bull run of 2005–2007.

Acknowledgements

I had never imagined that I would venture into the world of fiction so soon. One fine day, I found this story developing in my head and soon it caught such momentum that it was impossible to stop and I am happy and content that this work is now a published book.

It would have been impossible to do this without the unrelenting support from my wife, Manisha and kids, Aryaa and Chaitanya. God knows how many hours of family time they sacrificed for me to focus on my writing.

I am grateful for the blessings from my parents, Aruna and Lal Mohan Mishra as well as my in-laws Meera Rani and Dr. Mrinal Chandra Jha.

Special thanks to the wonderful team at Jaico Publishing led by Akash Shah. They have worked with me on this project like their own.

Sraddha Venkataraman edited and worked with me in fleshing out critical parts of the book so that it was fit for submission to the publishers.

Manisha Mishra and Varsha Naik provided initial critical feedback that helped me in refining the story.

Many thanks to Rakhi and Shivalik Prasad, Prachi and Saurabh Jambhekar, Rohit Basu, Shrishti Nahata, Paavni Varma, Ankur Shah, Bhavna Manwani, Vishal Joshi, Chetna Tekchandani and Sangeeta Mall for taking the time to read the manuscript and commenting on it.

Deeply indebted to friends like Shivendra Parihar, Dolphy D'Souza, Robin Bannerjee, Tushar Khese, Jitendra Jain and Matthew Antony for their support in this journey.

Finally, I am thankful to all my banking colleagues and the banking profession for teaching me so much about life. They definitely don't teach this at Harvard!

JAICO PUBLISHING HOUSE

Elevate Your Life. Transform Your World.

ESTABLISHED IN 1946, Jaico Publishing House is home to world-transforming authors such as Sri Sri Paramahansa Yogananda, Osho, The Dalai Lama, Sri Sri Ravi Shankar, Sadhguru, Robin Sharma, Deepak Chopra, Jack Canfield, Eknath Easwaran, Devdutt Pattanaik, Khushwant Singh, John Maxwell, Brian Tracy and Stephen Hawking.

Our late founder Mr. Jaman Shah first established Jaico as a book distribution company. Sensing that independence was around the corner, he aptly named his company Jaico ('Jai' means victory in Hindi). In order to service the significant demand for affordable books in a developing nation, Mr. Shah initiated Jaico's own publications. Jaico was India's first publisher of paperback books in the English language.

While self-help, religion and philosophy, mind/body/spirit, and business titles form the cornerstone of our non-fiction list, we publish an exciting range of travel, current affairs, biography, and popular science books as well. Our renewed focus on popular fiction is evident in our new titles by a host of fresh young talent from India and abroad. Jaico's recently established Translations Division translates selected English content into nine regional languages.

In addition to being a publisher and distributor of its own titles, Jaico is a major national distributor of books of leading international and Indian publishers. With its headquarters in Mumbai, Jaico has branches and sales offices in Ahmedabad, Bangalore, Bhopal, Chennai, Delhi, Hyderabad, Kolkata and Lucknow.

SINCE 1946